MW00634006

365 UNSOLVED MYSTERIES

First published in 2018 by

An imprint of Om Books International

Corporate & Editorial Office
A 12, Sector 64, Noida 201 301
Uttar Pradesh, India
Phone: +91 120 477 4100
Email: editorial@ombooks.com
Website: www.ombooksinternational.com

Sales Office
107, Ansari Road, Darya Ganj, New Delhi 110 002, India
Phone: +91 11 4000 9000
Fax: +91 11 2327 8091
Email: sales@ombooks.com
Website: www.ombooks.com

ISBN: 978-93-85031-29-8

Printed in India

10 9 8 7 6 5 4 3 2 1

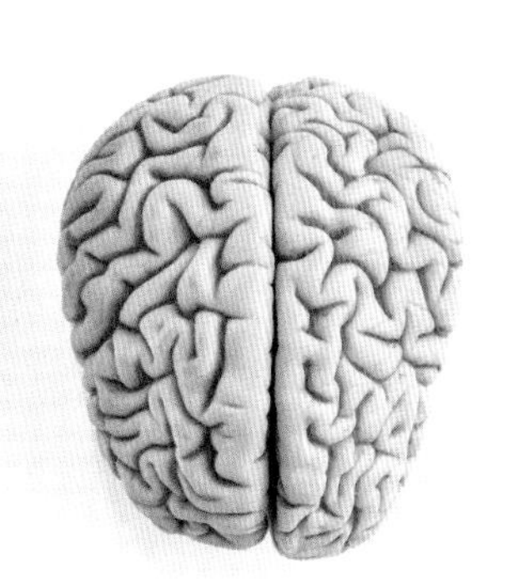

365 UNSOLVED MYSTERIES

Om KIDZ
An imprint of Om Books International

Mysteries in History

Mysteries in Archaeology

LIBRARY OF ALEXANDRIA

Mysteries Around the World

Mysteries of Mother Earth

Mysteries of the Human Body

Unsolved Mysteries of Science

Mysterious Unsolved Crimes

Mysterious in Pop Culture

Mysteries in History

History is the record of our past. We look at the past for answers and wisdom. But there are some questions in our past that no one knows the answers to. Several mysteries are yet to be resolved.

There are lost islands, strange disappearances and unfound treasures that have puzzled historians for decades. Sadly, the answers might forever be lost to us.

1. Dance Fever

Did you know that people could **die from dancing**? In 1518, a city in Strasbourg, France was struck by an unusual plague. It all began when a woman named Frau Troffea stepped into the street and suddenly began to dance.

She wasn't performing a beautiful ballet or an energetic Macarena, but she was shaking her arms and legs around wildly. The whole thing looked scary. Her body was twisting and turning and she couldn't seem to stop. She kept dancing for a week and what's strange is that more and more people began to join her.

It was called the 'Dancing Plague', and it killed nearly 400 people in the city due to heart attacks or exhaustion. Doctors put it down to a hot blood disease and asked the patients to keep dancing until they stopped. No one knows how this bewildering plague started or ended.

2. What happened to Amelia Earhart?

The mystery surrounding the **disappearance of Amelia Earhart** continues to boggle people even today.

Amelia was born on July 24, 1897 in Kansas, USA. She was the first woman to fly solo over the Atlantic Ocean. Around 1936, she started making plans to fly around the world and began her journey in June 1937.

On June 2, 1937, she disappeared over the Pacific Ocean along with her airliner 'Lockheed Model 10 Electra'. She had been accompanied by Fred Noonan who was also an experienced flight navigator.

Even though rescue workers started looking for them hours after they went missing, they were unable to find their bodies or even the airliner. The US Navy and Coast Guard made it their mission to find the missing people. They launched a large and expensive air and sea search. However, their search turned up nothing. Earhart's husband, George Putnam also launched a search, but he too
was unsuccessful.

It was as if Amelia Earhart had vanished into thin air! Even after decades, nothing of the airline has turned up, although, there have been many alleged sightings. This great mystery has produced many theories.

Some believe that Earhart and Noonan were American spies working for the American leader Franklin Roosevelt and that they were sent to find information from Japan. Others say that they were attacked by Japanese forces and that their bodies along with the airliner were hidden away. These theories are unlikely. But the fact remains that nobody knows what really happened to her or the airline.

FACT FILE

Before 1928, Earhart was working as a social worker who learned to fly as a hobby. She then turned the hobby into a paying career.

3. The Lost Princes

King Richard III was crowned King of England in July 1483. He died in the battle of Bosworth in 1485. But his remains were only found in 2013 in Leicester, England. He was hastily buried during a battle.

Interestingly, it is said that he had locked his two young nephews Edward V and Richard in the Tower of London for their own protection. But to this day, nobody knows where they vanished.

Historians are unable to find evidence that they were kidnapped or killed as their bodies have not been found. Suspicion fell on many of their relatives including King Richard. It has been 500 years...will the mystery of their disappearance ever be solved?

4. The Crystal Skulls

What is your skull made of? Not crystal for sure! So, imagine the surprise when **crystal skulls** were suddenly displayed in auctions around the 1800s.

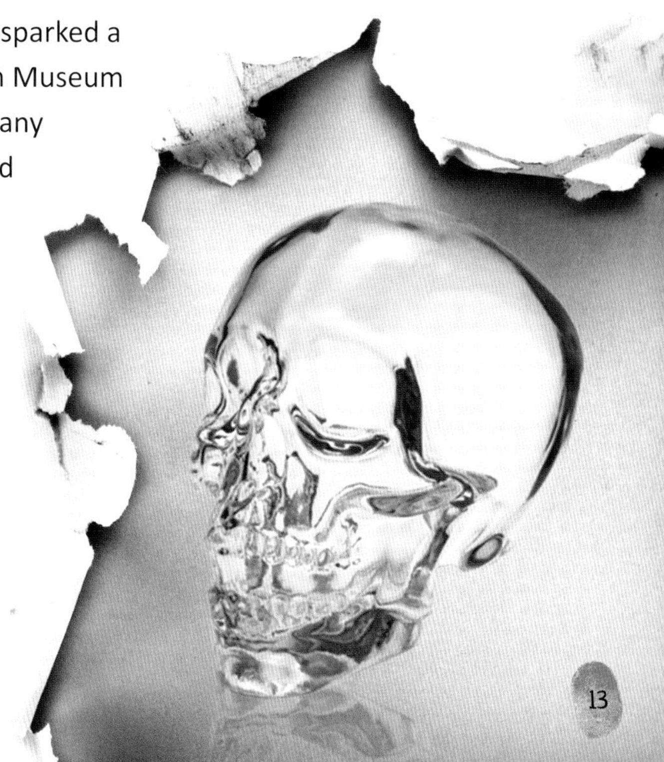

Where did they come from? This question sparked a lot of interest among history buffs. The British Museum and the Smithsonian Institution performed many tests and found markings on the skulls that led them to believe the skulls were from the 1800s.

During the 1800s, people were very interested in learning about ancient cultures and went to museums to look at unique pieces. It is quite possible that these museums created these skulls and gave them a fake backstory. But nobody knows for sure.

5. The Kennedy Assassination

Who hasn't heard about **John F. Kennedy**? He was one of the most beloved presidents of the USA. Sadly, he was assassinated by a shooter named Lee Harvey Oswald while touring with his wife along with a motorcade in Main Street at Dealey Plaza. Oswald was later killed in the police station. The judges of the Supreme Court recognised him as the murderer.

But the events of the murder raised suspicion among the public. Even today, people believe that he was not the real killer because he was too far away from the moving motorcade. Apparently, another shooter was spotted in the area who must have run away after firing the gunshots.

6. The Babushka Lady

John F. Kennedy was publicly assassinated. At that time, there were many people around the motorcade, including the media who recorded the incident. Those who had come to see the Kennedys had brought along cameras.

That is why there are many photographs of the tragic assassination. One such photo showed a woman taking pictures of the assassination. She was wearing a headscarf so her face was hidden in the photos.

Nobody knew who she was, but she was nicknamed as the '**Babushka Lady**' because of her headscarf, which is commonly worn by Russian grandmothers or 'babushkas'. The FBI had asked her to come forward and share her photographs but she never did.

7. The Killing of Robert Kennedy

Isn't it strange that President Kennedy's brother, Robert Kennedy, was also **assassinated** while he was running for the office of the president in 1968? He was in California for the presidential primary elections.

Robert was leaving the Ambassador Hotel accompanied by a former FBI agent named William Barry. He also had two of his personal bodyguards accompanying him. His style during the campaign season was to walk down to the long line of people waiting there to see him and speak to him.

A man named Sirhan Sirhan walked before him. The man hid his gun behind a large poster. Sirhan Sirhan pulled out his gun and fired the shots. He was immediately arrested and put in prison.

Years later, a witness claimed that a second shooter was involved in the killing and that Sirhan's bullet did not kill Robert Kennedy. So, many similarities in the two cases have led people to believe the witness.

FACT FILE

Sirhan Sirhan's lawyers have said that he was framed and that Sirhan did not remember assassinating Robert Kennedy.

8. The Lost Crew

Captain David Morehouse was sailing aboard his brig, Dei Gratia, when he spotted the Mary Celeste. He was puzzled to find the ship sailing in Portugal as it should already have reached its destination in Italy.

MISSING

He sent a boarding party to search the ship. He received a surprising report; the ship was in a bad condition because of heavy weather and water logging, the luggage, food and alcohol was untouched, the lifeboat was missing and the **crew had disappeared**.

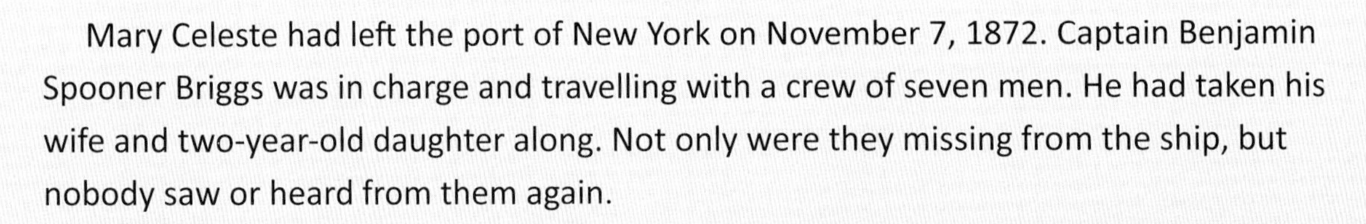

Mary Celeste had left the port of New York on November 7, 1872. Captain Benjamin Spooner Briggs was in charge and travelling with a crew of seven men. He had taken his wife and two-year-old daughter along. Not only were they missing from the ship, but nobody saw or heard from them again.

In 1884, Sir Author Conan Doyle, who had heard of the mystery of Mary Celeste, published a fictional short story. In the short story, a survivor from the crew talks about what happened to the ship. This inspired readers to come up with their own theories about the ship.

Did pirates raid the ship? Was it attacked by a sea monster? Was there a serial murderer aboard the ship? Did the crew drink all the alcohol and start a mutiny? Although mystery still shrouds the disappearance, it has inspired many movies and novels.

FACT FILE

The Mystery of the Mary Celeste is a movie based on this mysterious case. It was released in 1935 and then again in 1936 as *The Phantom Ship.*

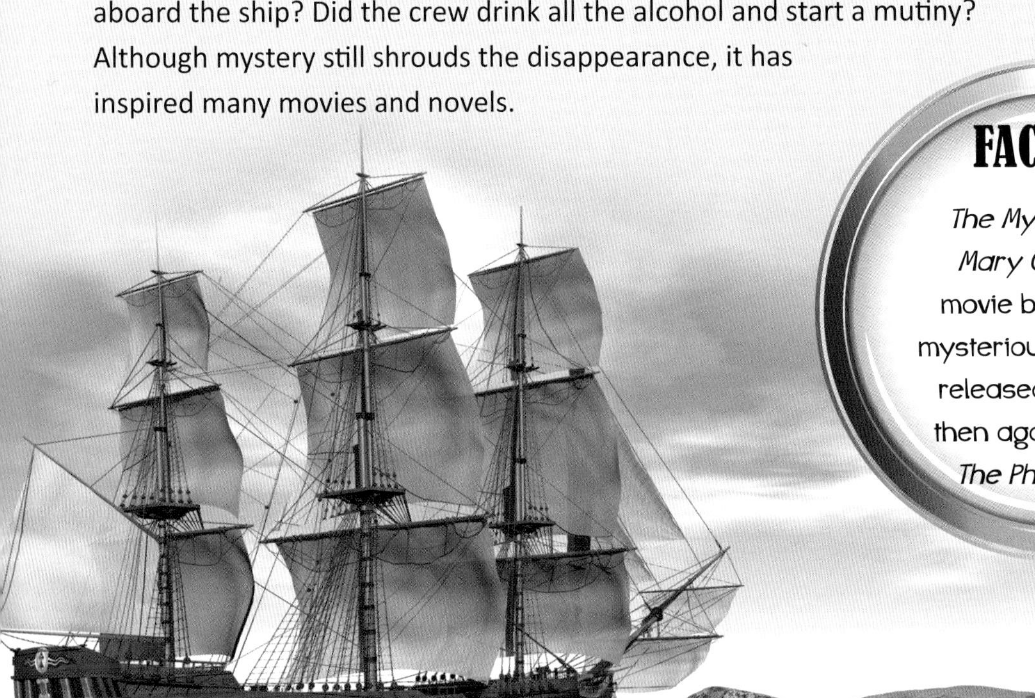

9. The Apostles

Have you seen the *Last Supper*? It is a painting by Leonardo Da Vinci in which Jesus Christ is seen having a meal with the Twelve Apostles. They were the **twelve followers of Jesus Christ**. They had ordinary occupations like a tax collector and fishermen.

Their names were Peter, Andrew, James, John, Phillip, Bartholomew, Thomas, Matthew, James, Thaddeus, Simon and Judas Iscariot. The twelve apostles are said to have watched the crucifixion, resurrection and ascension of Jesus Christ. They then spread out to different parts of the world to speak about Christianity.

Did these men really exist? Or were they a work of fiction? If they did not exist, how did people learn about Christianity and the teachings of God?

10. The Holy Earthquake

Back in 750 BCE, a man named Amos predicted that there would be a giant earthquake that would shake the Earth. He predicted it to be the 'Day of the Lord'. Usually, predictions of natural disasters that stem from religious thought don't come true.

But Amos must have known something that others didn't, because there was an earthquake that took place nearly two years after he predicted it. He was a prophet that later inspired other prophets to write about this incident.

It is possible that **Amos saw the earthquake** in advance, but we cannot be sure if it was because of religious belief or scientific knowledge. It could also be a weird co-incidence.

11. The Mysterious Spaceman

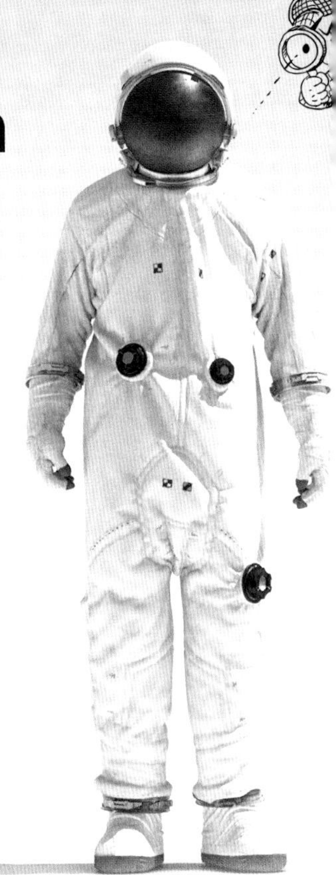

Imagine having a picture **spoiled by a spaceman**! That's exactly what happened to a man named Jim Templeton when he took a photo of his daughter in a place called Solway Firth.

He did not notice anything unusual while taking the photo. He took it to a chemist to be processed. This is when the chemist told him about the mysterious spaceman in the picture behind his daughter.

The man had a white suit, a white helmet and a visor. He looked like a NASA spaceman. Mr Templeton took the photo to the Kodak company to see what the problem was. But to this day, he has no clue to the appearance of the mysterious spaceman in his sensational photo!

12. The Mysterious UFO

There have been many UFO (Unidentified Flying Object) sightings in the past. But one of the earliest ones occurred on June 24, 1947 when a man named Kenneth Arnold looked up to find **nine mysterious flying bodies** shooting across the sky at high speed.

He was standing at the Cascade Range near Mount Rainier in the US. He was interviewed by the newspapers and after reading his account, many people reported their own UFO sightings.

The US Air Force, at the time, was taking such sightings very seriously. They launched an investigation into Arnold's report in September. Investigators, with Arnold's help, made up sketches of the nine UFOs. But this is the most progress they've made on the case.

13. The Renaissance UFO

Can you imagine finding an **UFO in a painting from the medieval times**? It is true! Many people believe that UFOs were spotted even back in those days and that artists captured them with their paintbrushes.

One such artist is Giovanni Bellini. He was a Renaissance painter from Italy. The Renaissance Period was the name given to a time in history when western civilisations produced classic pieces of art and literature. Many playwrights, actors, sculptors and painters became popular from this period.

Giovanni Bellini was famous for painting nativity scenes which was a trend of the time. One of his paintings was titled *Madonna with Saint Giovannino*. It captivates the viewer to this day and not just because of its beauty...

This painting appears to have an UFO in the background. There are those who enthusiastically believe that Bellini was trying to convey a message through the painting about how he could communicate with aliens.

But this theory is bizarre so most people dismiss it. In fact, some believe that the painting was trying to share a religious message rather than a message from aliens. The mysterious object could have been an angel.

This is reinforced by some other paintings from the time that show similar nativity scenes with celestial objects in the background. Nobody knows the answer to this mystery.

FACT FILE

It is possible that this painting is wrongly credited to Bellini as the artist could also be Domenico Ghirlandaio.

14. The Missing Aircraft

Have you ever heard of Roald Amundsen? He was a Norwegian explorer and one of the first people to have crossed the Arctic by aircraft. He had a deep interest in exploring the polar regions. He also wrote books about his expeditions which made him famous.

In June, 1928, he took on a rescue mission to the Arctic Circle. He was accompanied by a five-person crew. The mission set out to rescue crew members of an airship named Italia, which had crashed while travelling across the North Pole.

While flying over the Barents Sea, Amundsen and his crew met with heavy fog. Due to low visibility, their aircraft experienced a severe crash.

The exact date is unknown, but it is believed that Amundsen either died during or very shortly after the aircraft crashed. A search team was immediately sent for Amundsen and his crew by the Norwegian Government.

However, the search was unsuccessful. The bodies and the aircraft **have not been recovered** to this day. Late in 2004 and again in 2009, the Royal Norwegian Navy sent crew to find the wreckage of the aircraft. This created a lot of interest in the findings. But the crew were unsuccessful. While a wide area has been marked, the location of the wreckage remains a mystery to this day.

FACT FILE

Roald Amundsen was one of many who made their mark during the 'Heroic Age of Antarctic Exploration'.

15. Death of Alexander the Great

Alexander the Great was the King of Macedon who created a large empire by conquering parts of Asia and Africa. What's even more amazing is that he managed to do this by the age of 30.

His death came as a great surprise to his subjects. Some of them shaved their heads as a mark of respect and sorrow. But the reason behind his death is a great mystery. The exact date is pinned down to June 10 or June 11, 323 BC.

It is suspected that he was either poisoned or assassinated. There are also accounts that he died of malaria or typhoid fever. He is said to have displayed symptoms of fever for a week leading to his death.

16. Finding the Lost Tomb

It's not just the reason of his death, but also the location of his tomb that is a big mystery. It is known that Alexander the Great died in Babylon. After his death, Perdiccas, Ptolemy I Soter and Selecus I Nicator decided the **burial site**.

Although, Babylon seemed the logical choice, they later decided on Aegae. On the way, Ptolemy I Soter changed the location. This is where it gets confusing!

Ptolemy first buried Alexander's remains in Memphis but later they were transported to Alexandria for a reburial. However, despite more than a hundred search attempts, we do not know where exactly his remains are actually buried.

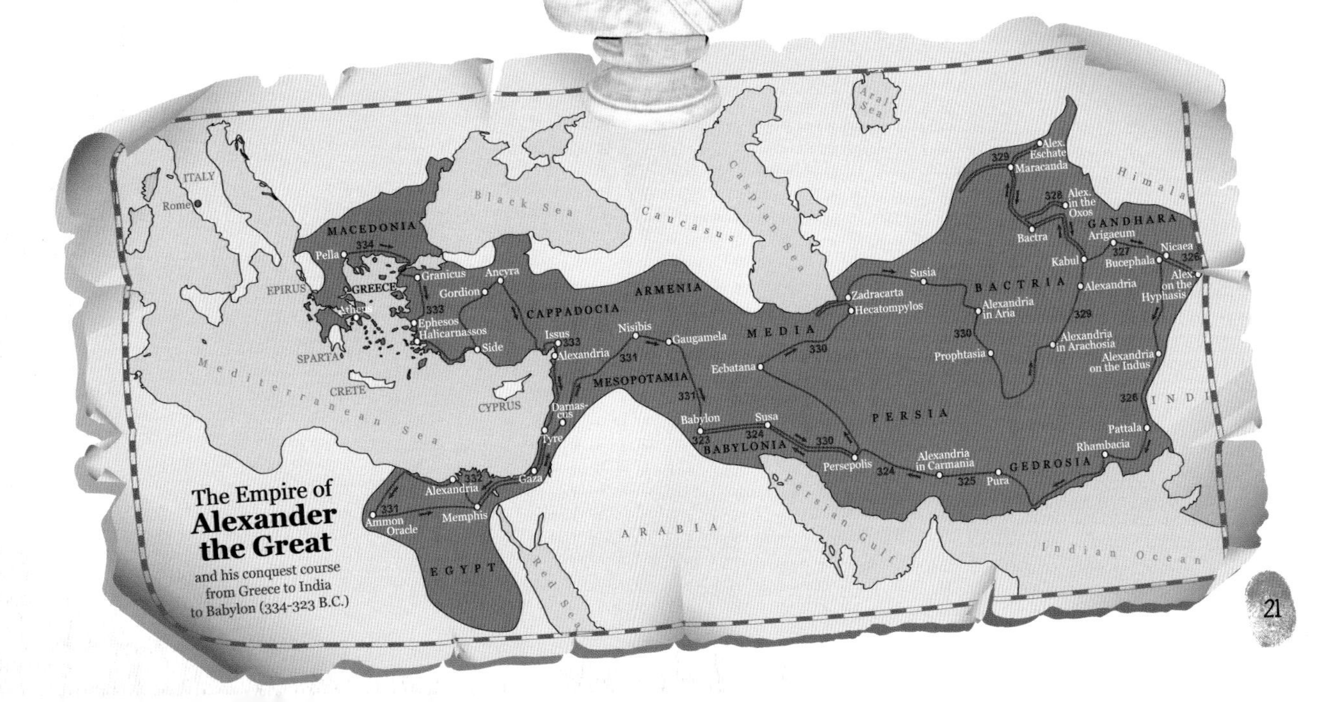

The Empire of **Alexander the Great** and his conquest course from Greece to India to Babylon (334-323 B.C.)

17. What happened to IX Legion? 

One of the most mind-boggling mysteries from the past is that of the missing IX Legion. They were a brave army of 5,000 Roman soldiers. The IX Legion was trained alongside the VI, VII and VIII Legion and was later inherited by Julius Caesar.

With the leadership of Emperor Claudius, not only did they conquer England back in 43 AD, but they also managed to keep Rome in power for 74 years, crushing every rebellion that took place in England.

Can you imagine why such a powerful legion would suddenly be wiped out of historical records? Strangely, the **entire legion disappeared** seemingly without a trace after 120 AD. It is said that they were all killed during a north England rebellion against Roman rule.

Another theory suggests that the legion marched into a region of Scotland called Caledonia in 108 AD. Nobody knows what happened next, but this is when they disappeared from historical records.

However, scholars suggest that the legion had simply established a base there as there are some inscriptions found up to 120 AD. Nobody seems to agree if the disappearance of the legion can be blamed on one rebellion or many rebellions that kept reducing their strength.

FACT FILE

Emperor Hadrian built a border wall Britannia (north England) soon after the legion disappeared.

18. The Elusive Giants

Mysteries occur in every country. Some however, seem so similar that it makes you wonder, is there actually a connection? Have you ever heard of the mysterious Yeti, Big Foot, Sasquatch, Almasty or the Abominable Snowman?

These are the names given to hairy, **giant human-like beasts** that are spotted in remote areas. People have spotted such beasts in the Himalayan mountains, Russia, North America and even in certain parts of Africa.

Nobody knows if these beasts exist or if there is any relation between the beast from one country to another. Often, people report seeing huge footprints while trekking in the snow. Some even claim to have seen the beasts themselves!

19. The Loch Ness Mystery

There's yet another beast whose existence itself is a mystery...the **Loch Ness Monster**! People have been reporting sightings of this monster since 1871. Back in 2011, a man named George Edwards reported that he had seen a 'slow moving hump' in the Loch Ness waters.

This creature is so popular that it has its own website and nickname, 'Nessie', given to it by a research team from the US. They deployed a submarine to the very bottom of the Loch Ness lake, nearly 300 feet deep.

However, they just found all the golf balls nearby golfers lost while practicing. Yet, the mystery of the Loch Ness Monster lives on!

20. Peter Gibb's Bad Flight

It was a dull Christmas Eve in 1975 on the island of Mull. Peter Gibb, an English Royal Air Force flying ace, decided to fly his Cessna plane after supper. His friends were surprised to hear about his sudden decision and asked him to reconsider. Yet, he insisted on it.

He took a companion named Felicity Granger to the runway and instructed her to guide the takeoff with torches. A strange thing happened here: Felicity insisted that she was the only one guiding the plane, other witnesses said that there were two torches moving at the runway.

While in the air, Peter Gibb caught a sleet storm that lasted for three days! **He went missing** for months. Then, his body was found lying on a nearby hillside. The reports said that he had died of exposure. His plane was missing.

Authorities were baffled. Finally, in 1986, a small aircraft was found that looked like the Cessna plane. It was in a terrible condition. It had obviously been in a violent crash. Even more surprising was that the doors were locked.

If Peter Gibb had jumped out of his plane to save himself, at least one door of the plane would have been unlocked. Besides Peter would have suffered terrible injuries. Nobody knows what happened.

FACT FILE

Peter Gibbs' body only had a small cut on the leg. It looked like the crash did not affect him.

21. The Wild Walrus

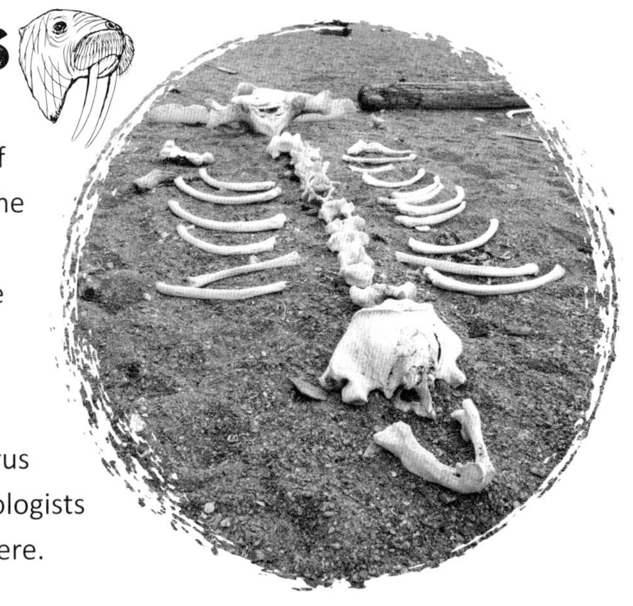

It all began as a regular work day for a group of London archaeologists. They had to excavate the graveyard of St Pancras Old Church. But much to their surprise, when they opened one of the coffins, they **found a walrus**!

Its remains dated back to the 19th century. Now, to those who might not know this, a walrus is a rare sight in London. Naturally, the archaeologists wanted to know why the walrus was buried there.

They searched past records but could not find any mention of bringing a walrus to the city. Where did the walrus come from? Whom did it belong to? This will probably always be a mystery!

22. An Alien Base

There is a military base in Nevada, USA that has been a source of inspiration for many conspiracy theorists. To the United States government, this base is simply the 'Nevada Test and Training Range'. But to conspiracy theorists it's the **mysterious Area 51** located near Extra-terrestrial Highway (Nevada State Route 375), which was a popular UFO spotting site.

Though the location of this base is well-known, no common citizen or visitor is allowed inside the base. There are many signs and guards preventing snooping eyes from entering the base. So, people believe that the government is hiding scientists who are testing aliens or researching alien technology. Could they be right?

23. The Devil's Triangle

Imagine if a ship **suddenly disappeared** while sailing across an area of water. Imagine if the same thing happened to a plane – in fact, several ships and planes. This area that we are referring to is none other than 'Bermuda Triangle' or 'Devil's Triangle'. The area of water is bound by Bermuda, Puerto Rico and Florida. It is been a topic of interest for many scientists, explorers and conspiracy theorists for years.

Some believe that the ships and planes disappear because of methane gas explosions. Methane gas is flammable and there are pockets of gases under the sea. It could be possible that extreme weather like lightning brings the methane gas to the surface and cause a reaction.

As per another theory, the accidents happen because of 'compass variation'. This means that when a person uses a compass in the area, the magnetic compass points to the true north rather than the magnetic north. This variation causes great confusion among pilots and captains. However, this theory has been debunked by the US Navy.

An author named Larry Kusche believes that there is no great mystery behind the Bermuda Triangle. He wrote a book named *The Bermuda Triangle Mystery – Solved* to disprove all the theories surrounding the phenomenon.

Still, theories shroud this area. The latest disappearance linked to this area is that of the Malaysia Airlines Flight MH370. There is a great fear among people because of this theory. They actively avoid the Bermuda Triangle while flying or sailing.

Some also believe that the ships and planes disappear in the Bermuda Triangle due to an UFO.

FACT FILE

It is estimated that over 100 years, 1,000 lives have been lost in this area.

24. The Exploding Fireball

On June 30, 1908, more than a century ago, a **wild explosion** took place in the Tunguska forest of Siberia. The explosion was so horrendous and powerful that it felled 80 million trees. That one explosion cleared nearly 2000 km^2 of the forest area. Even a town 60 km away could feel the tremors. It crashed many windows in nearby towns.

It all started when a giant fireball exploded above the forest. It is believed that the fireball was 50-100 cm wide. The strangest thing about it? Nobody knows what created the fireball and what caused the explosion. It has been a mystery for more than a century!

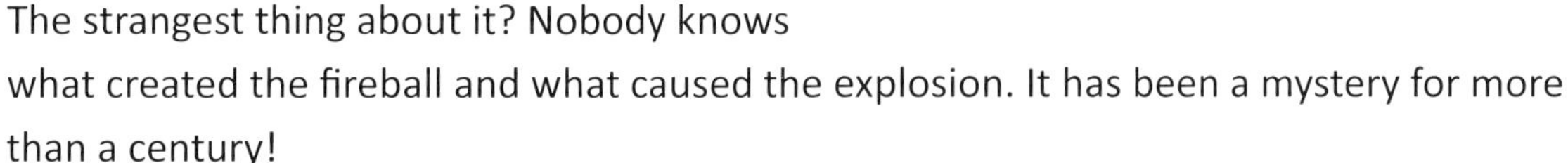

25. The Poisoned Astrophysicist

Have you heard about the **first murder at the South Pole**? Well, it hasn't been proven to be a murder. But many believe that is the case when they hear about an astrophysicist named Rodney Marks. He died of methanol poisoning while researching at the South Pole with a team of 49 scientists.

Even though he died on May 11, 2000, it took nearly six months for his body to be autopsied because flying in and out of the South Pole during winter is dangerous. His body was kept frozen until it could be flown to New Zealand.

Strangely, the police not only ruled out suicide, but also accidental poisoning or foul play. So, how did Marks get poisoned? This is still a mystery!

26. Shakespeare's Skull

In a play called *Hamlet* written by William Shakespeare, we see a gravedigger dig up the skull of a dead court jester named Yorick. The gravedigger holds the skull in his hand as he recites a thought-provoking monologue about death.

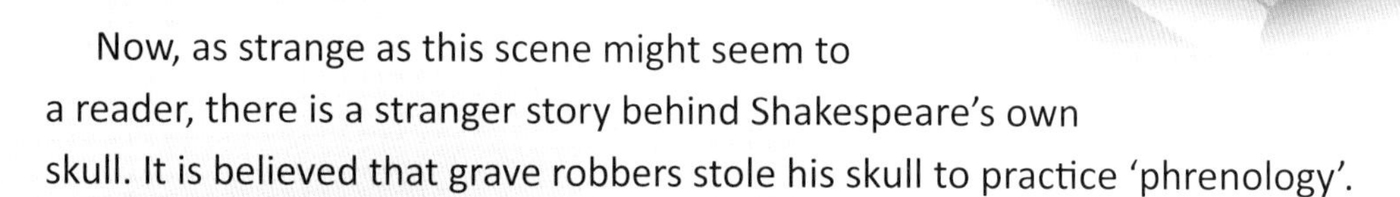

Now, as strange as this scene might seem to a reader, there is a stranger story behind Shakespeare's own skull. It is believed that grave robbers stole his skull to practice 'phrenology'.

Phrenology is the study of the size, shape and features of the skull. Apparently, by doing this, one can tell the mental traits and intelligence level of the person the skull belonged to. The skull could also have been stolen for medicinal purposes to enhance the brain.

Some historians believe that the skull was taken by a surviving family member as at that time, family members took the skull to place it in someone else's grave. While we don't know, who took the skull and why, over time, people have found skulls that might belong to Shakespeare.

It's easy enough to determine if the **skull is Shakespeare's or not**. So far, no skull has turned up. Some even believe that the skull is not missing at all and is inside Shakespeare's own grave above his neck.

Researching Shakespeare's grave where his remains have been resting for 400 years alongside his wife's grave might help to solve the mystery.

FACT FILE

The Tragedy of Hamlet, Prince of Denmark is a tragedy. It has the famous line "To be or not to be...that is the question".

27. Who Wrote Shakespeare?

Many authors choose to write with a pen name. It is possible that William Shakespeare was a **pen name**. Now, if that is true, then who was the real Shakespeare? A doubt arose in the minds of readers as far back as the 19th century about the real Shakespeare.

Some believe that this is just a conspiracy theory, but there are many who ask for proof that the actor from Stratford is the same man who wrote the plays and sonnets that continue to inspire writers to this day.

If you think that this mystery is unimportant, remember that Shakespeare came up with many English words. Understanding who came up with them and when, helps us understand the history of the English language itself!

The Shakespeare Authorship Coalition released a 'Declaration of Reasonable Doubt' to invite people to solve the mystery. While some are baffled by the identity, others think this is much ado about nothing.

28. What Caused the Decline?

We have all read about ancient civilisations in Rome, Greece and Asia. Usually, the collapse or decline of these civilisations is documented. However, there are some **civilisations that collapsed** and we still don't know why.

The Bronze Age was a period in which civilisations were thriving in the Near East, Mesopotamia and Egypt. These civilisations existed from 3300 BC to 1200 BC.

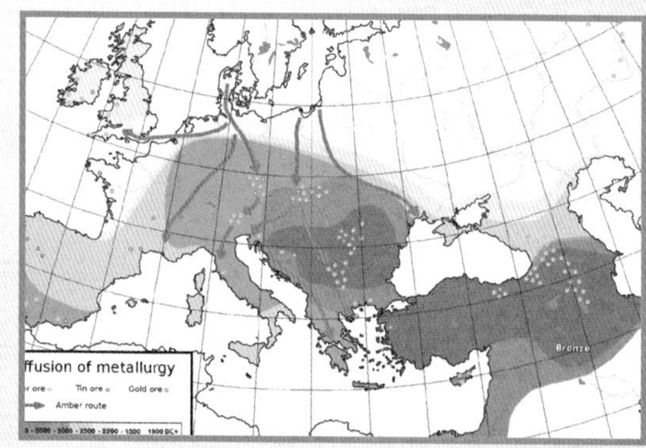

The decline started when cities like Pylos and Gaza experienced violent storms that forced people to migrate. After 40 years of such continuous and unexplained events, nearly every major city in the Mediterranean was destroyed.

Nobody knows what truly happened, but researchers like to credit extreme climate change for the collapse of the Bronze Age. Harsh weather changes affected the agricultural produce which slowly led to famine. Then, wars across the region took place to procure food.

People also believe that gradual change in cultural practices led to the decline of the Bronze Age. Tools and equipment improved with the invention of new metals.

Though historians disagree on the cause, they agree that it took nearly a century of continuous changes that led to the decline of the Bronze Age.

29. The Rainmaker

Have you heard of a rainmaker? This title is given to a **person who can make it rain**. Such a person existed more than 100 years ago, and his name was Charles Mallory Hatfield.

The state of California, USA has always experienced terrible droughts. More than a century ago, when it was having one of its worst droughts, the city of San Diego hired Charles Hatfield to make it rain. Only one-third of the Morena Reservoir was full. Without immediate action, the crops would dry out and the city would experience a horrible famine.

Hatfield was 40 years old. He made a living selling sewing machines. The city was taking a huge risk by relying on him. But he promised that he would accelerate the moisture in the skies and overflow the Morena Reservoir within a year. If successful, the city was to pay him 10,000 dollars in cash. Hatfield was so successful in San Diego that he caused floods.

He had pulled similar stunts in Los Angeles and other parts of California. The newspapers began to chase him to find out what his secret was. But Hatfield always told the people that he did not make it rain. He simply had the formula to attract the clouds.

Though modern technology has been able to manipulate the atmosphere to some extent using special technology, nobody really knows what Hatfield's exact formula was.

FACT FILE

'Rainmaker' is also a name given to a person who brings new business to a failing company.

30. UFO on the Berwyn Mountain

The **Berwyn Mountain UFO crash** is one of the greatest unsolved mysteries from Britain. It occurred on January 23, 1974. People observed some strange light and sound patterns. On further investigation, scientists linked the incident to the Cadair Berwyn UFO sightings.

In fact, during the sighting an earthquake had occurred that registered a 3.5 on the Richter scale. As residents of the nearby areas were fleeing their houses, they felt tremors, saw bright lights over the mountains and heard a loud crash.

Some like to brush off the incident as a meteor crash occurring at the same time as an earthquake. However, nobody knows for sure what happened.

MISSING

31. Up in the Air

Air travel can be fun but there are many who fear it because of dangerous incidents like the one that occurred in March, 2014.

A **Malaysian Airline** travelling from Kuala Lumpur to Beijing suddenly disappeared in thin air without any trace. The airliner was called MH370. It was transporting about 239 people. All of them went missing.

But the strangest part is that nobody has even seen the airline since. Some believe that it went missing while flying over the Bermuda Triangle. But reports suggest that it was just over the Indian Ocean.

32. Sinkholes in Siberia

Siberia is a beautiful place, but it does have some strange, unexplained mysteries. One such mystery is the **three giant craters or sinkholes** discovered by reindeer herders back in July, 2014.

Though we don't know why these sinkholes exist, scientists have been able to come up with reasonable theories. Some believe that when the surrounding ice melted away, the material beneath the ground collapsed to form the sinkholes.

Others believe that the sinkholes were caused because some underground matter was ejected. This probably happened because of extreme built-up pressure from natural gases like methane. Though both theories are equally credible, the truth is a mystery.

33. The Suspicious Submarine

Sweden and Russia have always had a strained relationship. Back in the 1980s, Russia would sneak its submarines into Swedish waters to establish control in the Baltic region. That was years ago, but Sweden never forgot!

In 2014, when reports showed that a **rogue submarine** was lurking in the waters of the Stockholm archipelago (overseen by the Swedish Navy), Sweden immediately pointed fingers at Russia. The Russian embassy denied any involvement and tried to pass the blame on to a Dutch submarine. But this turned out to be false.

Who is sending its submarine to the Stockholm archipelago? Sweden is trying to figure it out but the answer is still unknown!

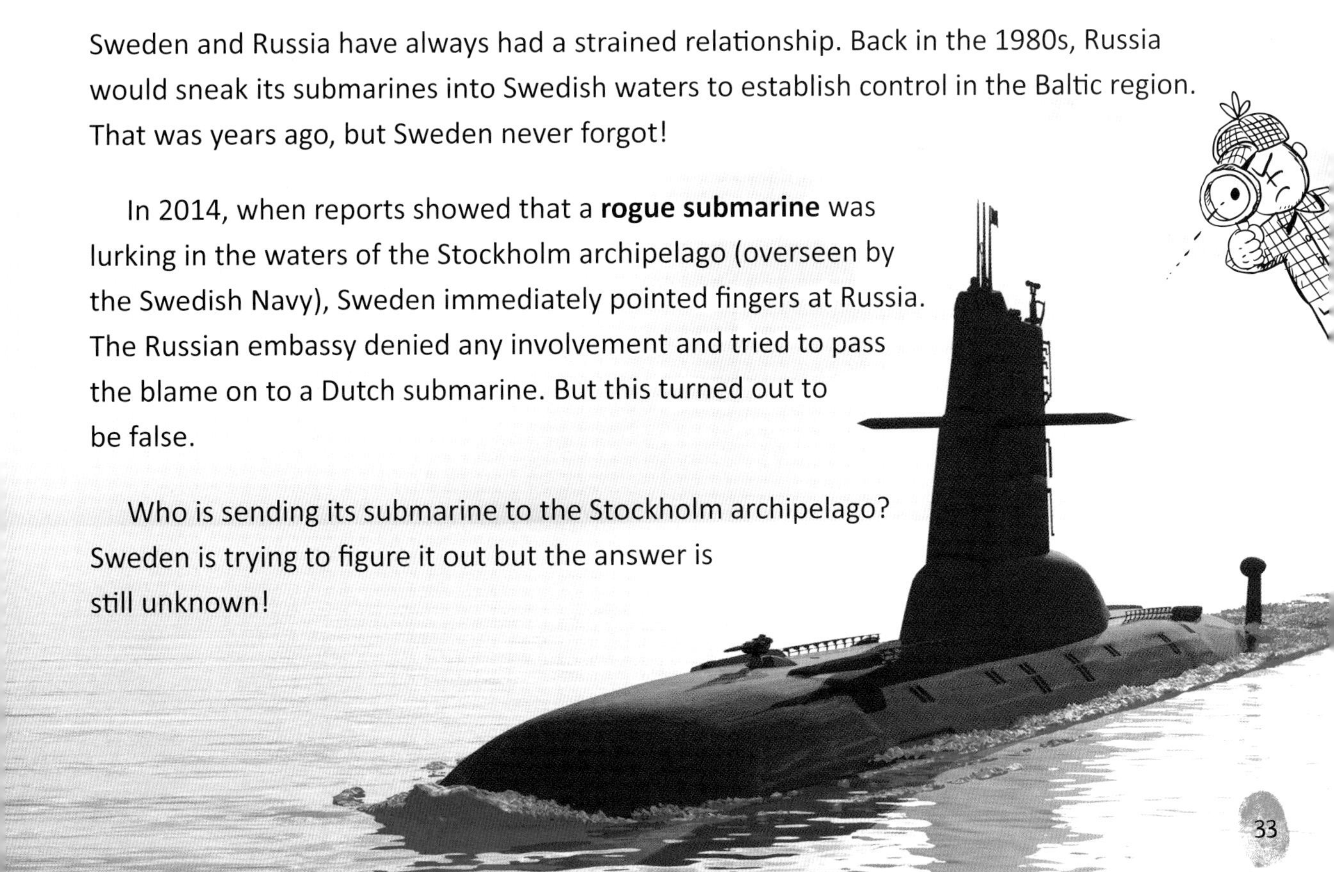

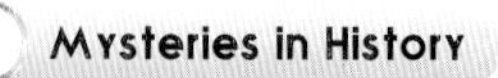

34. Missing Lighthouse Keepers

Have you seen a lighthouse? It might look lonely but there is always a keeper looking after it. This next mystery is about **three keepers** who looked after the Flannan Isles Lighthouse on a small island named Eilean More in Scotland.

On December 26, 1900, a ship stopped at the island to deliver supplies. A new keeper named Joseph Moore was to start work on reaching the island. The captain, James Harvey, along with Moore was surprised to find that the island was isolated.

They tried to call the keepers to the shore but nobody responded. Feeling worried, Moore checked the lighthouse. He felt very nervous as he got closer.

He saw that the door was unlocked. He scanned the area for the keepers but they were all missing. The kitchen clock had stopped, a chair was upturned and two of the three coats were missing.

He realised that a dreadful accident had taken place. He was too worried to wait around, so he wrote a letter to the authorities and fled. An investigation was conducted. This time, they checked the log kept in the lighthouse.

Apparently, a storm had hit the island. But this should not have troubled the three experienced keepers as they could have locked themselves in the lighthouse. Where did the keepers go? Why haven't their bodies turned up? The answer is still a mystery over a 100 years later.

FACT FILE

The final log entry was made on December 15th and read "Storm ended, sea calm. God is over all."

35. Mansion's Owner

After the Buckingham Palace, the second largest home in London is the Witanhurst Mansion. But who is the owner of **Witanhurst Mansion**?

Through research, we know that the mansion was purchased by a foreign company named Safran Holdings. Arthur Crosfield and Yelena Baturina were mistakenly named as the owners.

The mysterious owner has developed the mansion to include a large swimming pool, a modern spa and cinema hall. It is rumoured that the owner has spent more than the original price of the mansion. But why won't the owner come forward in public? This might always be a mystery!

36. Strange Lights

World War II was an extremely tense time. In most countries, citizens could look up to see fighter planes. Strangely, during World War II, there were **many UFO sightings** reported around the world.

For example, there was a Royal Air Force pilot who spotted strange lights that were flying directly towards his aircraft. He wasn't too sure where the lights were coming from, but he noticed that they were following his aircraft while maintaining a safe distance. He tried to evade the lights, but they seemed to be following the aircraft carefully. After some time, the lights disappeared.

Similar incidents were reported by pilots in the Solomon Islands. As the lights were not coming from aircrafts, they were reported as UFOs.

37. Erebus and Terror

Some ships have as much of a personality as their captains. Two such ships are the HMS Terror and HMS Erebus. These ships were used to conduct the Ross Expedition of 1839.

Once the Ross Expedition was completed in 1843, the ships were retired until 1845 when they were used for the Northwest Passage exploration. The Northwest Passage is a sea route that connects the Pacific Ocean and Arctic Ocean to northern Atlantic.

Both HMS Terror and HMS Erebus met a cruel fate while on this expedition. The ships were carrying nearly 129 men and three years' worth of supplies when they went missing. It took more than 160 years to find the ships again. While the search continued, many authors wrote tales about the ships.

The wreck of HMS Erebus was found in 2014, while HMS Terror was found in 2016. Surprisingly, HMS Terror was found in perfect condition. It was submerged in Terror Bay. HMS Erebus had undergone some damage.

Nobody knows exactly **what happened to the ships** or their crew. Researchers were only able to find two or three bodies that were perfectly preserved before they found the ships.

Apparently, both ships had an internal pipe system that supplied drinking water from melted ice. The water may have undergone lead poisoning. This is just a theory and nobody knows for sure what happened to the ships or their crew.

FACT FILE

Some researchers think that the poor maintenance of the ship killed the crew.

38. King Alfred's Remains

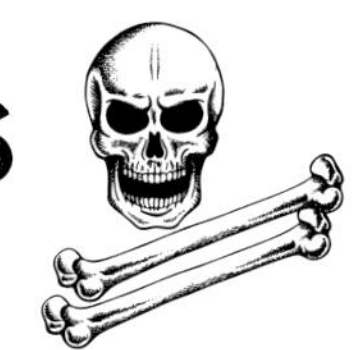

King Alfred the Great was a British monarch who died in 899. This was a long long time ago. But even today, historians are **in search of his remains**. He was first buried in Winchester's Old Minster. Then, his remains were moved to New Minster.

In 1098, New Minster was demolished so his remains were moved yet again to Hyde Abbey. Here they were left in peace until 1788, when convicts ransacked the coffins to find whatever riches they could sell. The bones were scattered out of the coffins and on the grounds. They might have ransacked King Alfred's remains.

Since then, archaeologists have tried to identify King Alfred's true remains. But so far, its whereabouts is one great mystery.

39. Hitler's Loot

Hitler was an infamous dictator who amassed a lot of wealth during his reign in Germany. Today, his **wealth** is estimated to be 19 billion dollars. But, nobody knows where it is.

He had stored his valuables in the German Reichsbank. After his death, his wealth disappeared from the bank. Some of the registered items were found spread across Europe.

So, where did all of Hitler's wealth go? As per one theory, it was Hitler himself who told his followers to take the wealth to maintain control over Germany. Another theory suggests that he buried it somewhere in a secret location. This location is still a secret to this day.

40. The Abandoned Lifeboat

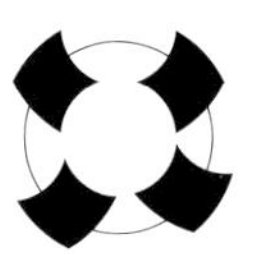

Have you heard of Bouvet Island? It is known as the **remotest island in the world**. This means that the island is so far away and isolated that you cannot find people there.

The island is covered in ice and is surrounded by the coldest ocean in the world. It doesn't support plant life so naturally; no human beings have settled there. The only time it has seen human life is when researchers travelled there for expeditions.

A strange thing happened there in 1964. Lieutenant Commander Allan Crawford, a British-born veteran, was sent to Bouvet Island to study a newly created lagoon. He took his team and reached the island by helicopter, which is the only way to enter and exit the area.

Here, the team saw a lagoon with an abandoned lifeboat. There were no markings on the lifeboat to give the team a clue as to where it came from or who it belonged to. Funnily, the boat moved with oars rather than a motor.

As he was on a mission, the Lieutenant decided to report the lifeboat and continue with his work. He also reported that there were no people or dead bodies on the island.

Years later when another expedition team was sent to the lagoon, there were no reports of the lifeboat. Which means that by this point the lifeboat either got destroyed without trace, disappeared or was moved. To this day, nobody knows what happened to the lifeboat or who it belonged to.

FACT FILE

Bouvet Island was named after Jean-Baptiste Charles Bouvet de Lozier who spotted the island in 1739.

41. Missing Cyclops

The Bermuda Triangle is an unsolved mystery. But, many disappearances from that area can be explained. This is not true for the **USS Cyclops**, one of four Proteus-class colliers that disappeared around that area during World War I.

The USS Cyclops was on its return from Brazil after supplying fuel to British ships in South America. After a stop at Barbados, it took off for its final destination in Baltimore when it disappeared. The date of its disappearance was recorded as March 4, 1918.

Along with the giant ship, its crew of 306 members and all its supplies went missing without any trace.

42. Wow! Signal

In 1977, technology was not as advanced as it is today. A researcher for the SETI was controlling the **Big Ear radio telescope** when he heard a very strong signal from the Sagittarius constellation. It was so strong that it lasted for 72 seconds.

Other researchers have tried to hear it since, but the signal was never reproduced again. After recording the signal, the researcher printed it out on paper, highlighted it and wrote "Wow!" That's how it came to be known as the "Wow!" signal.

Since then, scientists have floated many theories for the signal. Some point to aliens, others point to a passing comet 266P/Christensen. But the reason behind this signal is still unclear.

43. The Rohonc Codex

Have you ever tried to read a book written in an unfamiliar language? That's what it feels like to read a book that is filled with pages and pages of **mysterious code**. It's called the Rohonc Codex.

There are scientists who have spent decades trying to decode the book. They believe that the book is from a city called Rohonc in Hungary. The first time this type of coded language appeared in history was in 1743. It was written within the pages of a catalogue found in the Rohonc library. Here, it was kept within the prayer book section.

Again, in 1838, the Rohonc Codex made an appearance in the books donated by a nobleman living in England. He was a Hungarian by birth. However, it seemed that the man had acquired or purchased the book, because he could not share any information about the book's origin.

Researchers have tried since then to translate the book to either the contemporary Hungarian language or to the English language but all efforts so far have failed. In fact, over time researchers met with so many dead ends that they put up sections of the book on the Internet for amateur translators and sleuths.

Some believe that the Rohonc Codex was a book written by a prankster trying to create something like the Voynich Manuscript which is another strange book. Simply put, it either is a complicated book with a secret language or a hoax. Nobody knows for sure.

44. The Anonymous Poet

Many of you may have read the Christmas poem titled *Twas the Night Before Christmas*. This beloved poem is known to many around the world. But **nobody knows who the author** is.

When it was first published in a newspaper, the editor wrote that it was sent to them from an anonymous source. The poem gained some fame and then nobody read it again until it was published in a book written by a man named Clement Clarke Moore.

Some believe that the poem was written by him while others think that it was written by someone at the newspaper that first published it. The real author is unconfirmed.

45. The Gold Fort

Imagine a fort that has **170 billion dollars worth of gold**. Wouldn't you want to visit it? Well, this place might not have any gold at all. It's a real mystery. The Fort Knox, located in the US and named after Henry Knox, is impressive with or without all the rumoured gold.

It's about 109,000 acres in area and has lots of barriers and protection. The fort has been around for more than seven decades and is supposed to be America's only gold depositary.

The reason behind the big mystery is that few people have actually entered the vault. We don't know if they found gold there or if it is just a rumour to hide something else.

46. The Ancient Calculator

Can you imagine seeing a **mechanical calculator in Ancient Greece**? The technology seems out of place, as one of the earliest forms of calculators was an abacus. But there really was a complex calculator built in Ancient Greece.

The device is dated between 150–205 BC. It was discovered in 1901 from a shipwreck along the island of Antikythera in Greece. It is displayed in the National Archaeological Museum in Athens.

The Antikythera Mechanism is an ancient calculator. It is about the size of a shoebox. This device can show the user the date as well as the time in terms of the position of the moon and the Sun. It follows the lunar cycle and can predict the eclipses. Ancient Greeks used the device to find the date of the ancient Olympic Games. It was useful for astrological readings as well.

Just by reading its function, we can tell that it was a complex device. It was built with an intricate gearwheel system made of bronze. The system was packaged inside a wooden box. Historians are puzzled by the existence of the device. No other device of the kind had been seen until the 14th century with the invention of the mechanical clock.

Researchers have been pouring over every fragment of the device. Over time, the device broke into many fragments of which 82 have been recovered. Slowly, the function of each fragment has been learned.

FACT FILE

The Antikythera Mechanism is such a complex device that people could not believe it was from Ancient Greece.

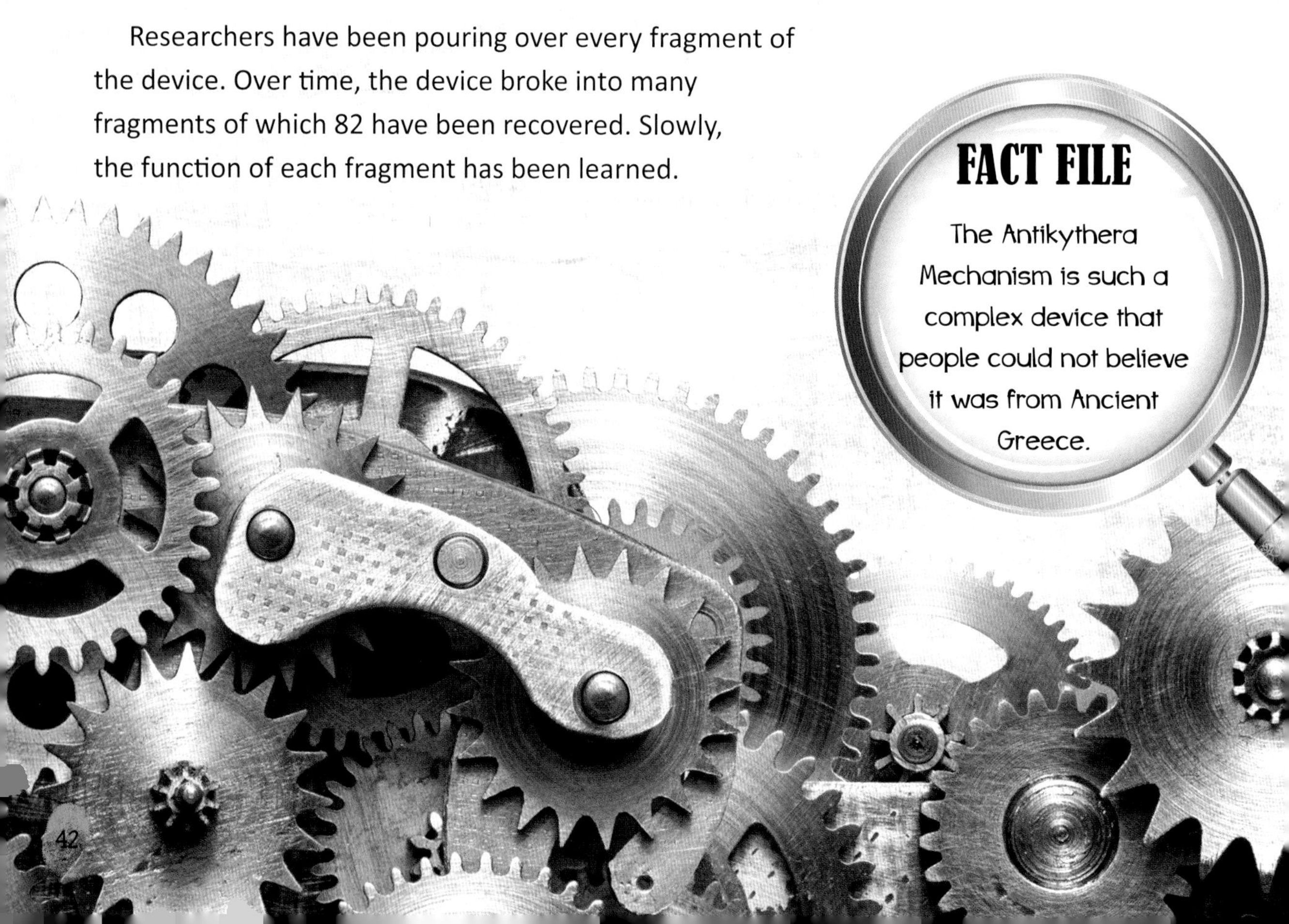

47. Underwater Sightings

Imagine spotting a dangerous creature while you are hundreds of kilometres away from land! That is exactly what the crew of HMS Daedalus sighted.

On August 6, 1848, Captain McQuhae of HMS Daedalus spotted a large **unidentified sea serpent**. This scared him and a few other crew members. They reported the sighting to the newspapers and described it as a large, four-footed creature that swam with its head above the water.

Though they could not see its body, they estimated it to be about 60 feet long. Was this a real creature or just their imagination? Nobody knows for sure!

48. The Stolen Plane

You've read about aircrafts that go missing or fight bad weather. But have you heard about a stolen airliner? Doesn't it seem very difficult to steal aircrafts? That's what happened on May 25, 2003 when an airliner that took off from Quatro de Fevereiro Airport in Angola was stolen.

The aircraft was **stolen in broad daylight**. Nobody knew who had cleared the aircraft for take-off. The Air Traffic Control, which was to look after the airliners, were clueless about how it all happened.

The biggest mystery about this case is who stole the airliner and why. That's right, nobody even knows what the motive behind stealing the aircraft was!

49. A Message from Aliens?

In 1977, something really exciting happened to a local news station in the UK. Its broadcast was overridden by a person who claimed to be heading the 'Ashtar Galactic Command'.

As the newscaster, named Andrew Gardner, was reading the bulletin, he felt a disturbance in the broadcast. While viewers at home could continue to view Gardner, his voice was muted and instead they could hear another voice delivering a strange message.

The voice reading the message identified himself as 'Vrillon' and went on to talk for **six uninterrupted minutes**. Meanwhile, the news station, the broadcast station and every transmitting team involved was trying to figure out what was happening. It was clear that they had been hacked! Authorities got involved into finding out who Vrillon was but nobody could solve the case.

There was another similar incident that took place in the US ten years later. The broadcast was taken over, this time by audio and video with a man named 'Max' speaking a similar message.

Again, a similar incident took place on the radio three years later. But this time instead of speaking a clear message, the intruder made strange noises and played sound-effects. He sang jingles from advertisements. People are not sure if Vrillon, Max and this person are connected.

However, it has been many years since these incidents, but nobody knows who they are, why they shared their message or what their agenda was.

FACT FILE

Vrillon's message was strange and it scared many viewers. This is partly how the mystery began.

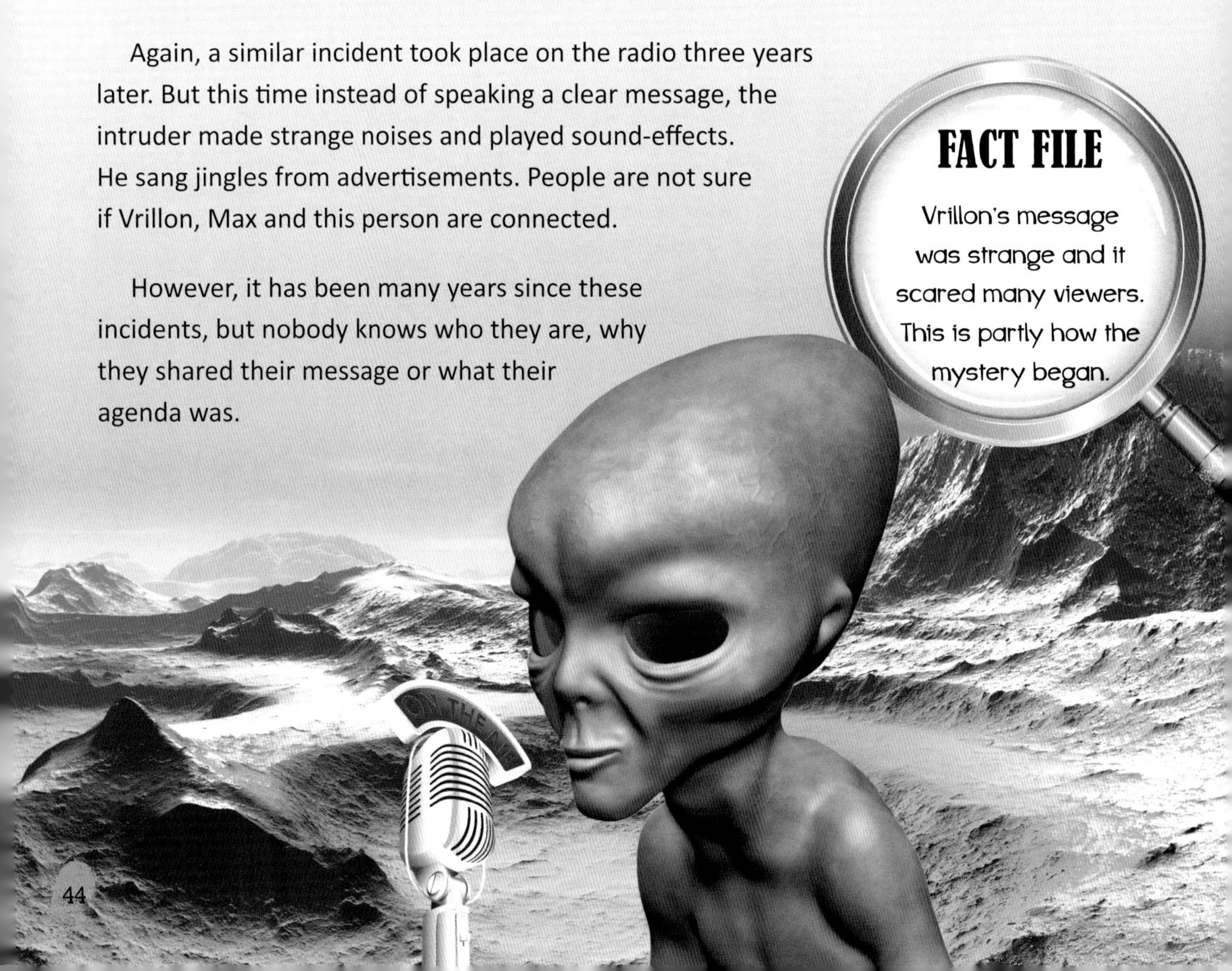

50. A Sunken Rose

King Henry VIII of England came into power in 1509. He was a fierce warrior who battled England's enemies with gusto. He built a large fleet of military ships to conduct battles and expand his territories.

The Mary Rose was one such military ship. In 1545, the Mary Rose was involved in the Battle of the Solent. Mary Rose was under the command of a man named George Carew who reported to King Henry VIII.

He led Mary Rose into a battle with French ships. Sadly, **Mary Rose sunk** during the battle. However, there are many conflicting reports as to what happened to the ship.

51. The Lost Rose

It is believed that **Mary Rose** sunk either because of unskilled seamen or that it was understaffed. It may be that Mary Rose was not only battling French ships but also bad weather. Later accounts of survivors say that the ship experienced terrible weather during the battle.

Another simple theory is that the French attacked the ship and it sunk. But this theory has been disproven by researchers who found Mary Rose in 1836.

The wreckage showed no signs of attack, but researchers retrieved several guns from it. So, people believe that the Mary Rose was overloaded with guns and canons. While these theories are plausible, none of them have been proven correct.

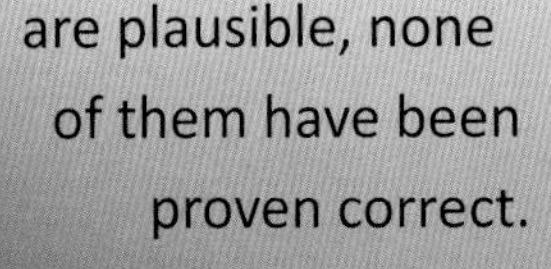

52. Roanokes Missing Colony

We all know about the colonisation of continents by Europeans. Often, people went missing in these colonies. But once, believe it or not, an **entire colony went missing**!

It happened in the August of 1590 to the Roanoke Island colony in North Carolina. It was established in 1587. It originally had 115 people. It was set up by a man named John White, a governor. He had to return to Europe for supplies for the colony.

It took him three years to return to Roanoke, but when he came back, the entire colony was missing, along with his wife and daughter. The only thing he could find was the word 'Croatoan' etched into a tree.

53. Jimmy Hoffa Disappears

It was a quiet evening in July. A man named Jimmy Hoffa stood outside a restaurant in Michigan, USA and made a phone call. He hung up the call and **disappeared forever**. No one heard from him again.

As he was a famous union leader and author, his disappearance shocked the country. The FBI has been looking for him since July 30, 1975, which was the date that he disappeared.

Could he have been kidnapped or murdered? Or did he simply decide to walk away from his life? It has been more than 40 years since he disappeared, but nobody knows where he went or what happened to him.

Mysteries in Archaeology

Archaeologists work tirelessly to find fossils and relics that could give us a glimpse into life in the past. These objects are supposed to answer our questions like, did we evolve from apes? How did the ancient civilisations collapse? How did people communicate?

But there are some objects that raise more questions than they answer. It's easy to dream up stories behind these relics, but difficult to find the truth. What's even more difficult to accept is that these questions might remain unanswered.

54. Stone Spheres in Costa Rica

If you go to the Osa region of Puntarenas, Costa Rica, you will see giant stone spheres scattered around the wild. Researchers believe that they were **created** in the Pre-Columbian between 500-1500 BCE.

Locally known as 'Las Bolas', these spheres have a diameter of 2.5 m. They were made from gabbro, a smooth rock formed from molten magma.

Some believe the rocks had religious purposes, while others think they may have been used to study astronomy. The truth is, nobody knows why these rocks were created.

55. Antony and Cleopatra

Cleopatra is a legend. She was the ruler of ancient Egypt – the very last in a long legacy of the Ptolemaic dynasty that ruled between 305 and 30 BCE. She was married to Mark Antony. Her life has been a subject of great interest. But there is an unsolved mystery around her death.

A common belief is that **Antony and Cleopatra were buried** together. They committed suicide after they were defeated in the Battle of Actium, by Octavian, in 31 BCE. After their death, it is believed, that they were buried together in a location in Alexandria. Nobody is sure exactly where the burial site is.

Plutarch, a Roman historian, came up with this theory based on his studies on the couple. He supported his theory by saying that Cleopatra had built a tomb for herself (a common practice among Egyptian rulers) and she was to be buried there after her death. The tomb was located close to her royal palace.

Historians believe that the tombs were lost when ancient Alexandria sunk beneath the ocean floor. An archaeologist named Kathleen Martinez, challenged this idea by saying that their tombs were buried in the temple of Isis and Osiris at Taposiris Magna. It is located about 45 km to the west of Alexandria.

It seems like a logical place for Cleopatra and Antony's tomb. It was a significant temple place for them. The real location of Cleopatra and Antony's tomb is still unknown, but there are several such possibilities.

FACT FILE

At the end of Cleopatra's reign, Egypt was captured by the newly established (Ancient) Roman Empire.

56. Mysterious Band of Holes

Archaeologists are interested in the strangest things. One of the mysteries that they have been trying to solve for decades is how the 'Band of Holes' came to be. These are a **series of holes** found on the rocks of Pisco Valley which is a part of the Nasca Plateau in Peru.

Locally known as 'Monte Sierpe' or 'Serpent Mountain', they are about 6000 holes carved into the rock. Nobody is sure about who made these holes or what their purpose could be. However, researchers suggest that they were either made for defence against approaching enemies or to mark graves. It is possible that they were also used for storage.

57. The Stonehenge Mystery

The Stonehenge has a very mysterious aura. At first sight, it's just **large pieces of stones** in the shape of horseshoes. They were laid out in concentric circles on a field called Salisbury Plain for nearly 4000 years.

Yet we know very little about why the Stonehenge was created. Historians believe that the Stonehenge could either have had astronomical or healing purposes.

While there are theories that the Druids built the Stonehenge, this cannot be confirmed. One clue to understanding why the Stonehenge was made would be to know who exactly made it. So, although we can estimate when it was made, we cannot confirm till date who built it or why.

58. Strange Nazca Lines

One of the biggest archaeological mysteries of Peru is the existence of **Nazca Lines'**. They are geometric designs made to look like humans, monkeys, spiders and birds. These are made with swirly and straight lines and shapes like triangles, rectangles and even trapezoids.

Archaeologists have spent decades trying to understand how these lines were made, who made them and for what purpose. So far, they have found 800 straight lines and 300 geometric figures that represent animals and plants. The designs are called 'biomorphs'.

The lines themselves are called 'geoglyphs'. Geoglyphs are drawn on the ground on a surface like rocks or earth. They might have been created nearly 2000 years ago by the Nazca people who lived from 1 to 7000 AD.

The lines could have been created for astronomical studies. A researcher named Johan Reinhard thought that this was a false explanation. Instead, the lines were supposed to point to places nearby where the Nazca people held their rituals.

Despite there being so many unproven theories out there, researchers are not disheartened. Reinhard once said that since so many archaeologists, anthropologists and historians were on the case of solving this mystery, slowly, but surely, it will be solved one day.

FACT FILE

Maria Reiche moved to a nearby area to protect the lines from stomping visitors.

59. Decoding the Voynich Manuscript

The Voynich manuscript is an **ancient document** dating back to the 15th century. Though its origin is unknown, researchers believe that it was from the Italian Renaissance period.

It has been more than a 100 years since its discovery and people have been trying to find out what the manuscript says. However, the words and illustrations of the manuscript are yet to be decoded for their meaning.

So far, all we know is that the document has six parts with information on medicine, herbology, astronomy, biology and cosmology. The final part is said to contain recipes. What are they about? That is as much of a mystery as the rest of the manuscript!

60. The Lost Collection 

Back in 332 BCE, Alexandria was one of the major cities of the world. It was the capital city of Egypt and a centre for Hellenic studies. Scholars travelled from different parts of the Mediterranean to study science and other subjects. The **Library of Alexandria** was a major part of the research institute of Alexandria.

A scholar could walk into the library and find a scroll among the many millions written about subjects like science, history, drama, philosophy and poetry. But then a man named Hypatia or Peter the Reader burned down the library for unknown causes. Now the entire collection of scrolls is lost to us. Researchers are trying to piece it together from what survived.

61. Sinkhole Full of Money

Sinkholes are formed when land collapses gradually or suddenly leaving behind pits or craters in the ground. Like the sinkholes in Siberia, there is a very famous sinkhole in Canada. It is located on Oak Island in Nova Scotia. It is called the '**Oak Island Money Pit**'. After inspecting the pit, people decided that it has a treasure buried deep inside.

Their first clue was that the sinkhole was surrounded by little signs and flagstones. The catch is that such signs were discovered more than 200 years ago, and the pit fills up with water every time it rains!

Someone seemingly dug deeper into the sinkhole once though. People have been digging this sinkhole for the treasure ever since. It is still not confirmed if the pit actually has treasure or not!

62. The Rongorongo Code

The Rongorongo code is an ancient language that archaeologists have been trying to decode for decades. **Decoding a language** helps unlock the wisdom, knowledge and secrets of an ancient world. There are several languages like the Rongorongo code that have yet to be decoded.

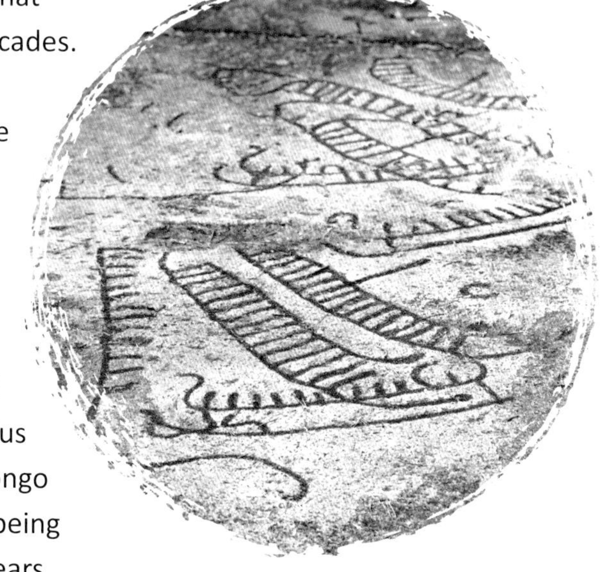

The Indus Valley script, which is the language used by the sophisticated people of this ancient civilisation, is another such language. It was used to document the lives and experiences of the Indus Valley people. What's strange is that the Rongorongo script is quite like the Indus Valley script despite being found near the Pacific Ocean. It was used 5000 years after the Indus Valley script.

How are the two scripts similar and what do they say? This is still an unsolved mystery!

63. The Mysterious White Horse

To archaeologists and historians, the **Uffington White Horse** is very important. Lying close to the mysterious Stonehenge, it is an elegant chalk drawing etched onto the fields of Oxfordshire. It is nearly 400 feet long.

This horse has been lying in the same place for 3000 years or more and dates back to the Bronze Age. If you are on the ground, you might not consider it very impressive, but try looking at it from a helicopter!

Everything about it is a mystery, including if it really is a horse! Could it be a dragon or a lion? Who built it and how? What was the reason? This is all unknown!

64. Secrets of the Sphinx

We have all seen the **Sphinx** in photos. Standing tall, it is a unique structure that has the head of a woman and the body of a lion. In mythology, it was said to be a creature without mercy that asked riddles to travellers. If they could not answer the riddles, they were eaten.

Today, the Great Sphinx of Giza poses one of the biggest riddles to the world. It is made entirely of limestone. The Sphinx has attracted the interest of archaeologists, geologists and Egyptologists (those who study ancient Egypt).

But none of them have been able to figure out when, how and who built this structure. No one's even sure about what it is supposed to be and what its use is!

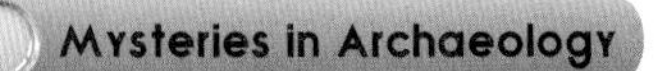

65. Big Mysterious Circles

Speaking of circular patterns, there's another one in Jordan that has researchers confused. It is appropriately named 'Big Circles'. It has a **diameter of 400 m**. There are many structures of this kind and 11 have been found in Jordan itself.

What's strange about these circles is that their walls are short and don't cover the entire structure. Archaeologists are not sure if this was purposely done. Any animal or person can walk in and out of the structure freely. Therefore, people think that it was used either as a settlement or for livestock or farming.

Researchers are trying to find out what exactly these circles were used for and who is responsible for them.

66. The Concho Stone

Sometimes archaeologists are bewildered with what they might find at an excavation site and how they should decipher what they find. That's what happened to a group of archaeologists who went digging in Glasgow. They found a **giant stone slab** which was at least 5000 years old!

The Concho Stone was massive with a height of 43 feet and width of 26 feet. It had intricate patterns described as 'cup and ring marks'. These same marks were found on other stones in other parts of the world, which helped archaeologists draw a connection.

Now many researchers are pouring over the Concho Stone to figure out what it's all about. Maybe one day they will solve the mystery!

67. Messages on Stone

'**Petroglyphs**' is an ancient method of writing which required a person to carve, pick and create incisions on the surface of a rock to draw symbols.

While there have been some efforts to understand this script, no one has been able to decipher it. Yet it appears on many stones. In North America, archaeologists discovered a curved soapstone structure with petroglyphs carved on the surface called 'Judaculla rock'.

People believe that the petroglyphs on this rock relate a message for future generations of humanity – this could mean the people of today! The script on this rock is sometimes confused with other markings.

68. A Super Structure

If you travel 4 km from the Stonehenge site, you will find the '**Super-Henge**'. It is a line of stone monoliths lined up for display. The site was found in 2015. It was buried beneath the Durrington Walls.

Some parts of the Super-Henge were damaged over time. They were originally meant to stand upright and at a height of 4.5 m!

Just like the Stonehenge, nobody is actually sure why these monoliths were laid out on a field. The real reason for it could be astronomical or it could have been meant as a sort of border. One theory is that they formed a C-shaped ground that controlled the flow of river or spring water.

69. Kite Traps

Back in 300 BCE, people had to forage for leaves and fruits or hunt for meat. Naturally, they used tools and traps to hunt for catch animals. But were ancient people smart enough to make long, complex traps?

That's the mystery in places like Jordan, Israel and Egypt where archaeologists have discovered somewhat similar looking 'kite traps'. They are **large stones** that have been arranged like walls. These walls stretch for nearly 64 km in some places and were probably used to funnel herds of animals like gazelles and other hoofed animals into pits or traps to be killed.

The traps are completely abandoned and were first discovered by pilots. No one can truly confirm if these structures were actually used to trap animals or who made them.

70. The Khufu Mystery

Historians can spend years studying ancient Egypt and still feel like they have a lot to learn and a lot of mysteries to solve. Just like the Sphinx, archaeologists have some information about the **pyramids** but there is a lot left to learn.

We know that the pyramids were built nearly 5000 years ago. One example is a three-pyramid complex where the largest of the three pyramids is called 'Khufu'. It was built for an ancient Egyptian pharaoh who ruled during the Fourth Dynasty. Built upon the Giza Plateau, the pyramid is estimated to be constructed of around 2.3 million stone blocks. It is said to have three burial chambers.

Archaeologists are still finding new tunnels and passages in these pyramids and uncovering more and more mysteries. One of the biggest unsolved mysteries is who built these structures.

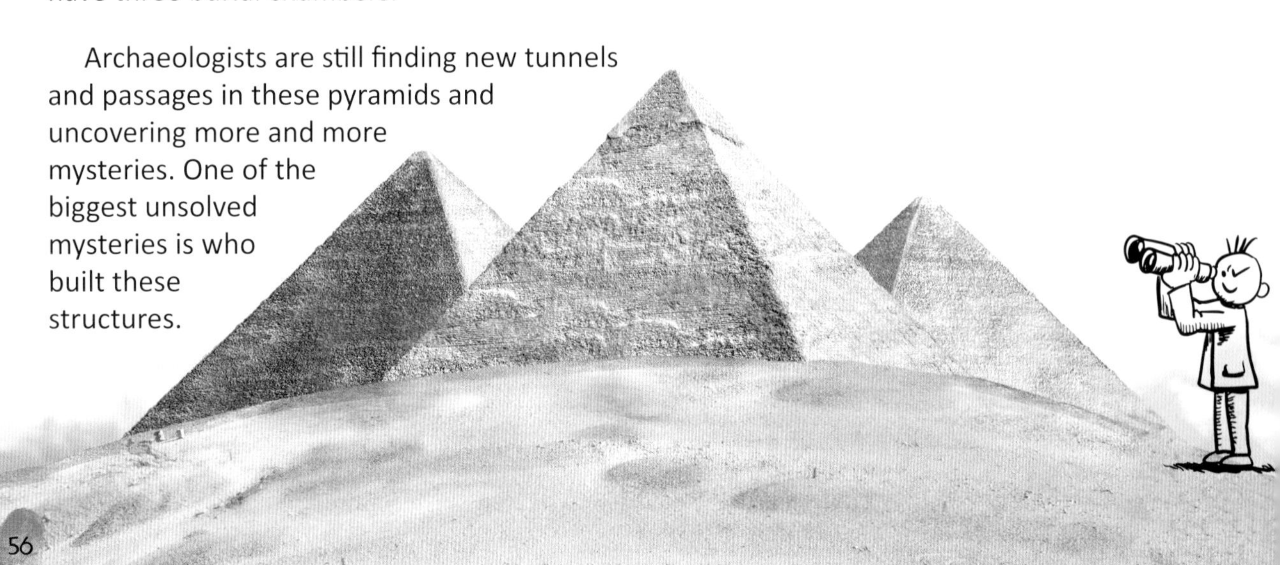

71. Shroud of Questions

Archaeology is not all about traps and jars. It is also about finding things that have religious value. One such archaeological find is the **Shroud of Turin**. It is a 14-foot cloth that bears a strange imprint.

It is been more than a century since a photographic negative of the cloth revealed the image of a body that seemed to have been tortured and bruised. To many, this image closely resembles that of Jesus Christ.

Indeed, the Shroud of Turin is said to be the burial shroud of Jesus Christ, in which he was laid after his crucifixion. Russ Breault was the first person who tried to confirm if the Shroud of Turin really bears imprints of Jesus. He had researched the subject for his college paper and since then has given many speeches about it.

The Shroud of Turin dates back to 1260 to 1390 AD. This possible date was determined by experts who conducted tests in the US, England and Switzerland back in 1988. The date also matches the first references to the shroud in 'church history'. This proves that the cloth comes from the medieval times. Now all that is left is to connect the dots.

But an Italian physicist named Paolo Di Lazzaro believes that it will be impossible to prove that the cloth is the shroud of Christ using scientific tools. Mystery will continue to shroud the shroud of Turin!

72. Jar of Secrets

What would you do if you suddenly discovered a **jar full of holes**? Who would make such a jar and what would you keep in it? That's what researchers are trying to figure out after finding a jar full of holes in a bomb crater outside of London during WWII.

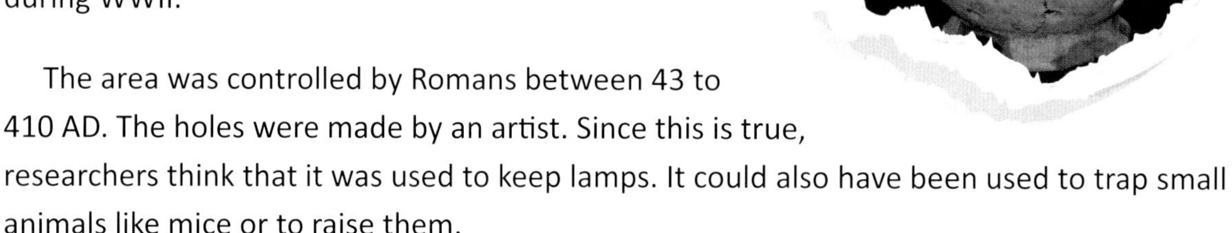

The area was controlled by Romans between 43 to 410 AD. The holes were made by an artist. Since this is true, researchers think that it was used to keep lamps. It could also have been used to trap small animals like mice or to raise them.

But these are guesses. This jar is kept on display in a museum in Canada where people are still trying to find out what it was used for.

73. The Lost Treasure

Imagine the joy of discovering a **treasure map**! That's exactly what people experienced when they went digging into a place called Qumran. In 1952, a copper scroll was found. It apparently led to a treasure of gold and silver.

Here's the strange twist; the map has proved to be useless in finding the treasure. Nobody knows where the treasure is and if it even exists. What makes the copper scroll so important is that it was found next to the 'Dead Sea Scrolls'.

Both maps are said to have been created more than 2000 years ago when the Roman Empire controlled the Qumran area. It is possible that the treasure was hidden from the Romans but it might be lost to us forever.

74. Temples and Settlements

For a long time, historians believed that human beings first began living in farming settlements, and only later built temples for worship. But there is an archaeological site in Turkey that challenges this idea.

In 1994, archaeologists came across **Gobekli Tepe**, an archaeological site which looks like a temple. It has huge stone pillars with animal carvings on them. The stones follow a ring layout. It is considered the oldest temple site in the world.

This site dates back to the 10th millennium BCE when nomadic tribes were still hunting and foraging for food and were still to discover farming techniques. The mystery here is who came first, the temple or the settlements?

75. Underground Cities

In ancient times, rulers built underground cities or pathways that led to **secret dwellings**. These served as a sort of backup plan in case they lost a war. Invaders could be brutal enough to wipe out the losing side's citizens. And that's exactly what the First Emperor of China did. That is also what the Byzantine ruler of the Cappadocians did.

In 2013, while working on a housing project, construction workers found the hiding place of the ancient people of Cappadocia in Turkey. While this area is still unexplored, it is possible that it had housed almost 2000 people.

Archaeologists believe that there are such underground tunnels and cities hidden around the world. They just need to find them!

76. The 'Lost' City of Atlantis

Just like Noah's Ark, it is possible that the city of **Atlantis never really existed**. Yet people have spent years trying to find it. Atlantis was mentioned in the writings of an ancient Greek philosopher named Plato. It is been 2300 years since his death, but people have tried and failed to find Atlantis, or prove that it doesn't exist.

In 360 BCE, Plato wrote about a city made of concentric islands that was connected by moats and canals. It was built by a half god, half human figure. The city was rumoured to have many precious metals. It had a thriving plant and animal life. The capital was at the centre of the concentric islands.

Plato claimed that Atlantis really existed 9000 years before his time. It was destroyed by a dangerous volcanic explosion and violent floods. His writing indicates that he believed the city to be real. Some believe he was talking about human conditions.

The description matches an area in the Aegean Sea in Greece in the medieval times. It was home to the Minioan civilisation and endured a great volcanic explosion after which its people suddenly disappeared. But there is very little conclusive evidence that links Atlantis to this civilisation.

A researcher named Charles Orser thinks that Atlantis is a hoax that people have fun with simply because every place on the map is said to be the location of Atlantis!

FACT FILE

The story of Atlantis was about how a rich civilisation was sunk by the gods as punishment for the unchecked greed and loose morals of its citizens.

77. Chest of Secrets

Have you heard of **the Ark of the Covenant**? It is written about in the Book of Exodus. The ark is described as a gold-encrusted wooden chest that stored the stone tablets of the ten commandments.

The chest was kept in a temple in Jerusalem way back in 587 BCE. A violent army led by King Nebuchadnezzar II attacked and destroyed the area. Nobody has seen the chest since then.

From the time of its disappearance, there have been several real and mythical searches for the chest. Some say that it was taken to Babylon by Nebuchadnezzar's army. Some say that it was buried in debris in Jerusalem. Others say it was destroyed. No one knows what happened for sure.

78. Screaming Mummy

When archaeologists discovered a mummy that looked like it was screaming, they immediately tried to **find out who it was**. They believe that it was Prince Pentwere, the son of a pharaoh's wife who was accused of killing the pharaoh.

This is yet to be confirmed. There are many contradicting clues left behind by the mummy for them to explore. Firstly, mummification was only for important people.

The mummy was covered in sheepskin, which means that the person did something wrong. It had an 'E' marking, which means it did not deserve an afterlife.

Could it possibly be that someone wanted the mummy to be honoured while someone else wanted it to be shunned? There lies the mystery!

79. The First Emperor's Tomb

Imagine being the person who discovers the lifelike statues of the terra-cotta army. You've made it! This marvellous display has attracted the interests of several researchers and archaeologists from across the world.

It has been four decades since its discovery, but this site still has many mysteries that are unsolved. One great mystery is about the creator of this intimidating army. His name is **Qin Shi Huang Di**. He was known as the First Emperor of China.

Have you heard about the Great Wall of China? It was built by the First Emperor. He was such a strong leader that he was able to unite all the feuding kingdoms of China under one country. He ended the feudal practices of his time. He died in 210 BCE.

The terra-cotta army display was his idea as well. No wonder his subjects wanted to honour him with an extravagant mausoleum to show their respect even after his death. It's actually at the same site as the terra-cotta warriors and is estimated to be about 98 km^2.

The problem is that the mausoleum is sealed completely by a pyramid-shaped structure. No one has entered the mausoleum or seen the emperor's tomb. This is because the mausoleum probably contains high levels of mercury, and it is unsafe for people to excavate the tomb. However, there are so many treasures and mysteries hidden there that someone is bound to find a way to enter the mausoleum soon!

FACT FILE

The site also has many graves that belong to labourers, prisoners, princesses and common subjects.

80. Mercury Life 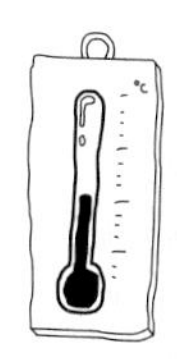

Will the First Emperor's tomb ever be explored? This is another unanswered question. This decision remains with the government of China. Though there are many archaeologists around the world who have shown interest, the Chinese government has held them off because of the high mercury levels found in soil samples around the area.

Whether it's true or a myth, many researchers believe that inside the mausoleum is a '**River of Mercury**' or something like it.

In Ancient China, people believed that taking liquid mercury could make them immortal. In reality, the First Emperor died at the age of 39 because he took mercury pills!

81. Mysterious Looks 

Historians rewrite or exaggerate truths about powerful leaders once they die. The same could have happened in the case of **Qin Shi Huang's appearance**. He died at a young age, so some historic records say that he was a tall and handsome man while others say that he was short and ugly.

The first book that described his appearance was written by the Han Dynasty whose people did not like him. So, the writers themselves wrote different descriptions where some were flattering and some were unflattering. It is also possible that modern readers have misinterpreted the language or tone of the accounts about Qin Shi Huang's appearance.

82. A Linear Mystery

Hobbits are said to be members of an imaginary species quite similar to humans. They are small in size and have hairy feet. Many of the ancient civilisations communicated by writing. But their script looks nothing like the one you are reading about on this page. Two **ancient writing forms** called 'Linear A' and 'Linear B'. They were used in some of the Aegean civilisations thousands of years ago!

Linear A frustrates those who are trying to decode it because many have been on the case for decades. Sometimes the problem could be that there are not enough examples to understand the script. But there are 1400 examples of Linear A, and that's plenty to study.

Now, researchers have been looking to technology to help decode Linear A. Once this mystery is solved, it will uncover many more.

83. Vikings!

Everyone knows that America was 'discovered' when Christopher Columbus took a wrong turn on his way to India. Its history is traced back to this period. But, recent discoveries could change America's entire origin story.

Explorers have already found some **Viking settlements** in North America. This was a big deal for historians because it forced them to rethink some Norse legends. The real influence of Vikings in the Americas is still to be explored.

Researchers are trying to find other settlements near the Atlantic Coast to solidify their case that Vikings either lived here or passed by. Now the mystery is what were Vikings doing in North America and how does this change the history of the Americas?

84. When did Hobbits Exist?

Hobbits became popular because of 'The Lord of the Rings' series. Do they really exist? Some **archaeological evidence suggests** that hobbits could have actually existed.

In 2003, when archaeologists went digging in Indonesia, they uncovered bones from an ancient hominin 'Homo floresiensis'. The bones were apparently from an adult woman who was 3.5 feet tall.

At first, researchers looked for signs of illnesses. But when they found none, they concluded that Homo floresiensis were a type of human species that existed in the past. Researchers dubbed them as 'the hobbits'. The mystery is, when did they exist and what happened to them?

85. The 'Lost' Ark

We have all heard the Bible story about **Noah's Ark**. In the 'Book of Genesis' it is described as the vessel that saved Noah, his family, and the remaining animals in the world from dangerous floods.

Some people think that it is just a mythical ark while others believe that it really exists. Like UFOs, there have been many sightings of Noah's Ark. The most popular sighting has been reported in a place called Mount Aarat in Turkey.

This is a natural place of interest, as in the 'Book of Genesis', Noah's Ark is said to have come to rest there. But while some believe that they can find the ark, others doubt it was ever built. The ark remains a mystery to this day.

86. Elusive Gardens

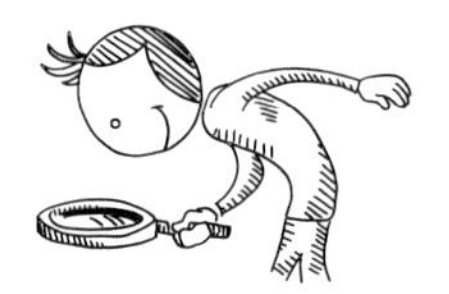

Near the royal palace of Babylon were said to be the beautiful **Hanging Gardens**...or were they? Their mere existence is a big mystery, and yet some researchers are very confident that they exist. They have mapped out the gardens, and created drawings of the structure and location. But these drawings varied from person to person.

While some thought that they were contained within the four walls of the royal palace, others thought that they were beautiful rooftop gardens. The latter explains the name 'Hanging Gardens'.

The key to finding the gardens is to discover the location and find out who built the gardens. There are several theories behind this as well like King Nebuchadnezzar II or Queen Sammu-ramat.

These names were found from the descriptions written by authors from the Classical period. Early theories explained how the gardens were built and how they were maintained. Apparently, the gardens were watered by an intricate irrigation system connected to a well and several chain pumps.

On the other hand, later theories say that they were false. Instead, they were built on sloping stones that were supposed to look like green mountains. The irrigation system was an early version of the 'Archimedes screw'.

FACT FILE

The Archimedes screw is an ancient machine that raised water at an angle.

87. Plain Old Jars

Most of you have all seen jars. But wouldn't you be amazed to see **giant stone jars spread across a plain**? The aptly named 'Plain of Jars' is a site in Xiangkhoang Plateau which has a large number of stone jars spread across it.

Found in Laos, it is one of the most interesting sites of the region. Archaeologists have named this site a 'megalithic landscape' which means that it's a site that has a lot of large stones constructed onto it.

Their origin is a big mystery. Who built them and why? Researchers think that it was a burial site. Those who dug into the jars have found human bones, burial goods and ceramics to support this theory. But who really built them?

88. Strange Extinction

Have you heard the term 'survival of the fittest'? Now look at a **mammoth** and try to guess why they went extinct. That's what a lot of researchers want to know because these ice-age giants ruled the world back in their time.

While some think climate change was the culprit, others think it was human beings that slowly killed them off until they all died. However, there are strong counter-arguments to both these theories. The problem is that there is not enough data to figure out what the real cause of extinction was!

Until researchers find more samples (that means uncover deeply buried mammoth bodies), the answer will remain a mystery.

89. The Boy Pharaoh

Few mummies have created so much excitement in the hearts of archaeologists. Once it was discovered, **King Tutankhamun's tomb** was rumoured to have a curse that killed anyone who tried to explore it. After people got over this fake belief, they carefully explored the tomb, as much as technology allowed them to.

They found that King Tut had a fascinating life where he came into power at the tender age of nine and married a relative. He spent a lot of his time trying to undo the religious revolution his father started, because he believed that the Egyptian gods were getting angry.

He apparently had some disease or abnormality growing up which meant that he was always sick. He surely had a walking disorder because several walking aides and canes were discovered in his tomb.

What's strange about the tomb is that the linen wrappings of his mummy caught fire years and years after his tomb was sealed. This, along with that fact that his death was supposed to be unexpected, gives researchers the idea that the tomb was originally meant for someone else.

He was probably mummified in a hurry, which is why the embalming oils that were meant to preserve the mummy failed and let nature take its course, in a tightly sealed tomb with reactive oxygen in the air. Will archaeologists discover other bodies if they continue digging?

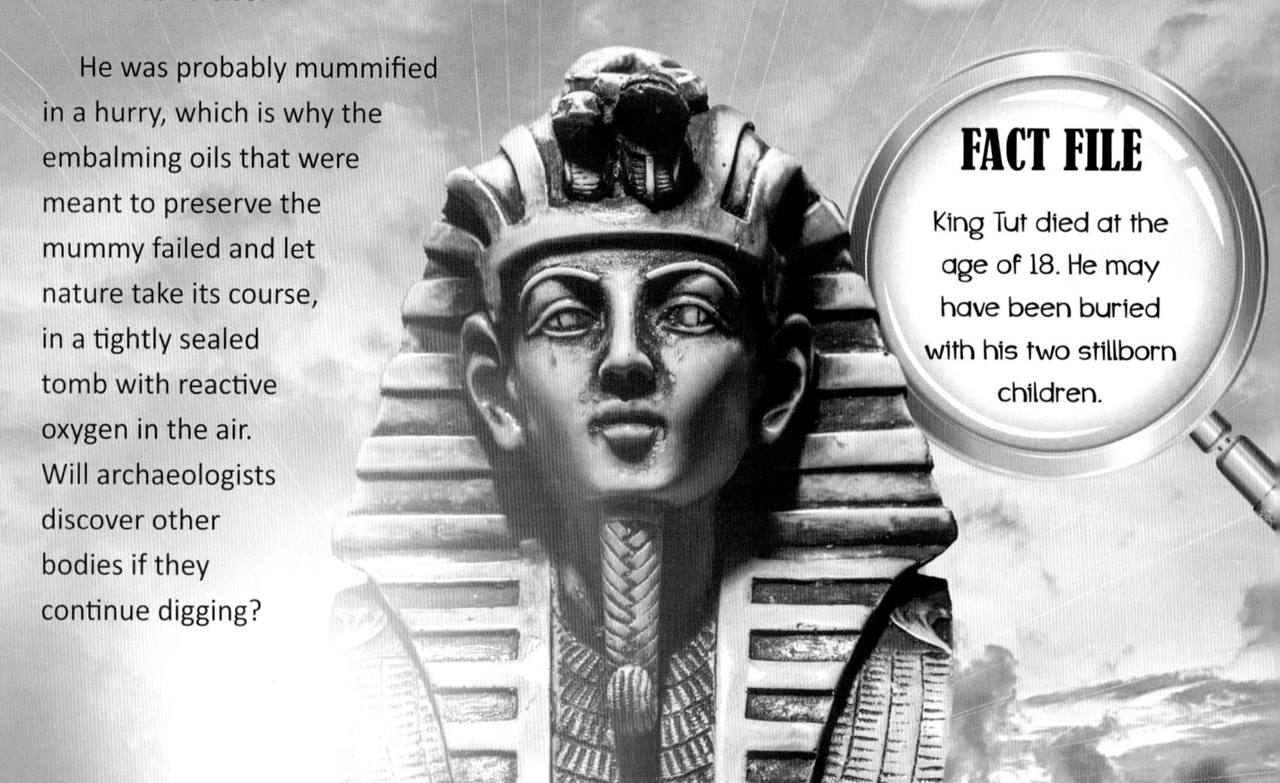

FACT FILE

King Tut died at the age of 18. He may have been buried with his two stillborn children.

90. Sanxingdui

'Sanxingdui' is the name given to an archaeological site that created a lot of confusion among researchers. Earlier thought to be a site for discoveries from the ancient Bronze Age, it was later found out to be the site of a big ancient Chinese city.

Today, this site can be found in Sichuan in China. All the artefacts found here so far have been remarkable and unique, so researchers have claimed that it is from a separate culture altogether known as the 'Sanxingdui Culture' which could have been a part of the Shu kingdom.

Such a unique discovery has challenged the traditional timelines and history of the ancient Chinese culture. The real story is still a mystery.

91. Strange Cairns

Not only do archaeologists dig, they also dive deep into the ocean to find mysterious treasures. Or at least, they hire divers to do it and wait patiently to find something like the **giant stone structure** found in the Sea of Galilee.

The stone is about 10 m in height and weighs 60,000 tonnes. It is a complicated artificial structure and has many small and big stones piled one on top of the other. Researchers want to know who built this structure, why and for what purpose. Those who have studied it believe it to be a cairn. The traditional use of a cairn is to mark a burial spot. The only problem is that they are usually found on land.

92. Lost Treasure

Long after the American Civil War was fought, historians and conspiracy theorists both had a common goal; to find out what happened to the **confederate gold**. This gold was worth millions of dollars, and it all went missing after the war. The treasurer, a man named George Trenholm, got arrested, but nothing was proven or found.

There were very few notes and coins that were saved. The rest of it went unaccounted for. Nobody knows what happened to the treasure. There are many myths about it. Some think that the southern states will rise again and the gold will turn up when they do. The real story behind the disappearance is unknown.

93. Moai Mystery

In 1722, an explorer was trying to find a place called 'Terra Australis'. He never managed to find that place, but what he did find was a really baffling island called 'Easter Island'.

The island was located literally in the middle of nowhere, or in the South-eastern Pacific Ocean. To his great surprise, it was inhabited by nearly 3000 people. What is even more surprising is that he found nearly **900 Moai statues** around for display. Each statue was nearly 82 tonnes in weight and 33 feet in height.

Researchers have long tried to find out how, nearly seven centuries ago, so many tall and heavy statues were built and carried to their destination. However, all attempts to find answers have failed.

94. Mayan Collapse

You might have heard of the **Mayans**. They were the ones who made the Long Count Calendar, which predicted the apocalypse or the end of the world. The Mayans belonged to the Maya civilisation. Their archaeological sites are mainly found in Central America today.

They were highly advanced people who created the hieroglyphic script. This script was the one and only developed writing system that existed in the Americas before Columbus accidently 'discovered' it.

They were known for their art, architecture and knowledge. Their calendars were made from an understanding of mathematics and the astronomical system. This great civilisation existed for nearly six centuries and then suddenly disappeared.

Archaeologists have been trying to find out why this happened. Early theories suggest that the collapse came about because of droughts. The ancient Mayans cut down forests to make room for more people and to build cities. This may have worsened conditions.

Other researchers think that the reason behind the decline could be slower and more people-oriented. The trade routes might have shifted while weak leaders were put into power. Historians report political unrest and conflicts that might have been worse than what is so far stated. It could be that the political conflicts and shifting trade priorities helped to bring on the decline of this civilisation.

FACT FILE

A cycle of the calendar ended at 2012 which people thought meant the end of the world.

The real reason for the decline or collapse of this civilisation is unknown. But, archaeologists might be able to find out because of the preserved sites.

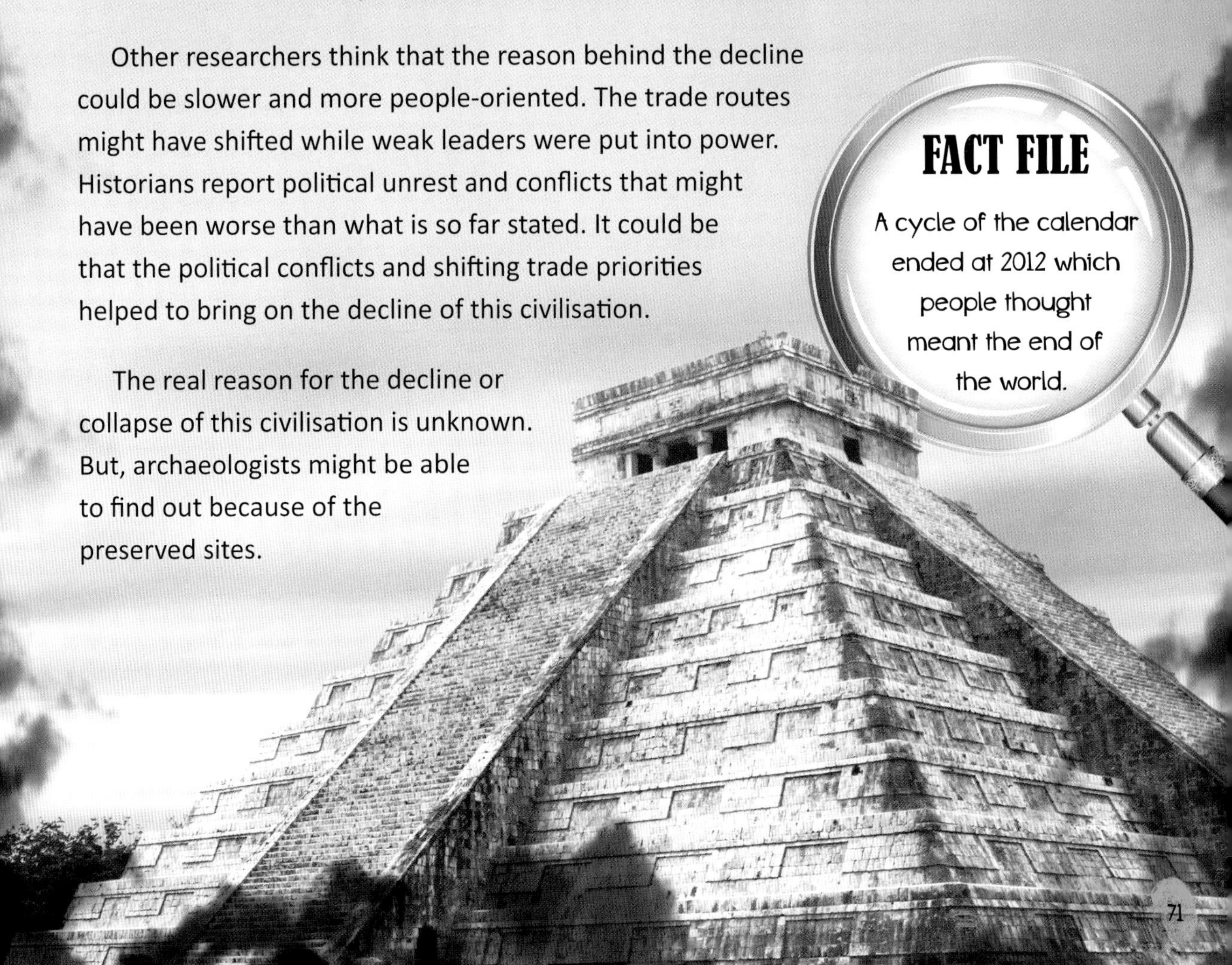

95. Genghis Khan's Tomb

Genghis Khan lived a very interesting life. He made sure that even in death, he remained interesting. Before he died, he apparently informed his soldiers that he should not be found. So, they **buried him in a secret location**.

Of course, some people might have figured out the area in which he was buried. Whoever tried to find the burial tomb was murdered by his soldiers. They even went ahead and killed the people who built the monument and tomb. Once they were sure that no one would find the tomb, they killed themselves.

It has been eight centuries and we still don't know where Genghis Khan was buried. This has not deterred the archaeologists who really want to know about Khan's final resting place. The desire to find his tomb increased a hundredfold when they found Genghis Khan's palace.

Not just archaeologists, but even common people are interested in finding his tomb. A lawyer from the US formed a dedicated team that opened 60 tombs of past Mongol warriors.

You might wonder why everyone is so determined to find the tomb. That's because there are reports that Genghis Khan was buried with unique treasures from his empire. Archaeologists however want to find the tomb to see if there are any documents and items that could help them understand the past better.

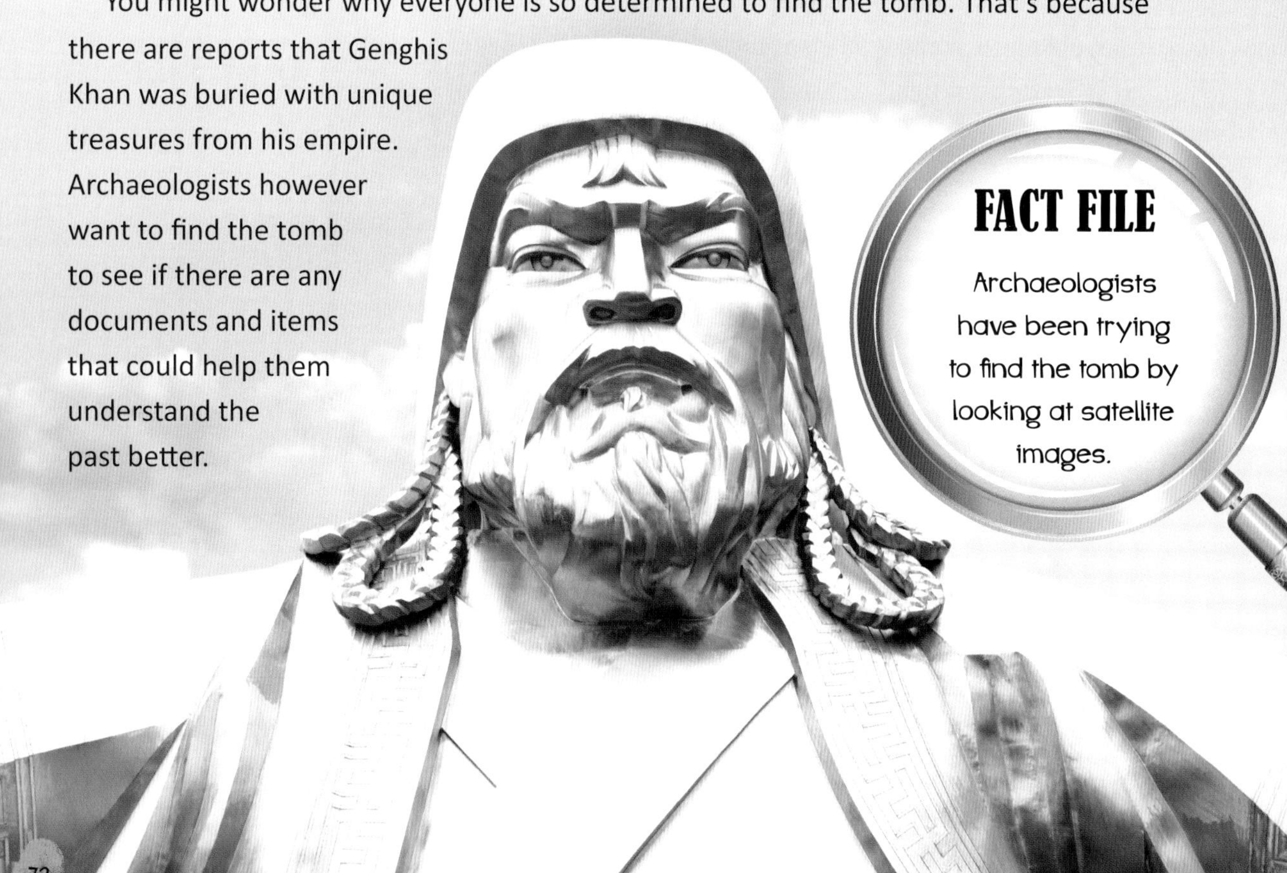

FACT FILE

Archaeologists have been trying to find the tomb by looking at satellite images.

96. Before Franklin 

Long before Benjamin Franklin tinkered with metal, people in the Mesopotamian region invented the '**Baghdad batteries**'. They were discovered by archaeologists in 1936, and were dated to 2000 years before the invention of the lightbulb.

The Baghdad batteries were clay pots that had iron nails wrapped in copper sheets. It is possible that they poured a liquid into the jar that had acidic properties and could generate an electric current.

The twist is that nobody knows if the pots were used for electricity, or if they were successful in generating an electric current. Did ancient people use a type of electricity? That still remains a mystery.

97. Sea People 

The **Bronze Age civilisation** was a time when the Minoan, Mycenaean and Canaanites ruled the Mediterranean and Aegean region. It was a very advanced time in ancient history when new scripts, languages and art forms were formed, and art, architecture and knowledge flourished.

Then the entire Bronze Age collapsed. Though there are many theories about this, there is one thing that is for certain. A mysterious group of people known as 'Sea Peoples' played either a minor or major role in the collapse.

Researchers believe that they were inferior and relatively illiterate people whose only interests lay in capturing land and increasing their wealth. Yet, they seemed to have set back the progress made by these cultures.

98. Gold Discovered

In 2014, a couple in California, USA, discovered that there was 10 million dollars' worth of **gold buried in their backyard**. It came from the 1400 gold coins that were hidden in eight tin cans. They were not at all sure who put those coins there, but after some tests they found out that it was put there nearly 100 years before they moved into the house. This could have been around 1901.

What is strange is that around the same time in 1901, gold coins of somewhat similar value were stolen from the US Mint. The mint was located in San Francisco, at the time. A man named Walter Dimmick was charged with the robbery of the gold, but he could have been falsely accused.

99. Phaistos Disk

Imagine finding an ancient 4000-year-old disk that has writings all over it, **but not being able to read it**. This was the case in 1908, when someone discovered the Phaistos Disk in the island of Crete, Greece.

The disk was traced back to 1700 BCE and was said to be a part of the ancient Minoan culture. A man named Dr Gareth Owens led the team that was trying to read what was on the disk.

In 2014, the team announced that they had cracked the code after six years. It could be a prayer to a goddess. Strangely, while we now have some idea of what the text says, we don't know what its purpose is.

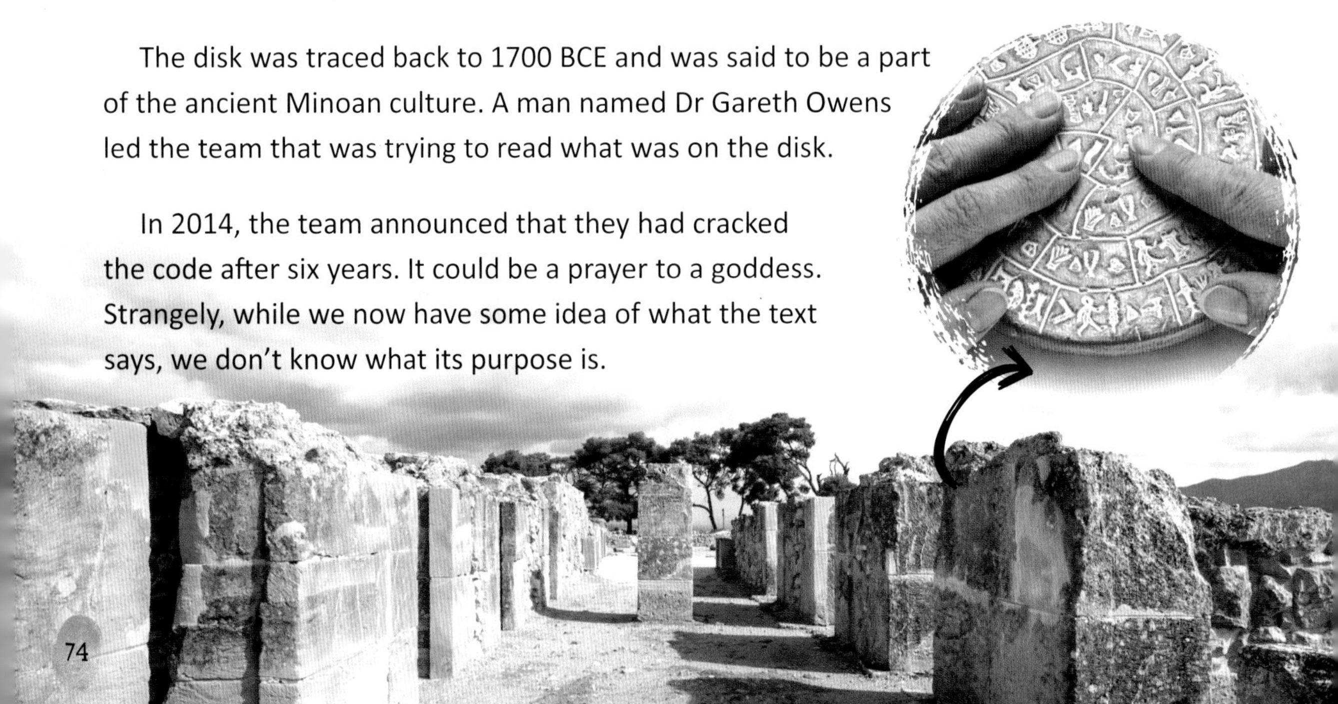

100. Bimini Road

In 1968, some divers went deep into the waters in the Bahamas and found something interesting. Off the coast of a beautiful island named **Bimini Island** the divers found a path laid of limestone slabs.

The slabs were spread over a kilometre. After some testing we now know that these slabs were not a work of nature and were in fact laid down by people. Yet, people still claim that it has to be natural because the alternate explanation is slightly weird.

People claim that the path leads to the lost city of Atlantis which may or may not exist. Others say that it was a secret path to an ancient civilisation. Which of these theories is true is still unknown.

101. Star of Bethlehem

What is the **Star of Bethlehem**? Is it just a religious myth, or can it be linked to a real star? This has been a question that many religious people and scientists have asked.

If you believe in the gospels, the Star of Bethlehem is the Christmas star that influenced the wise men from the East to travel to Jerusalem, where they met King Herod. According to a German astronomer, Johannes Kepler, the star is actually a series of three planets that seemingly came together. The star was also reported by ancient Babylonians.

Frederick further studied Kepler's claims to link the Star of Bethlehem to a triple conjunction of Jupiter with a star called Regulus. But this is still unconfirmed.

102. Columbus' Remains

Christopher Columbus had an eventful life. He also had a very eventful 'afterlife'. There are lots of controversies surrounding him and his past deeds. One such controversy is about his **final resting place**.

After his death, his remains were moved and sent to different places by his son and others. Because of this, and some mistakes in packaging, it is possible that the final place of his remains is a mystery. It is also possible that they may be scattered in two different places, namely Spain and the Dominican Republic.

While in 2006, a DNA test was performed to say that the remains in Spain were genuine, the tests were not performed for the other remains. Could it be possible that some part of Columbus still rests there?

103. Santa Maria

Santa Maria is the name of the flagship led by Christopher Columbus' small fleet. It was travelling from Spain to find a route from the west to China and India. On the way, *Santa Maria* **crashed into a coral reef**.

The crew got out and boarded another ship and managed to save the cargo. They continued their historic journey to find the new route. But they left behind the wreck which has fascinated so many researchers for years since.

In 2014, a man claimed to have found it, but his claim was declined by the UN which strongly stated that it was not the wreck. Finding the wreck could mean getting more information on Columbus' travels.

Mysteries Around the World

Sometimes, when you visit another country, you hear of some local tale or mystery that you haven't heard of before. That's because they are rarely reported and don't cross the border.

Instead, these mysteries are passed on from one person to another. At times a lucky tourist will hear about it and carry it with him or her to another country. Or, someone writes about it in a book. That is the only way you hear about them. And that is probably the reason why they remain unsolved!

104. Lost and Green

During the 12th century, the people of Woolpit, England were greeted with a strange sight when a boy and a girl came to their town. Their **skin had a greenish hue**, and they spoke a strange language that the people of Woolpit didn't understand.

They only ate raw beans. Eventually, the little boy died. But the girl survived. Woolpit's citizens taught her how to dress, what to eat and how to speak English. Then she told them about how she came from a place named 'St Martin's Land' where there were more green people like her.

Was she telling the truth or making things up from a hazy memory? It is hard to tell.

105. Robin Who?

The tale of Robin Hood, a man who stole from the wealthy to give to the poor, is popular around the world. When you think of Robin Hood, you think of a man wearing green tights and carrying a bow and arrow.

But do you know that this story was possibly **based on the life of a real person**? This is the lesser known mystery of Robin Hood. Seems a bit unreal, right? Robin Hood is popularly known as an outlaw who won the hearts of many because of his generosity. He was a talented swordsman and archer. He was always followed by a band of 'Merry Men' who helped him on his missions.

The first time he ever appeared in print was around 1370 in a poem called 'Piers Plowman' by William Langland. But he is more popularly known for fighting the corrupt Sheriff of Nottingham and the evil King John.

The idea that his character was based on a real person came from passionate researchers who tried to find a Robin Hood-like figure from the past. They found the 'King Remembrancer's Memoranda Roll of Easter 1262', which pardons an authority figure for confiscating the possessions of a man named William Robehod who was considered a fugitive. Could this be Robin Hood?

There are several such references in documents found in the 13th and 14th century of people whose names and backgrounds look like Robin Hood. But it is difficult to find out who the real Robin Hood was or if he ever existed.

FACT FILE

Some criminals changed their names to match Robin Hood's to get some sympathy or create confusion.

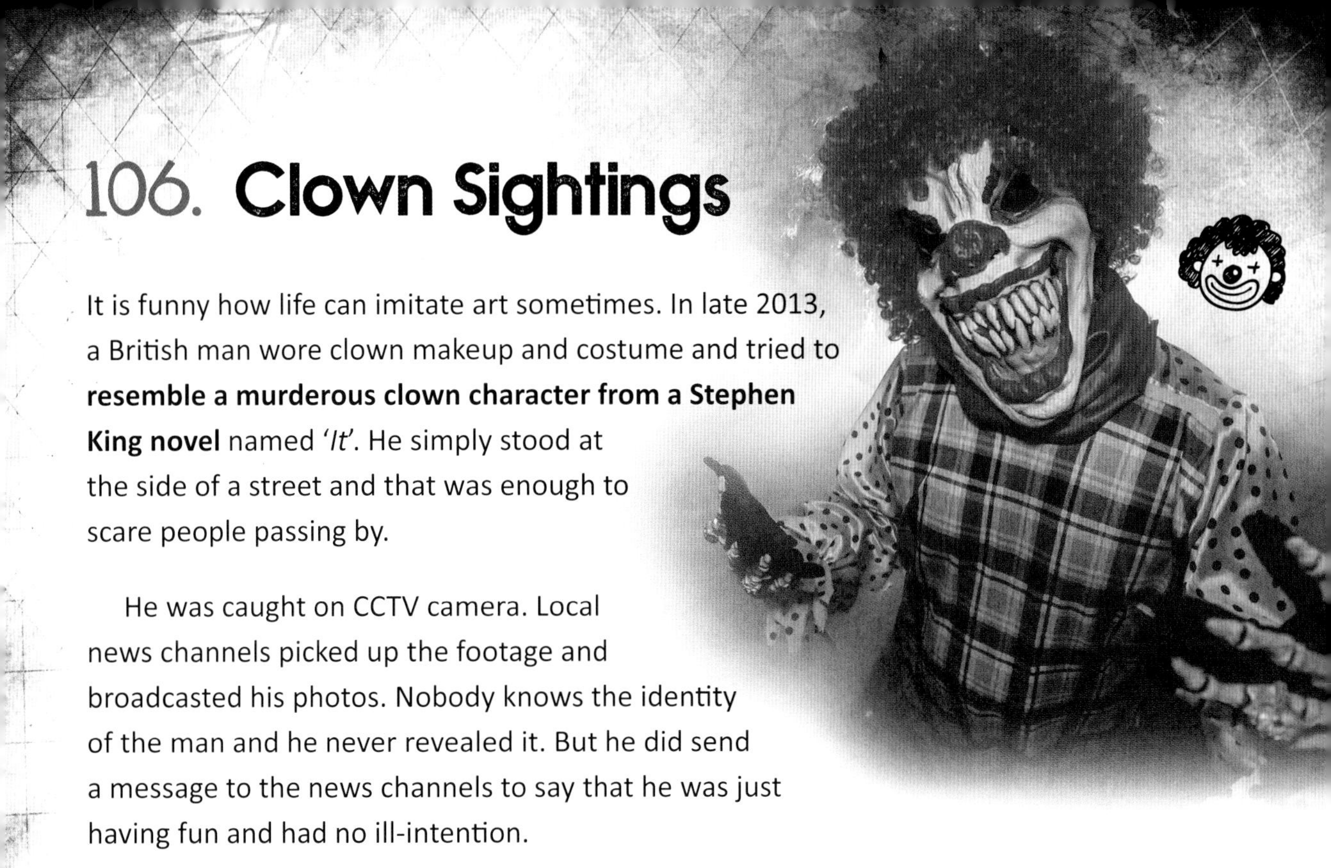

106. Clown Sightings

It is funny how life can imitate art sometimes. In late 2013, a British man wore clown makeup and costume and tried to **resemble a murderous clown character from a Stephen King novel** named '*It*'. He simply stood at the side of a street and that was enough to scare people passing by.

He was caught on CCTV camera. Local news channels picked up the footage and broadcasted his photos. Nobody knows the identity of the man and he never revealed it. But he did send a message to the news channels to say that he was just having fun and had no ill-intention.

107. Jumping Dogs

Overtoun Bridge in Scotland is home to a very peculiar mystery. Since the 1950s, several dogs have tried to **jump off the bridge** which is at a height of 50 feet. There is a waterfall below the bridge.

The jump is quite steep so only a few dogs can swim out to safety or are rescued. What is strange is that there is at least one dog that jumps off the bridge every year. They all do it from the same side. Another unusual fact is that the dogs are breeds that have long snouts.

While the local people would love to solve the mystery, it is so strange that they just don't know where to begin!

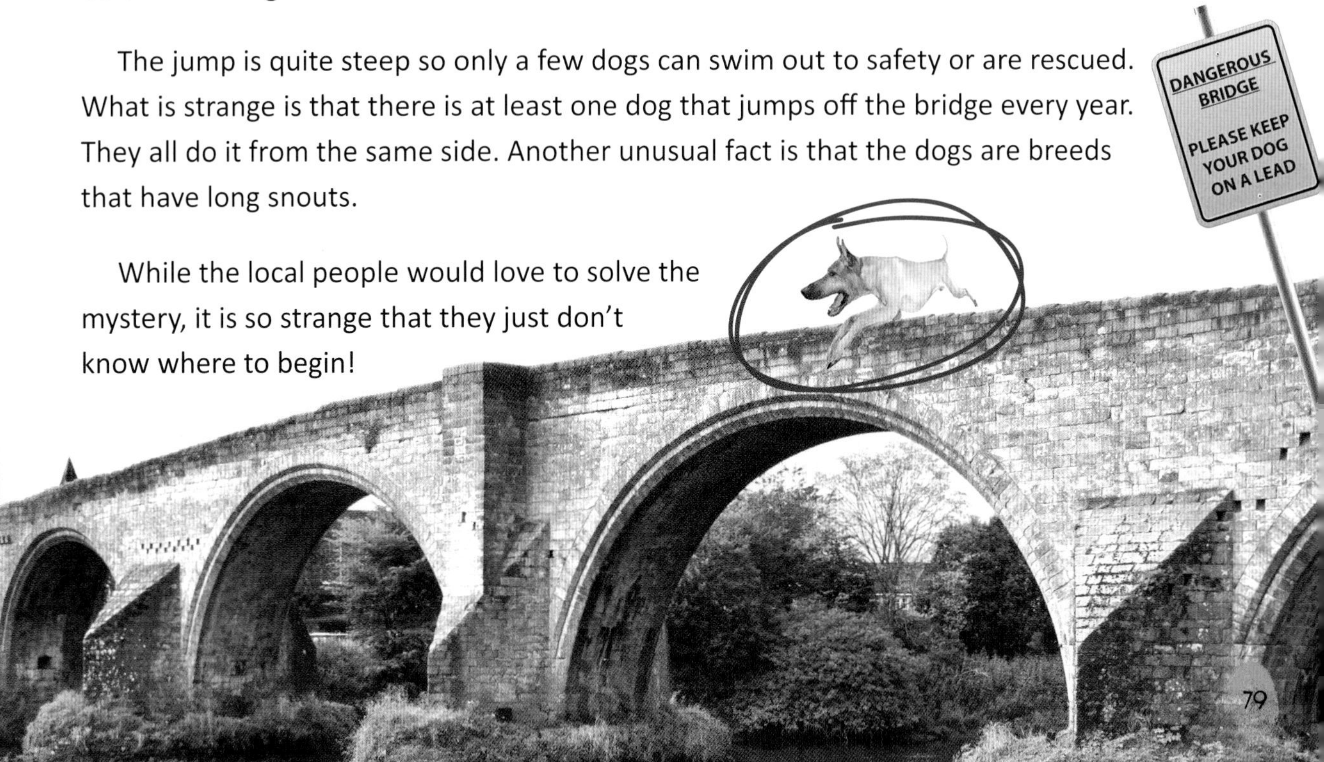

108. Strange Kaspar

Kaspar Hauser had a very strange and well-documented life. It all began on May 28, 1828, when he was walking down a street in Nuremberg. He had a letter on him that he took to a military captain.

What was strange was that he was barely able to walk. He was unable to use his fingers and he could not talk at all. When someone gave him food, helped him wash himself or cleaned his clothes, he would act like he had never seen such actions being done before. He was impressed by everyday things.

The letter he had on him was supposedly written by a labourer who had taken the boy into his custody in the year of 1812. There was also a letter from the boy's mother which stated his name and date of birth. His mother's letter claimed that his father was a deceased cavalry officer.

Kaspar was taken in by a man named Georg Daumer who taught him how to write, speak, talk and walk properly. He began to work and live a respectful life. Years later he died in an accident. But, strangely, the last words that he ever spoke could be translated to "I didn't do it myself."

This sentence could mean that the accident that caused his death, which was claimed to have been his fault, could really be someone else's. Kaspar's life was full of unsolved mysteries like where he came from, where he spent his youth and if he was killed.

FACT FILE

People made up tales about Kaspar's past and claimed that he was an exiled heir.

109. Cooper's Escape

A man named D. B. Cooper once hijacked a plane with a very clear plan in mind. He demanded **200,000 dollars to release the plane** and of course, parachutes. Once they were delivered, he asked for the rear door of the plane to be left open as they flew to Mexico.

He also asked for the plane to be flown low and slow. The plane was to make a refuelling stop in Nevada, so while they were descending, Cooper jumped out of the plane with the money and a parachute. The pinch was that he did it during the night time. There were no witnesses who saw him jump and despite heavy scrutiny, none of the policemen were able to find him ever again!

110. Devil's Mark

Imagine that it is very early in the morning and you are living in the year 1855. What would your reaction be to seeing **footprints** outside your home? The people of Devon were in for a similar surprise when they found marks that looked like the hooves of a strange animal in the snow.

These marks were spaced out at 64 km distances, and people were sure they were made during the night when everyone was sleeping. Nobody was able to find out who made these marks, but there were many theories which ranged from a prank to the work of the devil! What is strange is that the footprints were only from one foot.

111. Mothman

In 1966, four teenagers in America met with a hideous sight. They saw a man who looked **part human, part bird and part moth**. This man had really red eyes. Or so, said the teenagers as they only saw the man passing by on his way to another road.

The teenagers say that the man saw them, then began to pursue them by spreading his wings. They immediately reported the incident to the local police. Once news got out, the man was labelled 'Mothman'. Though the police looked for him, he was never to be seen again. A murder on the road where he was headed was linked to him and remains unsolved.

112. El Chupacabra

Have you heard stories from your parents about **scary creatures** that might come out at night and take away kids who don't go to bed on time? Or children who don't eat their vegetables? A lot of these creatures are taken from books and novels. Although not real, they are very useful when parents want to discipline their children.

So, imagine the surprise of some people in places like Mexico and Venezuela when they saw such a creature in the real world. Or at least, this is what they claim. Just like the Yeti and Loch Ness Monster, there is a creature out there called 'El Chupacabra'. It is hard to prove if the sightings were real or just made up.

113. Strange Lights

Sometimes, citizens of Texas, USA who live on Mitchell Flat see some strange lights called **Marfa Lights** floating in the air. Is it a trick of nature or are the lights artificial? This is a difficult question to answer.

The lights are big enough to be the size of basketballs. They are closer to the ground and would come up to the shoulder of an average-sized man. What is troublesome is that these lights keep moving quickly in strange directions. There is always a certain pattern that they follow.

Some people think that it is the work of aliens, while more rational thinkers claim that it is from traffic at the nearby highway. The real reason is still unknown.

114. Hessdalen Lights

Speaking of strange lights, have you heard of the '**Hessdalen Lights**'? They are seen in Norway in the Hessdalen Valley. They occurred for two years from 1982 to 1984. During these years, people observed the lights around 15 times every week. Nobody knew why these lights occurred.

What's special about them is that they are bright yellow in colour and sometimes, they float above the ground for more than an hour.

If you are lucky, you still might catch them as they occur around ten times every year. While no one knows why these lights occur, we can surely enjoy their beauty. They are quite rare and attract tourists from around the world who are interested in catching the Hessdalen lights at least once in their lifetime.

115. Mummies in China

We all know that important people were mummified according to Ancient Egyptian culture. Archaeologists have been studying mummies in Egypt for years. But the archaeologists who decided to settle in China and study the mysteries there, were in for a shock when they found some mummies there.

This is a lesser known fact about Ancient China. These mummies are called **'Tarim Mummies'**, because they were found in the Tarim Basin of a province in China. They were traced back to 1800 BCE. You would think that they were mummies of important Chinese people, but DNA tests reveal them to be of Indo-European descent. Apparently, the Tarim mummies belong to Caucasian people.

Today, the Tarim mummies, are displayed in museums in China. There are several Tarim mummies found near the Tarim Basin and other parts of China. What stands out about them is that they had reddish blonde hair. There were also some Mongloid mummies found around Ancient Chinese archaeological sites.

People were able to link the genetics of these specimens to the population of South Asia. It is possible that some of them were present during or lived in the Indus Valley.

Of course, very old texts from Ancient China tell us that they saw some foreigners from the West visiting them from time to time. But why were they mummified, and why were they kept such a secret? This is one mystery that is still to be solved.

FACT FILE

The interest in Tarim Mummies increased when it was mentioned on an American TV show called 'Bones'.

116. Taos Hum

This unsolved mystery is not well-known, but researchers from many different countries have been trying to solve it for years! In USA, United Kingdom and some countries of Europe, people sometimes hear a **low-pitched humming sound**.

This sound is described as a diesel engine left running despite the motor vehicle being idle. Is not it annoying to hear the sound and not know the source? That is why in 1997, researchers gathered Taos, in New Mexico, USA, to figure out where the sound was coming from but were unsuccessful. This sound came to be known as 'Taos Hum'.

Similar hums were heard in England called the 'Bristol Hum'. It was also heard in Indiana and was called 'Kokomo'.

117. Bird Mystery

A small village named Jatinga in Assam, India is home to a big mystery. Every year during the months of September and October, this village sees many '**bird suicides**'. Strangely, during the night, between 6 pm and 9 pm, birds simply drop dead from the sky.

The nights are usually without a moon and these birds seem to drop when they fly above a specific one-kilometre area. These deaths have been occurring for nearly a century, and the mystery of why this is happening is still not solved. It could be the result of a strong magnetic field or because of confusing night lights. But these are simply theories.

118. Alien Skulls?

A scientist named Vladimir Melikov of Russia found some skulls on Mount Bolshoi Tjach. This would not have been so strange if someone had not also found a Nazi briefcase nearby with an old map of Germany.

Another strange thing is that the skulls were misshapen and not like human skulls. Melikov reported that he hadn't seen skulls like these before. He also mentioned that the skull could resemble a bear's...or an alien's. That's how conspiracy theorists have found this report and spread it around the world.

However, when shown to palaeontologists, the reports were different. They said that the skulls could possibly have been buried or submerged for a long time under sand which could have led to their strange shape.

119. The Buzzer

There was once a Russian radio station named UVB–76 that only relayed buzzing sounds. It was first reported in 1982 when a person changed the station to hear this buzzing broadcast. For the entire day, all this radio station played was around **21 to 40 buzzing sounds per minute**. Each buzz lasted for a second and not more.

Strangely, the buzzing noises were interrupted by a man who simply read out some codes and Russian names. Was it some dangerous code? Was it putting lives in danger or helping heroes in need? Several people tried to solve the code but could not. The station still broadcasts today but the mystery is unsolved.

120. Dyatlov Pass Incident

A team of Russian **cross-country skiers** were going up the Ural Mountains in the Dyatlov Pass. They wanted to reach the Oroten Mountains in the Urals. It was supposed to take them a week. The entire team left together from their starting point on January 27, 1959. But they never completed their trip because they never came back alive.

They were found dead several days later. They had set up a tent on the way which was ripped apart. It was not that the entire team was found together, but they were found across the mountains. First, they found two bodies next to some woods. Their clothes and shoes were missing. It looked like they were returning to their tent.

Many months later, the other people in the team were found. They were buried beneath the snow. None of them had marks on their bodies and they looked peaceful and calm. Strangely enough, some of the bodies looked like they had exchanged clothes as they were wearing each other's clothes.

Some of the members died because of injuries done to them. While others died because of hyperthermia or extreme cold weather. Was it a murder or a big freak accident? All of the skiers were experienced, so what happened to them?

Conspiracy theories started spreading about the yeti finding the team and attacking them, but there is no proof of this. While the doctors said that an external force killed some of the members, nobody knows what the external force is.

LOST

FACT FILE

The Dyatlov Pass Incident has become a topic of interest in Russia and has been featured in movies and television shows.

121. London Stone 

Have you heard of the 'London Stone'? It is found in London at 111 Cannon Street. There is a gate that you must find on this street. The gate is in front of the wall of an old building that had office spaces.

If you cannot go to London right now, maybe you can look it up on Google Maps. That is what a lot of people are doing to figure out the origins of the London Stone. This stone is apparently thousands of years old. It is sometimes called '**Stone of Brutus**' because according to local stories, it was built by Brutus the Trojan. He was the so-called founder of the city of London (this is unproven).

The stone was written about by Shakespeare, Dickens and Blake in their literature. Apparently, the stone was used to measure distances from London to other nearby places. There is also an ancient myth that says that if the stone is safe then the city of London is safe.

That is why the stone has been moved several times by authorities. Surprisingly, the stone was safe even though a massive fire struck London. It might be moved again for safety. There are many superstitions attached to the stone.

While nobody has been able to find the origin of the stone, the mystery of its origin almost feels unimportant because people are very attached to the stone.

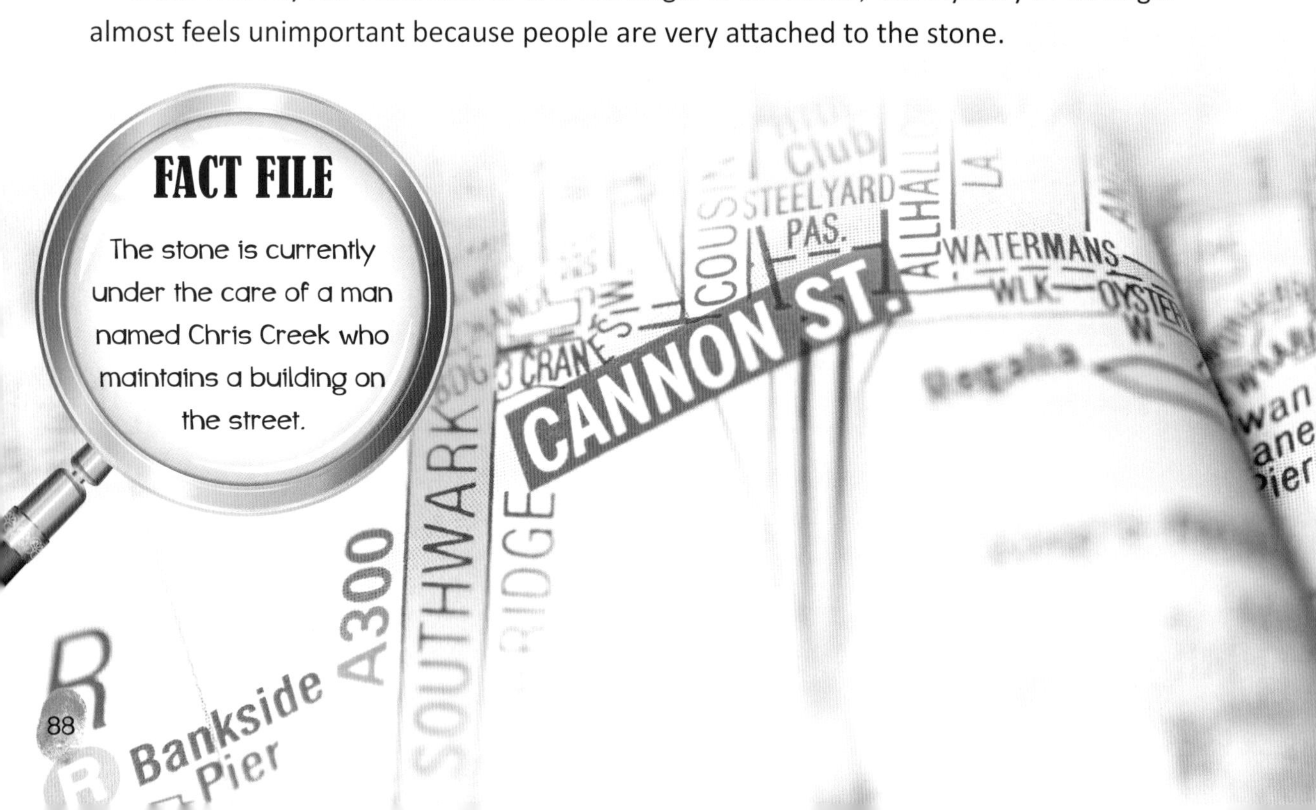

122. Message in Tiles

In various cities across the United States, and about four cities in South America, you could find tiles that have the same message written on them. They are called '**Toynbee Tiles**' and are made of linoleum. They have intrigued puzzle lovers across the country.

These tiles are about the size of license plates on cars. They are inscribed with variations of the text "TOYNBEE IDEA MOViE `2001 RESURRECT DEAD PLANET JUPITER". Not all tiles have the correct spelling or grammar.

At first, people thought the tiles were laid by James Morasco, who was a carpenter from Philadelphia. But the tiles kept appearing even after his death. So, the mystery remains unsolved.

123. Decode the Wall

If you get a chance to visit the Courtyard Plaza of the CIA grounds in Virginia, USA, then you must try to find the S-shaped sculpture named '**Kryptos**'. The sculpture was created by a very famous artist and sculptor named Jim Sanborn, in 1989.

The sculpture has four sections and each section bears a coded message. The messages attracted a lot of attention and three of the four messages are now solved. The fourth remains one of the greatest unsolved mysteries from the US. There are professional and amateur cryptanalysts (people who study encrypted messages in order to decode them) trying to solve the code.

124. Lost Library

Way back in 563 BCE, a man named St Columba came to the **Scottish island of Iona**. There, he built a monastery which became an important centre of knowledge and learning. It had a spectacular library with many books from the time.

Almost all of these books have vanished today. What is left is '*The Book of Kells*' which is now kept in the Trinity College library at Dublin. Researchers believe that the library (and the entire monastery) might have been destroyed by Vikings who raided it for goods and wealth.

They cannot agree if the Vikings destroyed all the books, or if some of the books from the library managed to survive and were transported to different parts of the world.

125. Stone Carvings

Have you ever heard of the special **stones from Scotland**? One type of stone is famous for the ring-and-cup designs carved on the surface. It has been said that the stones are nearly 5000 years old. The carvings on these stones might have a special meaning, but that is lost to us.

The other types of stones have different carvings that are similar to Egyptian hieroglyphs. They are called 'Pict stones' and are found all over Scotland. They portray people and animals doing regular things, as was commonly seen on the walls and relics from Ancient Egypt. It is possible that these carvings are a coded language that needs to be cracked. The scripts also have a similarity to other known ancient languages.

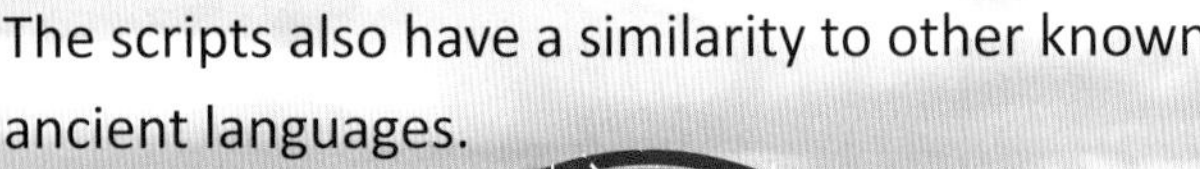

126. The Duke of Rothesay

We tend to think that Dukes and Duchesses live a privileged life. But **David Stewart**, the Duke of Rothesay, had a very unfortunate life. His father was Robert III, the King of Scots. He came to power in 1390. Or at least, he acquired the throne.

Robert III did not get the support that he needed to rule. Instead, his younger brother Robert Stewart was preferred among them. He was the Duke of Albany. He, too, was opposed to the rise of his brother to the throne.

When David Stewart was appointed by his father as the lieutenant in 1399, Robert Stewart (his uncle) opposed his position. He showed his lack of support by getting David Stewart arrested in 1401.

Here is where the mystery begins. What happened to David Stewart after he was put into prison? Did he die because no one cared for him? Was he starved to death? Did he suffer from some disease? There is even a rumour that he escaped and was able to survive.

Robert Stewart claimed that David died due to dysentery. However, there were rumours that he himself had given an order to have David Stewart put to death. After his death, he was to be buried in an unmarked grave.

Today, researchers are trying to find the grave in the reported location to find the body and investigate.

FACT FILE

Robert III was first named John Stewart and then changed his name to Robert, like his younger brother.

127. Hidden Treasure

Rarely do construction workers or labourers come across a **hoard of treasure**. But that is exactly what happened on June 18, 1812 when a group of construction workers were busy demolishing a building in London.

Below the brickwork of the building, they found a buried treasure that contained lots of jewellery, gems, figurines and sculptures. The treasure had precious gemstones like rubies, sapphires and emeralds. It also included a funny clock. There were about 500 valuable items packed within the treasure chest.

When it was reported, people tried to find out who it belonged to and why it was buried there. These two questions remain a mystery to this day. Since then, this treasure has been called the 'Cheapside Hoard', and is a subject of interest to many people in London. Some of the pieces from the treasure are displayed in museums in London.

When the labourers found the treasure, they took it to a man named 'Stony Jack' who was a jewellery dealer. Stony Jack took the treasure from the labourers for a respectable sum, and then sold them off to collectors and curators.

Then the items were dated back to the 17th century. There is a possibility that these items were collected during the English Civil War, and then lost during the Great Fire of London. The owners of the fire probably died during the fire. This disaster has in fact produced many unsolved mysteries in London.

128. Lord Lucan

Another great mystery from London is the **disappearance of Lord Lucan**, formally known as John Bingham, 7th Earl of Lucan. Suspected in a murder, he suddenly went missing nearly four decades ago. He was said to be a very handsome man, and there already was a lot of intrigue about his actions.

After he was accused of killing his nanny, he ran away. This created further suspicion. He was finally declared missing, and since then people have claimed to have seen him in London, India and even Australia. In 2016, his death certificate was issued, but the mystery of his disappearance lives on.

129. Beast of Sydenham

The citizens of England are used to unexpected rain. But, they are not used to unexpected beasts. So, imagine the uproar when some people spotted a **big black cat** walking around the streets of England.

A man named Tony Holder first spotted the animal in 2005 very early in the morning. He was attacked by the animal, but was fortunately able to escape without any serious injuries. After it was reported, a team of policemen scoured the area for the cat, but were unable to spot it.

Ever since there have been many alleged sightings of the animal. Since it was claimed to be as big as a Labrador, one cannot really call it a panther or classify it as any other animal.

130. Ivory Rush

We have all heard of the Gold Rush, but did you know that Europe once had an 'Ivory Rush'? It might have had something to do with the decision of the **Vikings to move to Greenland**. The reason behind this decision has always been a mystery.

Vikings looked for walrus tusks, as ivory art became more popular in Europe during the 11th century. Ivory was made into sculptures, jewellery and luxury items.

It is possible that the Vikings who thrived on agriculture moved to Greenland just for the ivory, because Greenland's vegetation was not suitable for agricultural life. The Viking economy also changed as a result.

131. Ivory Chess

Chess is a very old game that is been played for centuries. And that is one of the reasons why it is such a treasured game. In fact, archaeologists feel thrilled to find chess pieces and chess boards. Sometimes, they are simply works of art and sometimes they are a thing of mystery.

When someone found 78 ivory chess pieces tucked away in a buckle bag in the Hebrides, they immediately took it to some archaeologists to find out where it came from. These chess pieces are now called '**Lewis Chessmen**' and are the most famous in the world.

Nobody knows who made them and how they ended up in the Hebrides, UK, because research shows that they were made in the 12th century in Scotland.

132. French Figurine

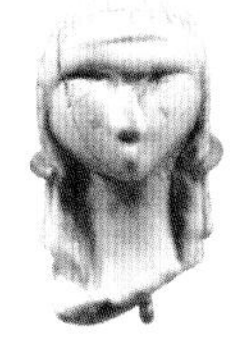

Speaking of ivory, another striking ivory piece was found in Brassempouy, France. It was a figurine of a woman's face. The face is not as detailed as it could be on a sculpture made today, but that is because it was created in 23000 BCE.

The sculpture has been named the '**Venus of Brassempouy**'. The figurine has eyes, hair, a snub nose and a small forehead but no mouth. The sculpture is made up to the neck and has a small crack which might have formed over the years.

Like the chess pieces, this sculpture mysteriously travelled from its original location in Russia or Siberia to France, because such figurines can only be dated back to the Lake Baikal area in Siberia.

133. Siberian Sculptures

Though it is not common knowledge, Siberia was known for its ivory figurines like "Venus of Brassempouy". When archaeologists found many figurines in Buret, Siberia in 1957, they first assumed all of them were figurines of women. So, they named them '**Venus of Furs**'.

Turns out, the figurines also showed men and children of either gender. In fact, it is possible that the unknown sculptor was trying to replicate real-life people of Siberia who were dressed to fight harsh winters. The sculptor tried to show different hairstyles on the figurines as well.

Such discoveries are not well-known outside of Siberia and only became a bit more popular after 'Venus of Brassempouy' was discovered in France.

134. The Valentich Mystery

A young lad named Frederick Valentich was flying an aircraft over the Bass Strait in Australia when he disappeared. It happened on October 21, 1978. Frederick Valentich was on a training flight when he felt that he was being followed by a UFO.

Valentich immediately radioed into the Melbourne air traffic control to report the UFO. He claimed that 300 m above his aircraft, a UFO was trying to get closer to his aircraft. He also said that his engine was being affected as a result.

FACT FILE

A UFOlogist studies the records and visuals of the UFOs sighted around the world.

Right after his disappearance, other people claimed to have seen a UFO. But the officials at the Department of Transport were not satisfied with these reports. Valentich, when asked by the people at the air traffic control, kept insisting that the flying body was not an aircraft. As the incident occurred at 7 p.m., it is possible that Valentich was unable to see the flying object clearly.

The controller that Valentich spoke to, named Steve Robey, was also quite sceptical. If you read the transcripts of their conversation, you will see that he kept asking a lot of questions and got many details out of Valentich.

Valentich was on his way to King Island when he disappeared with his aircraft. His last words on the transcript were "It's not an aircraft".

This story has interested many UFO researchers and conspiracy theorists around the world. There are several possible theories provided by people who have researched the mystery. Some even claim to have solved it.

Mysteries of Mother Earth

A long time ago, if people couldn't figure out why certain things happened in nature, they blamed it on the gods that they worshipped. For example, the Sun coming up in the morning and disappearing at night was only because someone was controlling it.

Today, we can't possibly use that excuse. And so, people have set out to solve mysteries connected with Mother Nature. With advanced technology and knowledge of the past, we've been able to solve many mysteries. Mother Nature still has some unsolved mysteries waiting to be solved.

135. Whistling Sand

If you spend enough time in the desert sands you might hear them whistle. That is not because you are hallucinating, but when sand falls down a sand dune, **it does make a sound**. The sound is quite soft and low. This sound can be heard in the deserts of California, Qatar and India.

Marco Polo and Charles Darwin have mentioned these sounds in their writings. Modern scientists claim that these sounds are caused by vibrations. The size of the grains must be a factor in the sounds.

While we now know why these sounds are made, we don't know exactly why these sounds seem to synchronise enough to sound like a musical note.

136. Bending Trees

If you are a child growing up in Poland, you might be confused about what a tree looks like. A forest in West Pomerania has an unusual collection of trees called **'Crooked Forest'**. There are about 400 pine trees in this forest that seem to curve or bend at the base. The angle of the bend is about 90°.

What is even stranger is that this crooked forest is surrounded by more pine trees that grow naturally with a straight base. So what has caused this mysterious bend in the trees of 'Crooked Forest'? Nobody knows. All the trees were planted around the same time in 1930, and it is possible that the bend was caused by some interference from the people planting the trees.

137. Eternal Eruption

Iceland's **Bardarbunga volcano** erupted in August, 2014. It continued to erupt for more than a year. The volcano's crater has been sinking steadily, and it has released a lot of sulphur dioxide while erupting.

The volcano managed to create a lava field that is more than 82 km^2. It is claimed to be the third largest lava field on earth. Everyone in Iceland has at least once, taken in some of the gases released by this volcano. The caldera of the Bardarbunga volcano has sunk 184 feet, and has even sunk the instrument that was placed to measure the sinking!

And through it all, it is still erupting. Why is it still erupting and when will it stop? That is a big mystery.

138. Jelly from the Sky

With great mysteries come great debates. And this next mystery has been a subject of debate between cynics and conspiracy theorists who have followed its progress. It all began when people in Scotland found soft and gooey white balls of jelly in parks.

These balls of jelly are called **'star jelly'**. A theory claims that these substances are the stuff that makes up the Sun, the stars and some meteors. When meteors and stars break apart, the gooey substance falls off and sometimes manages to land on Earth.

Star jellies have been spotted in other places like Texas and Canada. So, they have been collected by scientists for study. Many people have come forward to say that the theory that star jellies come from stars is impossible.

Firstly, because stars are not made of soft, gooey material. Secondly, because stars cannot break apart in a way that their insides come spilling out and fall down to Earth. Thirdly, because Earth's atmosphere would destroy this gooey substance before it reaches its lithosphere.

Another theory put forward is that these star jellies are the insides of frogs. When predators attack the frogs or toads in parks and other places, they rip their bodies apart. Sometimes, this means that the gooey ovum jelly in the frogs comes spilling out. If it rains, the substance absorbs water and swells in size. While this explanation is less imaginative, it certainly is more believable.

FACT FILE

Star jellies can also be a form of fungi or mould. Nothing has been confirmed yet.

139. How does Lightning Work?

Every second, nearly 100 lightning bolts hit the Earth. Possibly, it was a strong bolt of lightning that set off reactions that led to life on Earth. And yet, to this day, we do not know how lightning works.

We do know why lightning strikes. That is because of electrically charged storm systems or electrically charged clouds that generate lightning bolts. Each bolt of lightning is hotter than the surface of the Sun. The electrical waves zoom out in all directions. There is a brilliant and blinding flash of light.

But the big question is **how are clouds electrified?** We know that when positive and negative charges separate within the cloud, lightning takes place. A growing storm needs ice for there to be lightning.

We also know why lightning tends to hit tall objects like buildings, large columns, poles and trees. It is because the negative charges spread beneath the base of the cloud while the positive charges spread out under the storm and get concentrated over the tall objects.

The negative charges slowly make their way towards the ground and the positive charges move up in direct response. Whenever these positive and negative charges meet, the negative charges start flowing down while a strong electric current (the lightning bolt) goes shooting up to the cloud in the path of the positive charges.

So, what sets off this whole reaction? There are many possible theories to this but none of them have been able to answer the question satisfactorily.

140. Ball Lightning

Lightning is usually in the form of bolts, but have you ever seen or heard of **lightning that strikes in the form of a ball?** That is the phenomenon of 'ball lightning'. The 'ball' can be a few centimetres or even a few metres in diameter, and can explode and leave behind a sulphurous odour.

Until 1960, scientists thought that ball lightning was a myth. Then nearly 5 per cent of Earth's population claimed to have seen ball lightning. It even struck the Golden Temple in Amritsar, in 1877! Scientists can now reproduce ball lightning in a controlled atmosphere in laboratories. But strangely, they cannot tell what causes ball lightning. Nobody knows when or where the ball lightning will strike next or even where it will strike. It is infrequent and unpredictable.

141. Catatumbo Lightning

Infrequency is not the problem with Catatumbo lightning. It only strikes in one place – over the mouth of the **Catatumbo River in Venezuela**.

The lightning can strike the same place for 260 nights a year, for 10 hours a day and can occur almost 28 times in one minute. That is nearly 2800 times a day! There was a brief time in 2010, when the Catatumbo lightning did not strike the river for three months. Then it suddenly started up again!

While the lightning is easy to predict, it is difficult to say why exactly this phenomenon occurs every year at the same place. But this place, sure is the most electric place in the world.

FACT FILE

Lightning travels from the ground upwards though we think it travels from the cloud to the ground.

142. Red Rain

'Red rain' means that **raindrops are bright red** in colour. This red rainfall occurred in Kerala in 2001. The people who got soaked with rainwater looked like they were bleeding. People have also reported rainfall of other colours like black and yellow.

At first, people thought that the rains were caused by a meteor burst that had previously occurred. But the Government of India conducted research and said that it was caused by some specific airborne algae. This did not explain why the neighbouring states had not experienced such rainfall. Other theories about aliens and dead bats also popped up locally, but none of the theories so far are satisfactory.

143. Animal Rain

What if you look up one day and see that it is raining frogs and fishes? Animal rainfall has been reported many times in history and even in recent times. A man named Charles Fort wrote about this, in 1919, in his book, '*The Book of the Damned*'.

Apparently, he saw that it was **raining frogs**. He explained that the frogs were picked up by a rainstorm that started in Kansas and travelled to him. This phenomenon usually affects small animals like worms, ants and fishes.

Scientists claim that these rainfalls occur as a result of recent tornados or storms in nearby areas. But this explanation has many loopholes and thus this phenomenon remains a mystery.

144. Stinky Ape

You have heard of skunks and you have heard of apes. But did you know that there is a **skunk ape** hiding somewhere on Earth? At least, that is what some people claim. Sightings of a giant ape were reported in the US in the states like Florida, Arkansas and North Carolina between the 1960s and the 1980s.

Those who saw the skunk ape said that not only was it a big ape-like creature, but that it had a really bad odour. Officials at the United States National Park Service have declared the skunk ape to be a hoax. Researchers have stated that the reports were inaccurate, and possibly people saw an orangutan or black bear and claimed it to be something else.

145. Vampire Monkeys

When people claim to have seen or spoken to vampires, they are disbelieved. But what about vampire monkeys? They are **mythological creatures from China** inspired from the story of Jiangshi. That is a hopping vampire monkey that was written about in ancient Chinese legends.

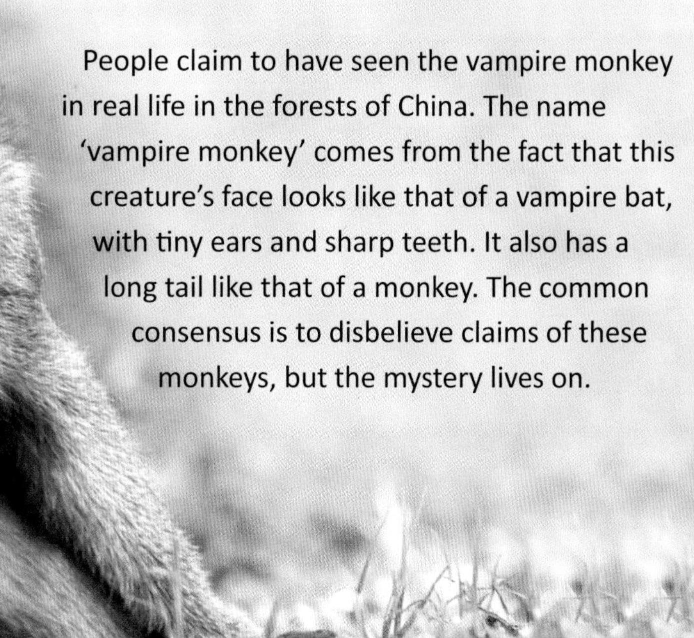

People claim to have seen the vampire monkey in real life in the forests of China. The name 'vampire monkey' comes from the fact that this creature's face looks like that of a vampire bat, with tiny ears and sharp teeth. It also has a long tail like that of a monkey. The common consensus is to disbelieve claims of these monkeys, but the mystery lives on.

146. Shark GPS

Speaking of big eyes, how is it that sharks can see underwater and move around? Sharks travel long distances for migration. A Great White Shark will start its journey from the Indian Ocean and swim all the way to the coast of Australia.

Do they know where they are going? What are the things under water that inform them about the direction and location? This is one big mystery that marine biologists have been trying to solve for years. It may be that sharks have evolved to have a developed sense of smell, sight and touch (of magnetic fields) that help them travel in water.

147. Moving Day

We don't know how sharks are able to migrate and we don't even know **why sharks migrate**. But marine biologists want to know more and more about their migration patterns. They have developed and used technology that tracks a shark and puts up all its travel information on their computers.

Sharks might be migrating because of temperature or shortage of food, but nothing is known for certain. Each shark tends to have a particular pattern of migration, even if it belongs to the same species as another shark. The only way to find out would be to follow many sharks of one species.

148. Whale Shark

A group of scientists began to track some whale sharks in Indonesia, in 2016, to find out their **migration patterns**. The whale shark is the largest fish species in the water. They found out many interesting and surprising things about the whale shark.

Firstly, that the whale sharks spend most of their time in the bay but also take long trips. Why do they take these trips? That is a mystery. Just like every other shark, why the whale shark goes to a certain place and what it does there is still unknown. Some sharks even dive down nearly 6000 feet into the water once every trip. Why? Still unknown.

149. Hammerhead Shark

The hammerhead shark is an interesting underwater animal. The most unique feature of this shark is the **shape of its head** which inspired its name. But the interesting shape of its head is also one of the biggest unsolved mysteries of the underwater world.

Why does the hammerhead shark have such a strange shape for a head? Everything in nature has a reason. So, scientists have come up with many reasons to explain this mystery. One theory says that the shark is able to swim faster and more easily because of this shape. Another theory claims that it allows for better vision. This is supported by many researchers. But none of these theories have been proven conclusively.

150. Cannibal Sharks

Can **sharks eat each other**? That is the question that came up when a great white shark was murdered. The shark was being tracked by researchers. Suddenly, they noticed that the shark dove deep under water to an area that it had never gone to before. Then they realised that it was attacked.

The researchers quickly came to the conclusion that the shark was eaten. But what could possibly attack and eat the great white shark? They realised that it had to be a really fierce and powerful creature. Maybe even one that we haven't heard of before.

It is not unusual to see one shark attack another shark. But scientists believe that a great white shark would win any match, unless of course, it is fighting against another great white shark. What really happened is still a mystery.

151. Strange Globsters

Do you know what **'globsters'** are? They are washed up sea bodies. Usually, people spot globsters on the beach or along the coast. They complain to an authority that then brings a team along.

The team clears up the globsters and sends them out to a laboratory for testing. Here, the globsters are checked to find out which animal it is. Sometimes, when a fish or other aquatic animal dies in the water because of natural or unnatural causes, the body keeps drifting and catching up with other materials that messes it up. This is a 'globster'. Most globsters have been identified. Almost every day, there is an unsolved globster mystery to solve.

152. Secret Dolphin Language

Like most animals, dolphins can communicate with each other. What makes them stand apart is that they might have a **"spoken language"** and can easily tell which dolphin they are speaking to. This language is said to be very developed.

Scientists have recorded numerous conversations between dolphins to crack the code. They are trying to figure out exactly what the dolphins are saying so that they can 'translate' it to human beings.

A Russian researcher, has even recorded a conversation between two adult bottlenose dolphins. He found out that dolphins don't interrupt each other when they are speaking. They communicate with each other with pulses, and the patterns show that they might be using words and sentences.

While this researcher sees similarities between dolphin conversations and human conversations, other researchers have difficulty in believing that dolphins can even have 'conversations' as they are not mammals.

In another experiment, scientists put dolphins in different aquariums (separated by a wall), and had a line connecting them almost like a telephone. The two dolphins began to communicate, and it seemed like they knew who they were talking to.

FACT FILE

Dolphins not only make sounds but also signals and actions with their fins and jaws.

153. Diversity at the Equator

As you go from the poles to the equator, you will see greater diversity in plants and animals. This means that there are more species of plants and animals that grow at the equator than at the poles. But why is this the case? Nobody knows.

The topic has been of interest to biologists for a long time. Even if for example, they choose to observe frogs, they will find that there is a much larger variation near the equator. This phenomenon is called **'Latitudinal Diversity Gradient'**. 'Latitude'refers to the distance from the equator and whether it is to the north or south. 'Gradient' refers to the number, as in how many species.

There are many theories for this. One theory is that there is more sunlight that reaches the equator. There is also more space or area at the equator than there is at the poles. The Earth is wider at the equator.

The need for solving why there are more species closer to the equator, is also motivated by the fact that there are more ingredients for medicines. With more species of plants and animals, researchers can find more things to use in potentially life-saving medicines.

There is a possibility that there are more species closer to the equator, because of no reason whatsoever. It could just randomly have happened that way. But scientists like to think that there is a reason and it is most likely related to the relative distance of the poles and equator from the Sun.

Low Diversity

Equator

High Diversity

Low Diversity

FACT FILE

The LDG phenomenon is not just true for land but also water.

154. Plankton Puzzle

Plankton is so small in size that you cannot even see it without a microscope. But plankton has caused a lot of grief to biologists. Lots and lots of different plankton species can live in peace and harmony in small spaces in lakes and oceans.

This is in **direct contrast** to the popular theory that when plants of different species are put together, they compete to get the most sunlight and water. So much so that any other plant species might die off.

One reason for such great cooperation could be the uncertainty of life under water. Species under water experience a lot of change almost on a daily basis. So, perhaps, the plankton species work together to survive.

155. Head Mysteries

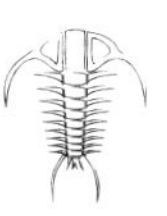

Have you heard of the **'Arthropod Head Problem'**? This is a debated issue among biologists. Animals like lobsters, spiders, crabs, millipedes and other eight-legged creatures belong to the family of arthropods. The head of every arthropod has different parts like antennae, mandibles and compound eyes.

But why is the head of an arthropod so complex? Despite the differences in species, every arthropod seems to more or less share these similarities when it comes to the head. Biologists want to know why. While many theories have been flouted like similarity in habitat, food type, reproduction process, none of them have been satisfactory. So the mystery is also called the 'endless dispute'.

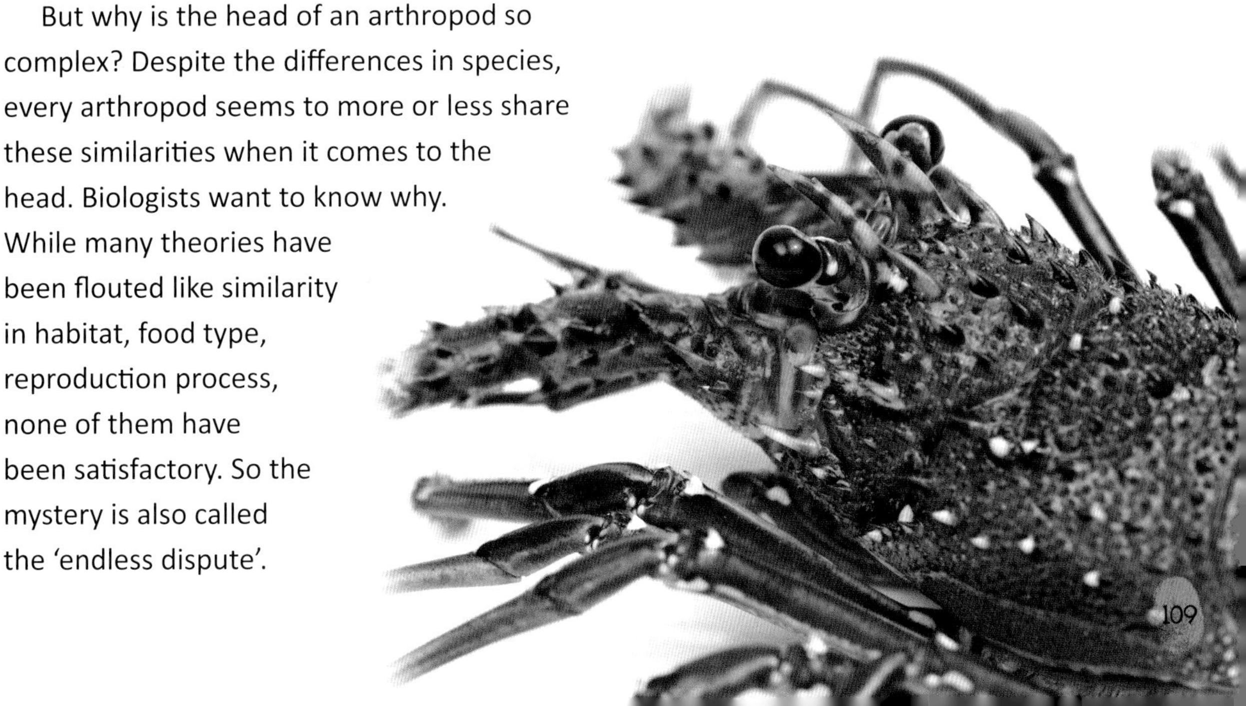

156. Hunting Tigers

If you have visited the Sundarbans, you should be familiar with the many warnings that you need to follow carefully. That is because **tigers in the Sundarbans** are on the lookout for human prey.

Nobody knows why these tigers so fiercely attack and prey on human beings, as this is not common with tigers. They rarely hunt for humans. But the Sundarbans tigers are skilful enough to wait until human beings on a boat are sleeping in order to attack.

At first, researchers thought that it must be a common thing among Royal Bengal tigers, which is the breed that is found in the Sundarbans. But the Royal Bengal tigers from other parts of India do not hunt human beings.

157. Taming Dogs

Before dogs were man's best friend, they were wolves. Nearly 15,000 years ago, human beings began to partner with **grey wolves and tried to tame them** from a wild animal to a domesticated pet.

That is how, over time, the grey wolves began to have smaller teeth and skulls and smaller paws. Their ears began to flop, and they became less frightening and aggressive and more docile.

While we know the story of the origin of dogs, we don't know exactly how these wolves came to be domesticated into dogs. How many species of wolves were domesticated and how many times? How did we get the different breeds of dogs we see today? These questions are still unanswered.

158. Titanium Boost

Titanium is a metal that has a lot of strength but very little density. It is strange to see that when applied in small doses, **titanium can boost a plant's growth**. When titanium is used on a tomato plant, it begins to act on the plant's metabolism and stimulates its growth activity so that it can take up more nutrients.

Nobody would look at titanium and think it could be so beneficial to plants, because titanium is used mainly in aerospace industries. But this beneficial use of titanium was discovered in 1930. Why titanium helps plants is anybody's guess, but it has started scientists thinking on how helpful other metals might be.

159. Placozoan Mystery

When you hear the word "animal" you probably think of four-legged creatures. But **"Placozoan"** is a multicellular animal. This organism is not a parasite. It is small and flat and has a body diameter of 1 mm. That's super small and can only be seen through a microscope.

Little is known about it. Though only one species is found, three variations identified on the bodies of the Placozoan show that there could be more.

The Placozoan was first discovered in 1880, on the glass wall of an aquarium. Since its discovery, the only progress made so far is to learn if it can be found in the wild (yes). Nobody knows what it eats, how it reproduces or what its contribution is to Earth.

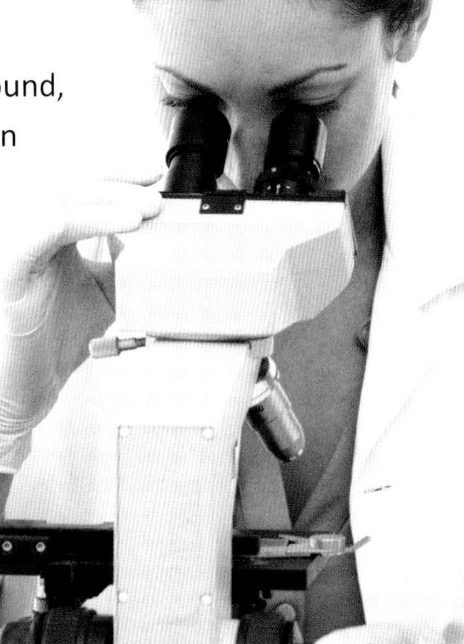

160. An Elephant's Purr

Did you know that elephants can purr? Or at least that is what the sound they make might sound like if humans could hear it. It is a strange sound to hear from such a giant and strong animal. Elephants communicate with each other by trumpeting. They also make low sounds that cannot be heard by human beings, but can be **felt through vibrations**.

So how are these elephants able to produce such a low vibrating noise? That's the mystery. Finding out how it works could help us understand how elephants, and possibly, other animals communicate with each other. Understanding the sound will also help us understand how elephants use different sounds for different messages.

After examining the larynx of an elephant, researchers thought of a few theories that could explain how and why elephants make the low sound. Firstly, elephants contract the muscles around the larynx to make that low sound. The other theory is that the sound is made from an elephant's vocal cords.

It is also important to study the mood of the elephant when it makes this sound. Is it frightened and worried for itself or another elephant in the herd? Is it happy because it spotted some delicious food? Understanding the mood can also help us learn what the elephant is trying to communicate by making the sound.

And if this mystery is solved, it opens the door to solve many other mysterious sounds made by animals like the giant whale whose sounds cannot be heard by humans.

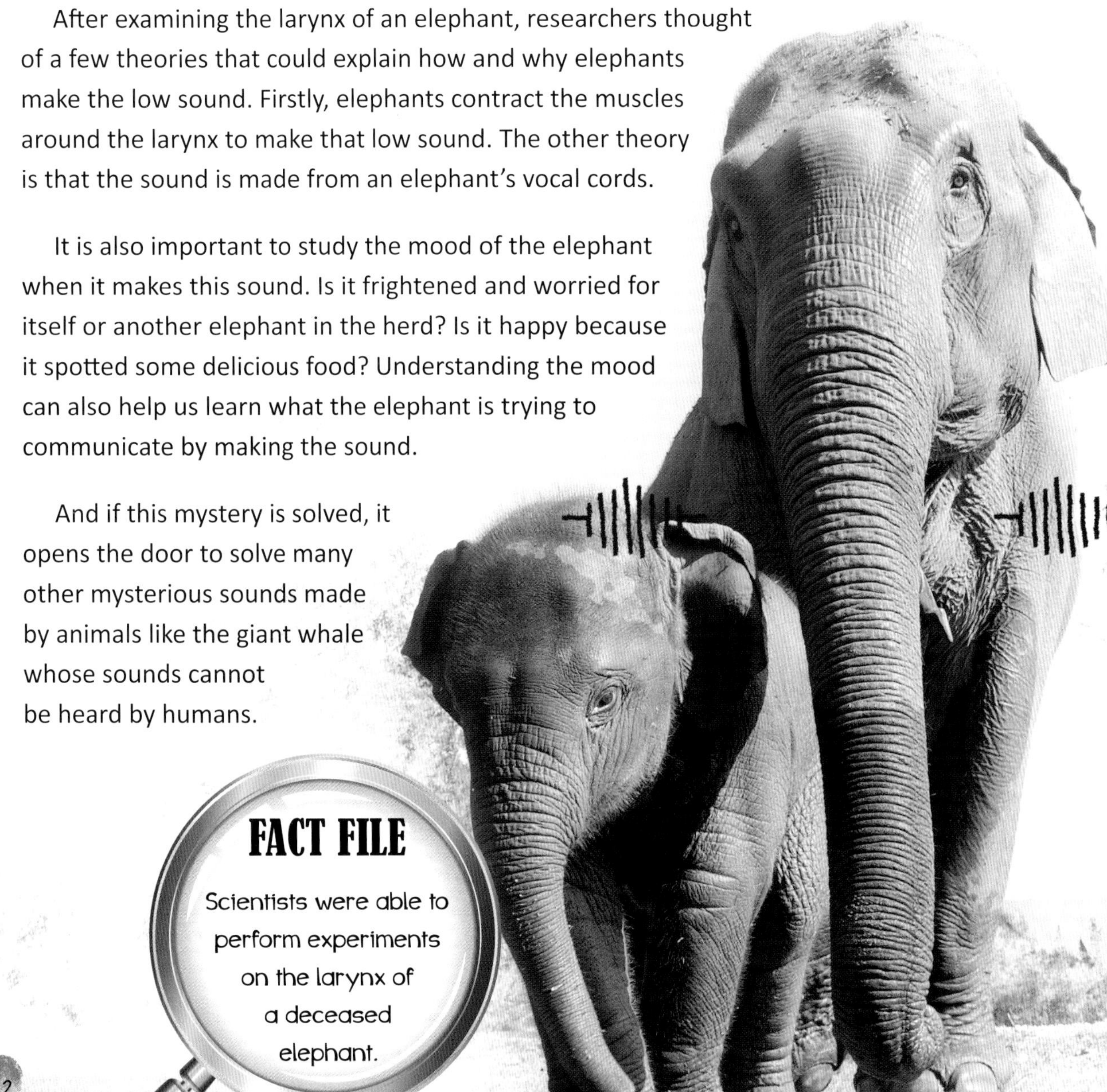

FACT FILE

Scientists were able to perform experiments on the larynx of a deceased elephant.

161. Water on Earth

We all know that Earth has a lot of water. But **where did water come from**? Water needs two hydrogen molecules and one oxygen molecule. Earth is about 4.543 billion years old. Scientists believe that at the time of its creation, Earth was a dry rock with no water or wetness. But it did have a lot of hydrogen.

What about oxygen? It could have come from comets or asteroids that collided with Earth. Due to the collision, oxygen atoms were released. These oxygen atoms merged with hydrogen atoms to form oceans of water. So, it is quite possible that the water in the ocean is about 4 billion years old!

162. Origin of Life

While some scientists want to know if there is life on Mars, others want to know the **origin of life on Earth**. In the very beginning, there were no humans or large animals on Earth.

Then, 3 billion years ago, there were small microbes that evolved and became more and more complex which led to plants, animals and human beings. But how did these microbes come to be?

Scientists have come up with several theories to explain the origin of life. Some say life began after powerful lightning struck Earth. Others say that the molecules started on clay. But which of these theories is correct? Scientists are still trying to figure it out.

163. Desert Fairies 

Have you ever seen **small circles on the floor of a desert**? There is grass on the fringes of these circles. Some tribes believe that they are the footprints of Gods. Others believe that they are marks left by aliens.

They are called **'fairy circles'**. There are unproven theories that describe their origin. We know that there is some water in the desert. Researchers believe that this is the water that helps the grass grow around the circles. But why circles? So that the grass can keep soaking up all the water deep in the ground for months and months after the last bout of rainfall.

Usually, the area within the circle does not get enough water so the grass dies off, leaving little grass surrounding the circle.

164. Nabta Playa 

Somewhere in the Sahara Desert at Nabta Playa you will find a **megalith structure** that is 1000 years older than the Stonehenge. This structure has five rows of upright slabs (or tombs) standing tall in a ring pattern. Each stone is about 9 feet high and weighs 2 tonnes or more.

It dates back to the Stone Age which is 6000 years ago. But researchers are not sure exactly who could have placed these slabs in such a complicated pattern in the desert. The structure was built to practice astronomy, and it could possibly be the first of its kind. If we manage to find the accurate time and people who created this structure, then it could change history as we know it.

165. Atacama Deposits

The Atacama Desert is said to be the **driest place in the world**. It was once described by Charles Darwin as the place where nothing can exist. This however is not true. The Atacama Desert does have some plant and animal species, and it is very sparsely populated.

NITRATE

This desert is so dry that its soil has been compared to the soil on Mars. In fact, those who want to shoot outer space scenes in movies go to the Atacama Desert to film them. Most of the population avoids the interiors of the desert and instead sticks closer to the coast which borders the Pacific Ocean. The people who settle within the desert's interior are mostly male.

The Atacama Desert only gets 1 mm rainfall during the year. However, despite this, researchers have found lots of nitrate and iodine deposits in the desert. But what's strange is that the bacteria that help form the deposit is missing.

Researchers believe that the deposits were formed when sprays of water were received in certain areas from the Pacific Ocean. The deposits are, after all, about 50 km from the Pacific coast. In this way, the nitrogen that is present in the atmosphere forms nitrates when bound with salts and soil.

While this theory is considered to be the best explanation for it, there are other theories that could possibly explain what the nitrate and iodine deposits found suitable in the climate and location.

FACT FILE

The deposits themselves are only 700 km long and 20 km wide.

166. Zebra Stripes

Have you ever wondered why **zebras have stripes**? At first, researchers believed that zebras have stripes for camouflage. But this theory did not go well with a lot of people.

Finally, experiments were done to test out if predators truly are put off by the camouflage so that the zebras have time to run away. The results showed that even though the predators might get fooled by the stripes, they can smell the zebras from great distances. So, the stripes are of no use.

A new theory suggests that the stripes, along with the temperature of the body, are meant to scare away bloodsucking flies. But this has not been proven conclusively.

167. Chimpanzee Religion?

Are **chimpanzees smart enough to follow a religion**? That is a new mystery that has come up in the world of animals. There was some footage taken of West African chimpanzees that were banging rocks against trees and throwing them into holes.

The chimpanzees seemed to be following a certain sacred ritual. Before the stones were put into the holes of trees, the chimpanzees seemed to carefully find and assemble the stones into neat piles. Such behaviour was displayed by human beings very early on when religion and rituals were just developing. If scientists solve this mystery, they might even be able to solve another one about how human beings started to practice religion.

168. Exploding Toads

Toads have a funny ability of puffing themselves up to look bigger in size so that their predators get scared and run away. Strangely, back in 2005, many **toads began to explode** in Germany. That is right, they simply exploded. This started up suddenly in the month of April.

Scientists tried to come up with reasons for this strange behaviour. One veterinarian claimed that it might have had something to do with the neighbourhood crows that poked their beaks into the toads and took out their livers. When the toads saw the crows coming, they puffed themselves up and exploded when the beaks punctured them. But this solution seems quite far-fetched and so this mystery remains unsolved. There are several other theories on the mystery of the exploding toads but none of them seem possible.

169. Terror Beast

Animals follow certain patterns. They only attack when they need food or are under stress. There was one animal in the **Dowa district of Malawi** that seemed to attack people for no reason at all. A few villagers came across the animal and had to flee the place forever in fear.

The animal, which is unidentified to this day, killed three people in the group and injured 16. It did not feed on the people that it killed. The villagers were terrified. Later, they reported it to be a large, angry dog-like creature. It is quite possible that this was a hyena, but some of its behaviour didn't seem to match with that of a hyena.

170. Snapper Deaths

It is always strange when a big group of animals go missing or **die off suddenly** for unexplained reasons. Almost always, authorities find the correct reason for the occurrence but sometimes even they are bewildered.

One such incident happened at a beach in Australia. Many snapper fish washed up dead on the beach. There was no explanation provided after the investigation except to say that the deaths seemed 'deliberate'. Then, another similar incident occurred on the same beach two years later, with many snapper fish coming up dead on the shore.

The authorities blamed an illegal fishing boat's broken net. While this time, an explanation was provided it did not seem satisfactory.

171. Milky Sea

In the past, sailors would come across a body of water they described as **'milky'** and **'glowing'**. People thought this to be a fake story that sailors told each other. But then in 1995, a merchant vessel again came across a sea that was 'milky' and 'white'.

Researchers began to study the water to see what caused it to become that way. They found out that there are bacteria that give the water this glow. They are 'bioluminescent' which means that they give out a light from their bodies. The bacteria attract prey with this light. But it takes trillions of these bacteria to have this effect, and scientists still don't know the reason why so many bacteria gather in one place.

172. Were Dodos Smart?

The word **'Dodo'** has been used to describe someone who is not that smart. Dodo was the name of a bird that went extinct in 1662. When they first saw humans, dodos went about their normal routines. They were not aware of the predatory instincts of human beings. This made it easier for hunters to find and kill dodos. That is how humans began to think that dodos are not very smart.

Recent studies on the brain of the extinct dodo reveal that the bird could have had a bigger brain than we think, and that it could be as clever as a pigeon today. Pigeons are smart enough to remember human faces. They can be trained. The studies need to be verified, but they do challenge the traditional views.

I am Smart

173. Elephant Bird

Like the dodo, the elephant bird was a flightless bird that went extinct by the 17th or 18th century, if not earlier.

It is a mystery as to how these birds became extinct as they were 3 m tall and 454 kg heavy. They were strong birds. Scientists think that the usual culprits were to blame in their extinction – human beings.

It is possible that the elephant birds went extinct when they lost their habitats or when people began stealing their eggs for food. Diseased birds, like chickens and hens, raised by human beings were also to blame.

174. Gilbert's Potoroo

Australia was and still is home to many unique species of animals. But, many of them became extinct when Europeans formed settlements in Australia. Most of the animal extinctions were blamed on human beings as they began to clear forests and hunt them.

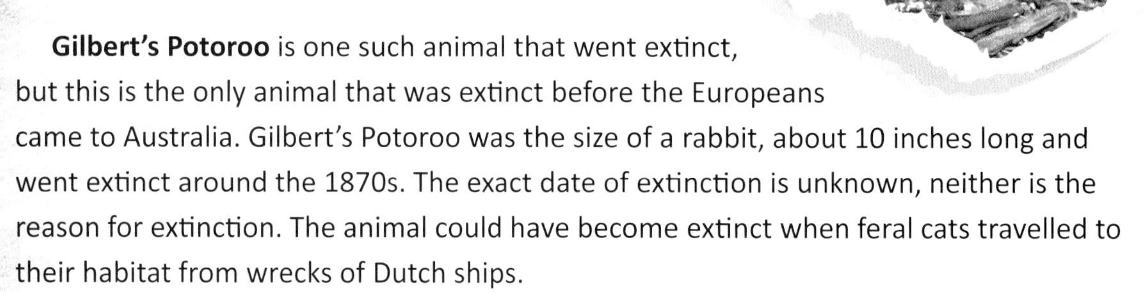

Gilbert's Potoroo is one such animal that went extinct, but this is the only animal that was extinct before the Europeans came to Australia. Gilbert's Potoroo was the size of a rabbit, about 10 inches long and went extinct around the 1870s. The exact date of extinction is unknown, neither is the reason for extinction. The animal could have become extinct when feral cats travelled to their habitat from wrecks of Dutch ships.

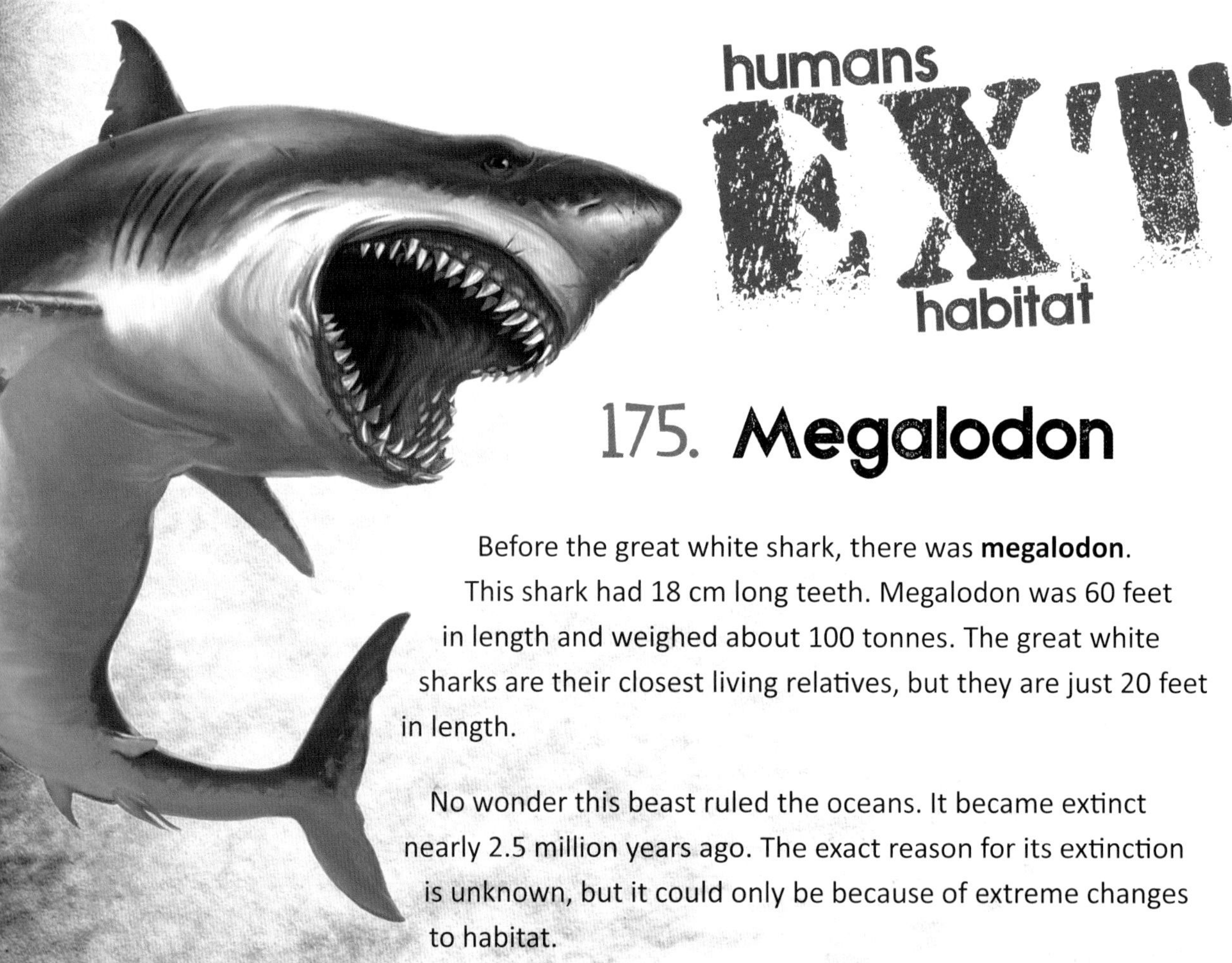

175. Megalodon

Before the great white shark, there was **megalodon**. This shark had 18 cm long teeth. Megalodon was 60 feet in length and weighed about 100 tonnes. The great white sharks are their closest living relatives, but they are just 20 feet in length.

No wonder this beast ruled the oceans. It became extinct nearly 2.5 million years ago. The exact reason for its extinction is unknown, but it could only be because of extreme changes to habitat.

The megalodon could not survive the massive changes that took place.

176. Extinct Neanderthals

Until 40,000 years ago, **Neanderthals** lived in parts of Europe and Western Asia. Nearly 45,000 years ago Homo sapiens, which are the early members of the species of human beings, migrated to Europe and Asia from Africa. About five years later, all Neanderthals went extinct.

Some researchers draw a connection between the migration of Homo sapiens and the extinction of Neanderthals to say that human beings drove the extinction. They are definitely the likely suspects in all extinctions in the past and present. Others think that this time, human beings were innocent of the charge. There are also some fossils found that could prove that Neanderthals went extinct even before Homo sapiens reached them.

Instead, ecological changes were to blame. Neanderthals were experts at hunting animals of the Ice Age period. When the climate began to change, their food became extinct right from the Woolly Mammoth to the sabre-toothed cats. And when food gets extinct it is only natural for the person who eats it to go extinct as well.

There was a time when scientists thought that a volcanic winter wiped out the Neanderthal population. This was caused by a super-eruption of an active volcano that the Neanderthals lived close to. Others may have died because of climatic changes.

Here is another idea, it could have been all these causes combined; the volcanic winter, competition with early humans and weather changes. The Neanderthals just got extremely unlucky.

FACT FILE

Recent studies show that Neanderthals had interbred with early humans.

177. Francis Leavy

Imagine if someone said they were going to die on a particular day and it came true? That is what happened to Francis Leavy, a brave firefighter from Chicago. He was cleaning the window at the fire department in a bad mood. When the others asked about it, he told them he had a feeling **he would die that day**.

Then they got a call about a fire, and he rushed to the site with his team. While rescuing people from the building, the roof caved in and Francis Leavy was trapped under the rubble. He died that day.

The next day, his colleagues noticed something strange on the window he was cleaning. It was Leavy's handprint. Despite cleaning it several times, the print never came off.

178. Jeannette DePalma

When a dog in New Jersey discovered the body of a teenage girl, the owner quickly informed the police. The police noticed several **strange objects around the body**. They thought that it was a part of some strange occult ritual.

When interviewers came to write about the story, everyone in the town refused to talk about it, including the police department. The police were trying to solve the case, and were getting lots of anonymous leaks from people. Everyone wrote about witches living in the area. For the first two weeks since her discovery, the murder was big news. Then, everyone went quiet and refused to talk about it. The killer remains unknown.

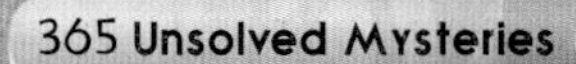

179. Hoia Baciu

If you want to shoot a horror movie in a forest, there is no better place than the **Hoia Baciu forest in Romania**, because it naturally looks scary due to the trees growing there. Besides, everyone who has visited the forest has felt scared by it.

The visitors to the forest have experienced rashes and felt like they have forgotten a few hours of their trip even though they usually don't have a bad memory. It all started in 1968, when a man took a photograph in the forest of something that looked like a UFO. Around the same time, a shepherd lost 200 sheep in the forest. Why these weird incidents occur in the forest is unknown.

180. Kalachi Village

Imagine a village full of people who are too sleepy to stay awake. A village in Kazakhstan, named 'Kalachi' is suffering from a strange disease. People in the village suddenly fall asleep during the day even if they have slept through the night and are not tired. They wake up hours, even days later.

It is been called a **'sleep epidemic'** but nobody really knows why this is happening and what the cause could be. Everyone in the village knows about the strange epidemic as someone or the other in their family has experienced it. Scientists have found high volumes of carbon monoxide in the air, which could be a reason for the sleep epidemic.

181. Sichuan Province

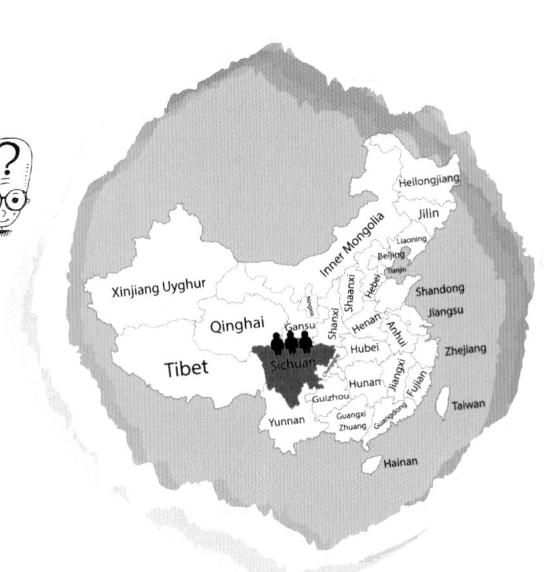

Imagine a village with just 80 residents. And imagine that about half of them are dwarfs. The reason this village in the Sichuan province in China, is not very populated is that for more than 60 years, children are affected by something that stunts their growth. The problem usually starts between the ages of 5 and 7.

The children only grow to a height of 3 feet, and also suffer from some disabilities. The Chinese Government has reportedly banned others from visiting the village because of this problem. People have been trying to figure out what happened, but the villagers themselves believe they have been cursed by ancestors. Luckily, the most recent generation of children seems to have escaped the 'curse'.

182. Sixth Mass Extinction?

Remember when people predicted that the world would end in 2012 and nothing happened? A similar dangerous warning has been issued by scientists around the world who claim that a **sixth mass extinction** will take place that will wipe out most of the marine life and animals by 2100. If this happens, human life will also be extremely threatened.

Scientists don't have to think too long about who to blame for this mass extinction. The blame lies solely on human beings who have been hunting, overfishing and carrying out deforestation leading to pollution and global warming. Could this prediction come true or will it be a dud like the 2012 apocalypse? Remember, prevention is better than cure!

183. Planet Nine

Not too long ago, we believed that there were nine planets in the solar system. Then, scientists shocked the world by saying that Pluto was not a planet, instead it was a 'dwarf planet'. All the textbooks had to be reprinted to reflect this change.

Now, textbooks might need to be updated once more because scientists claim that they are close to finding a ninth planet. It is not Pluto. This ninth planet is said to be hovering at the fringes of the solar system, just out of reach of the desperate scientists. And it could possibly be a deadly planet that destroys the entire solar system.

The entire theory comes from a branch of scientists who believe that the Sun will die in about seven billion years. And when the Sun dies, the distant planets like Jupiter, Saturn, Uranus and Neptune would be barely able to survive. But Earth would be swallowed up in the impact.

Scientists have worked the ninth planet into the scenario to create a really drastic scene. Apparently, the Sun's death would cause one of the planets to go shooting off into space. This could impact the distant planets like Uranus and Neptune which were earlier thought to be safe.

Scientists first thought that a ninth planet existed by looking at the movement of objects that are far away in the solar system. They are still trying to prove its existence, but believe they are close to solving this mystery.

FACT FILE

The mysterious ninth planet is also said to be blamed for four of the five mass extinctions.

184. Crop Circles

Have you seen a crop circle? It is been reported in almost every country on Earth. The mystery started back in 1970 when people saw strange, large circles on green fields. As time went on, the designs became more complex. Those who tried to investigate the origins believed that they were the work of aliens.

However, scientists claim that it is the work of extreme weather. There are some crop circles created by human beings. Researchers are sceptical as to who could have put these crop circles around the world. Scientists are still trying to figure out if crop circles are natural or man-made.

185. Ice Age Conquerors

About 14,500 years ago there was a massive population change that took place in Europe. This is way back when the Ice Age period was coming to an end. This **new mystery** was found when scientists conducted DNA tests on the bones of hunter-gatherers from Europe.

New genes, new techniques and even technology spread in Europe and other continents because of massive waves of immigration. The hunter-gatherers whose bones were tested were immigrants who came to Europe 40,000 years ago. Then 8000 years ago, immigrants from the Middle East came to Europe. This set off the farming period. In this way, modern Europe was a result of mass immigration. However, this is all speculation and not really proven.

186. Mysterious Eye

On a map, it is called the **'Richat Structure'**. But to befuddled scientists and conspiracy theorists, it is called the 'Eye of the Sahara'. This geological mystery is one of the greatest and most breath-taking mysteries of Earth. The structure is about 40 km in diameter.

When it was first spotted from space, people thought it was a crater or an area impacted by an asteroid. From further research, geologists found out that this is a geologic dome created from lots and lots of erosion. One mystery after another keeps emerging from this beautiful structure. Even the rock samples taken from the structure are misleading and confuse scientists.

187. Sailing Stones

We all know that stones are lazy and that they can stay in one place for several years without moving. Sailing stones, however, are another desert mystery that puts the lazy stones to shame. They are found in the Death Valley, USA at a place called Racetrack Playa.

These sailing stones move from one point to another without any help from animals or human beings. They even make right and left turns! Several theories have been put forward to explain this movement. It could be strong winds, evaporating water trapped beneath the stones or some other such cause. Nothing has been proven conclusively.

188. Blue Grotto

Somewhere in the island of Capri, Italy is the Blue Grotto. This is a sea cave that has water. The water is special and mysterious, because it reflects a brilliant blue colour. The cave has two openings that allow sunlight to pass through.

The sunlight is what gives the water this blue reflection which lights up the cave. The entire cave is about 50 m wide and 150 m deep. There is sand at the bottom of the cave. If the sea is not calm, the Blue Grotto becomes difficult to reach. Inside the cave, people found **Roman statues**. Where did the statues come from? That is still a mystery that is close to being solved.

189. Sand Sinkholes

Imagine being **swallowed up by sand**. Nope, this next mystery is not about quick sand but sand sinkholes. They are found in Mount Baldy which is the tallest sand dune near Lake Michigan. It is called a 'living' structure because the wind around the sand causes the sand to keep constantly moving.

Strangely, when the wind moves, it creates sinkholes in the sand. This is a new phenomenon because usually, sand fills up any holes created in the dune. But these holes remain exposed for some time even causing physical harm to people exploring the sand dune. This phenomenon has never been seen before and the mystery is still being solved. The trees growing on the dune might have something to do with it.

190. Hot Spots

The Hawaiian Islands are some of the most beautiful islands in the world. There is a big mystery surrounding the **formation of these islands** that still needs to be solved.

People believe that the Hawaiian Islands were formed when continental plates drifted over a hot spot causing magma to rise and form rows of volcanic islands. But what exactly is a 'hot spot'? This phenomenon is not well-known. Even the location of the hot spot is a mystery, as some claim it exists between the mantle and the inner core, while others think it is much closer to the surface. There is a good chance that hot spots actually don't exist, which means nobody knows how the Hawaiian Islands were formed.

191. Grand Canyon

The Grand Canyon has been around for a long time. Researchers want to know exactly **how old the Grand Canyon is**. It is one of the most famous geological structures on Earth. Many geologists study it and are fascinated by this structure.

A lot of them want to find out the age of the Grand Canyon, but so far there is no definite answer to the question. According to some researchers, the Grand Canyon is just six million years old. But others think this structure is so ancient that it existed more than 60 million years ago! One guess is to look at the Colorado River but researchers are not sure if the Grand Canyon was standing before the river formed.

192. Uturuncu 

A volcano erupted nearly 300,000 years ago in Bolivia. Since then, it has been a subject of great mystery. The Uturuncu volcano is a 20,000-foot-long volcano that has got a strange **growth problem**. The underground chamber of the volcano has been filling up for the past 20 years at a rapid pace. So every year, the floor near the volcano keeps rising by a couple of centimetres.

Scientists are trying to figure out what is causing this rapid growth. They also want to know what it means for the future. Will the volcano explode and result in massive destruction in nearby areas? It takes about 300,000 years between every eruption so the only option is to wait and watch.

193. Bubble-gum Lake 

Earth is called the blue planet, but not every water body is blue. Lake Hillier is pink. Located in Australia, it was discovered in 1802. The wildlife around the lake is threatened, and as a result, the only way to see this lake is from the sky.

That is why we know very little about this lake. This lake is therefore one of the biggest mysteries in the world. What we do know is that this lake has a lot of salt but it is safe to swim in. The pink colour is probably caused by the bacteria and marine life that live in the lake. Or it could be the result of chemical reactions.

FACT FILE

Boquila on the ground get eaten more than camouflaged Boquila on trees.

194. Boquila Mysteries

The Boquila (or Boquila trifoliolata) is a vine that has generated a lot of interest because of the mysteries it hides. Found in Chile and Argentina, the Boquila survives best in temperate rain forests. Like most vines, the Boquila also wraps itself around trees or crawls on the floor.

But what is surprising is that without support, the leaves of the vine look round and stout with a light green colour. Then when they wrap themselves around a tree, they become narrow and dark green. They also look longer. This means that the leaves of the vine actually change appearance to match their new surroundings. This has never been seen in vines before! Unlike the mimosa plant, the leaves don't need to have any contact to change appearance and shape.

Researchers found that all vines of this kind tend to change their appearance. The only difference is that the leaves become round and stumpy if the tree they have wrapped themselves around has such leaves.

But why does this happen? Maybe the plant feels like it needs to fit in with the cool leaves of the tree, or maybe it is some protective instinct to camouflage itself. Possibly because the vine does not want to be eaten by caterpillars. Or it wants to look like the scary, poisonous leaves that caterpillars crawl away from.

The mystery is what causes these leaves to change their appearance this way.

195. Desert Shine

Most desert rocks have a shiny, thin coat. The coat tends to look light orange or black in colour. It is like varnish on the rocks. Ancient people scraped lines on the varnish to create symbols and art. The desert varnish is a well-known concept. Yet, nobody can explain how this varnish is formed.

We know that varnish on rocks is formed from clay while the colour comes from iron or manganese. Though this might be the case, it doesn't satisfactorily explain desert varnish. Another theory claims that desert varnish is formed from microorganisms that live on the rocks. However, microorganisms don't normally produce varnish.

196. American Samoa

Global warming has threatened marine life, especially coral reefs. But there are corals in American Samoa that have been able to resist the damage caused by global warming. How they are able to do this is still a mystery. If the mystery is solved, it can help scientists recreate the environment for other coral reefs to be protected.

On one hand, scientists predict that coral life will come to an end by 2050. On the other hand, the corals in American Samoa have actually become stronger and have been able to survive the warm waters that might be deadly for other corals. They have also grown in size.

197. The Great Serpent Mound

One of the biggest mysteries in the world is the meaning and use behind 'The Great Serpent Mound'. This is a **1300-foot long** effigy that is about 3 feet tall. Located in Ohio, it happens to be the oldest surviving prehistoric effigy in the world. The name comes from the appearance of this breath-taking structure, because it looks like a giant serpent that is about to uncoil and attack.

The plateau on which the Great Serpent Mound was built is quite curved, and so is this effigy. The skill required to build such an effigy completely changes the view that people first had of the intelligence and capabilities of ancient people. There are seven coils on the effigy which curves and unwinds for 800 feet. The mouth of the serpent is open and there is a round structure to one side of it which looks like its egg. However, even its meaning is a mystery as different people choose to perceive it in different ways.

Researchers believe that prehistoric people built the effigy by first laying the base with ash and clay. Later, they filled it up with solid stones and strengthened the structure. This structure is dated back to 1070 BCE. The effigy could have been built by the Fort Ancient Peoples, who lived in this part of Ohio from 1000 to 1550 BCE. But testing on the material of the effigy shows that it is only 1000 years old. Therefore, there is a lot of conflicting data to get through.

FACT FILE

The Great Serpent Mount was once used for religious ceremonies.

198. The Twin Town

There is a village in Kerala, India named 'Kodinhi'. This small village in the district of Melappuram, has a very strange unsolved mystery. It has a **high concentration of twin siblings**. This is not common in the rest of the country. That is why Kodinhi has been nicknamed 'The Twin Town'.

The village has a population of only about 20,000 people. From this number, 500 siblings are twins of different ages and genders. Doctors have collected saliva and urine samples of as many twins as they can to find out what the mystery behind this is.

199. The Ghost Village

Another village in India named '**Kuldhara**' in Rajasthan is also known as 'The Ghost Village'. That is because two hundred years ago, an entire community from the village disappeared overnight with no trace as to where they went. That is nearly 1500 villagers who nobody saw leave.

Some of the villagers there think that they left behind a curse to kill all the remaining inhabitants of Kuldhara. It is considered both foolish and courageous to visit the village or even stay the night there. Rumour has it that a minister had fallen in love with a girl from the village and threatened the chief that if he didn't get to marry her, then he would kill everyone there.

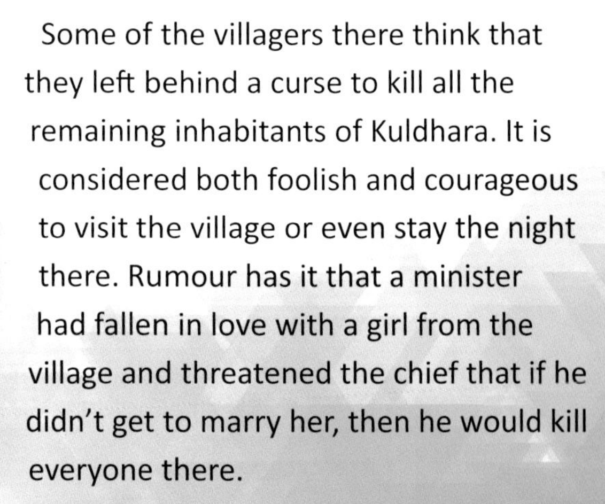

200. Hanging Pillar

In the **Veerabhadra temple** that was built in the 16th century, a strange mystery awaits all the worshippers. The temple has a 'Hanging Pillar', which is a stone pillar hanging from the ceiling. Its base does not completely touch the ground. Visitors amuse themselves by passing thin blankets or papers under the pillar from one side to the other.

The pillar did not always stand like this. Apparently, it was dislodged from its original position when a British engineer tried to move it to find out how it could support itself. Besides this pillar, the entire temple is a place of architectural and engineering wonder.

201. Breatharian

A man named Prahlad Jani from India, has claimed that he hasn't had food or water for the past seven decades. He has been dismissed by some as a fraud, but the Indian defence research organisation took him in to test whether he was telling the truth. They kept him under strict observation to see how exactly he was able to survive without any sustenance.

Such a person is known as a 'breatharian', a person **who can live on spiritual life-force**. Scientists of India's defence and research organisation think that by finding out his secret, they could teach their soldiers to survive at war without food or water for a long time.

202. Faults

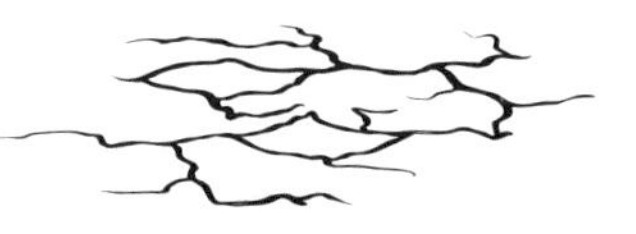

Have you heard of faults? They are cracks that form on Earth's surface over time, and are an interesting geological phenomenon. They are caused when rocks slide past each other and create friction. The part of the fault that rests on top is called the 'hanging wall'. The part below is called the 'footwell'. If a hanging wall starts sliding up or sliding down the footwell, the resulting fault becomes even deeper. They are called 'slip-dip faults'.

A normal fault that is observed around the world has a very shallow slope. The fault can be horizontal or it can have a very low angle. They are called 'low-angled normal faults'. It is strange to see such faults in the Earth because theoretically, they should not even exist. Instead, the faults should just get steeper. Geologists have been stumped by this mystery for years and have named it 'the greatest problem of tectonic plate theories'.

According to the theory, a normal fault should not move as the two sides of it should lock it in place. If a fault is locked in place, the friction will build up until there is a violent reaction like an earthquake. But low-angled normal faults don't cause earthquakes. At least, that is how the theory goes. This great gap in reality and theory is quite frustrating for researchers who have been trying to find answers to this problem for years.

FACT FILE

There are four main types of faults - normal, reverse, strike-slip and slip-dip.

Mysteries of the Human Body

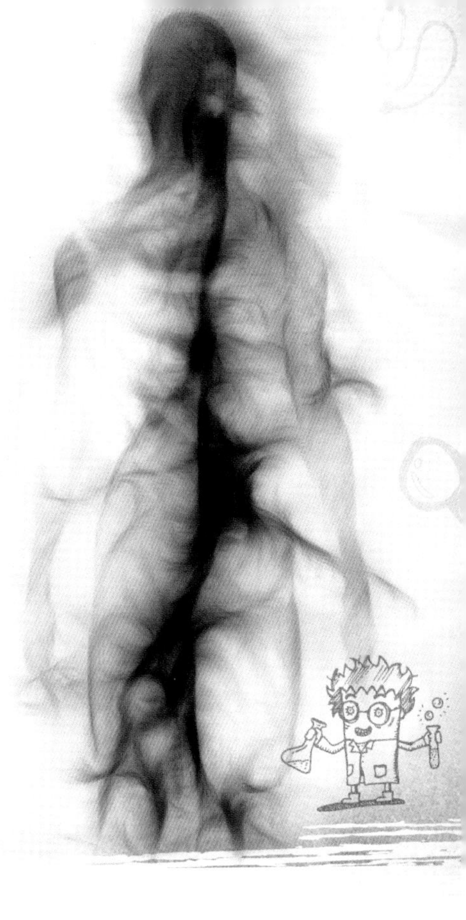

Human beings have been pursuing mysteries around the world in order to find answers. But there are some mysteries that are not too far away. The human body itself has many mysteries that are yet to be solved.

Our brain, heart, limbs, muscles and other parts of the body hide certain secrets that scientists are desperate to solve. The more we understand the human body, the easier will it be to fight diseases and find cures. Take a look at some of the unsolved mysteries of the human body.

203. Ape Strength

Chimpanzees are one of the closest primate relatives of human beings. There are certain resemblances between humans and chimpanzees. If you look at a chimpanzee's body from neck to waist, and compare it to a human body, you will observe a similar muscular build.

Yet, strangely, chimpanzees are three times stronger than human beings. A chimpanzee can snap the branches of a tree easily, but a human being would need a tool. It is a mystery why human beings do not match chimpanzees in strength despite a similar build. Scientists believe it is because of subtle differences in the way our muscles are attached or how dense our muscle fibres are. It is also because chimpanzees live in forests where such skills are more useful to them.

204. Brain Sickness

Why do people get malaria? Because they have been bitten by a mosquito. And why do some suffer from the flu? That's because of the influenza virus.

Now why does the **brain get sick**? Do you know the answer? One of the most scary and unsolved mysteries in the world is that we don't know why the brain gets affected by diseases like Alzheimer's. The brain is a very complex organ. If we don't know the cause of brain diseases, we cannot treat it effectively.

Researchers must find the answers by trying to fully understand how the brain functions. But even this is a big mystery that has puzzled scientists for years.

205. What are Emotions?

When you see a puppy, **what do you feel**? Hopefully, happy. In the same way, when you are in an argument, you begin to feel angry or annoyed. These are emotions that you could feel all over your body.

There is a big difference between emotion and feeling in that feelings are subjective among people while emotions are quite standard. People around the world have similar emotions but might feel things differently towards their neighbours or friends.

One of the big mysteries of the human brain is why and how we experience emotions, how we experience feelings and why do they vary from person to person.

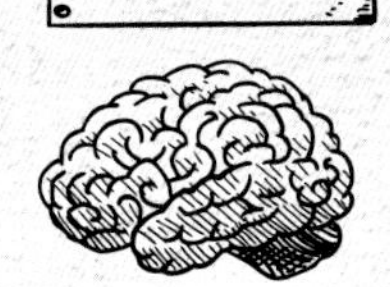

206. Does Size Matter?

Did you know that not everyone's **brains are of the same size**? That's right! Researchers have found that men have bigger brains than women. But this is because on an average men are physically bigger than women in size.

The size of the brain is a very important subject for scientists. Some believe that our brains become smaller as we age. Some believe that smarter people have bigger brains and higher IQ.

So, does that mean that men are smarter than women? Well, it depends on which scientist you ask. Some scientists have conducted tests with both men and women and found men scored higher points. Others found that women scored higher points.

Some scientists don't believe that the size of the brain matters as much as the size of parts of the brain. Einstein was said to have an average-sized brain. Yet, parts of his brain were bigger than average. Especially a part known as the "inferior parietal region" which helps us understand mathematics better.

Many cultures believe that bigger brains lead to higher intelligence and that you can change the size of your brain by eating certain foods. Some others believe that repeatedly performing certain activities will increase important parts of the brain.

Scientists have evidence that taxi drivers who drive more and more complicated routes show an increase in the size of parts of their brains.

207. Common Human Hair Colour

Most people have black hair. It is the most common hair colour observed around the world. The rarest hair colour however is red. In fact, red hair was once considered to be a sign of black magic, because of how rare it was. But why is this the case? That is still a mystery. The clue to understanding this might be in pigmentation.

The colour of one's hair depends upon the **pigmentation of the hair follicles**. There are two types of melanin called eumelanin and pheomelanin. If there is more eumelanin, then a person's hair is the darker shade of their hair colour. If there is less eumelanin, then the person's hair is a lighter shade of their hair colour. But this just shows, how dark or light the colour of the hair will appear to be.

208. Handedness

Did you know that out of every ten people, it is most likely that nine of them are right-handed? This means that they use their right hands to do things like write and eat comfortably. It is called the **'dominant hand'**.

The first mystery to solve is why are so many people right-handed rather than left-handed. The second is why do human beings have a dominant hand? Why can't they use both hands just as well? It might have something to do with which side of the brain is used for speech, which usually is the left hemisphere of the brain. However, some right-handed people don't use the left hemisphere to control speech, while many left-handed people do.

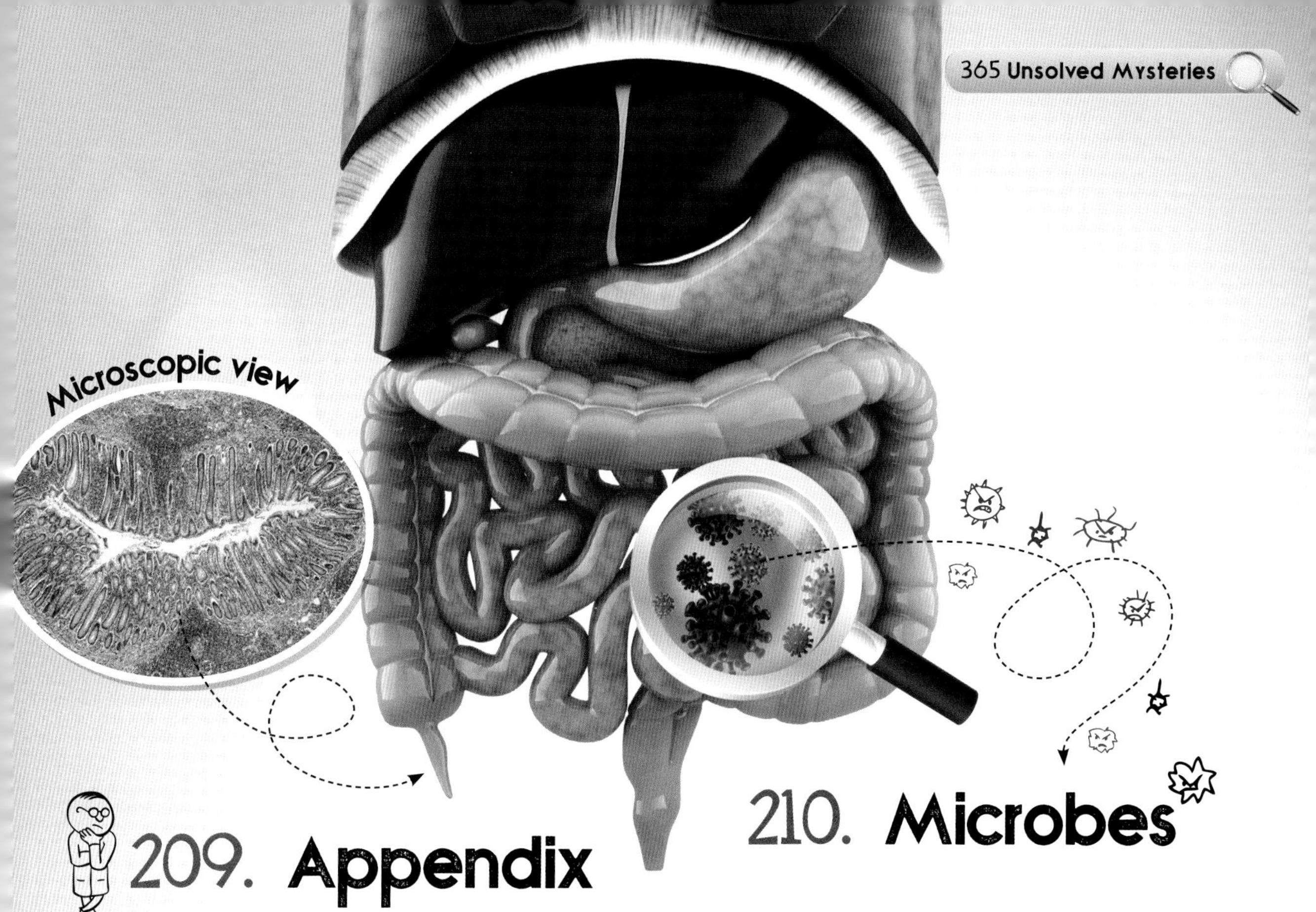

209. Appendix

There are some parts of the human body that are considered to be **'useless'**. Be it the wisdom teeth, muscles that help wiggle ears or the appendix. You must have watched a show or read a book where a person suddenly experiences pain, and it turns out they just need their appendix removed. In fact, the very name 'appendix' means 'add-on'.

However, scientists are now trying to find out if the appendix really is useless. Could it be holding a stash of microbes? In this way it could replenish the digestive system after a person suffers from diarrhoea or stomach flu.

The appendix might be training the immune system of the body while the foetus still grows in the womb.

210. Microbes

Find out your weight. Now subtract 1–3 per cent from your weight. This is the weight of the **microbes that are living inside you**. An average human body has 30 trillion cells, with 40 trillion bacteria. Most of the bacteria reside in the digestive tract.

These microbes are sometimes helpful. They help digest the food we eat, they help keep the skin clean or produce sweat. Most healthy people have viruses living in them that could be harmful, but instead these viruses actually help the body.

How and why these microbes live in and help humans is unknown. But if you try to get rid of them, you might end up with diseases like diabetes.

211. Pain

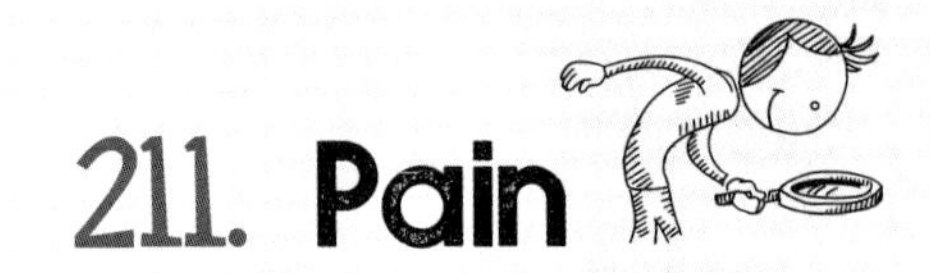

We all feel pain. It is experienced by both animals and human beings. We feel pain to some degree when we enter the world, and it is possible we will feel pain when we leave it. We can all describe pain as getting hurt or bruising. Pain is also felt when extreme pressure is applied on any part of the body. But **what exactly is pain**?

One of the bigger mysteries of the brain is which region of the brain tells us we are in pain? Is it the same region that tells us when different parts are in pain or are there different regions for different parts? Do we all feel pain the same way?

212. Anaesthesia

Anaesthesia is a drug used on patients before surgeries. The goal of anaesthesia is to numb pain artificially so that the patient cannot register the pain. When it is administered, anaesthesia can shut down parts of the brain.

However, here's something strange...if too much of it is administered then it means that you won't wake up. If too little of it is administered then it means that you will feel pain through the surgery. Just the right amount means that the chemicals work correctly. But how do they work and how do they affect the body? That's a mystery.

213. Armpit Hair

Even though primates are distant relatives, human beings have many differences from primates. One major difference is how much **hair grows on the body**. Human beings, through evolution, have evolved and lost a lot of hair on their body.

Instead, there are smatterings of hair on the hands, fingers and legs. Some areas do, however, still have a lot of hair. The armpits are where a lot of hair grows freely. Nobody knows exactly why the hair grows here. Is it to keep these parts free from friction? Is it to protect them from harmful bacteria? The purpose of the hair is unknown.

214. Super Smell

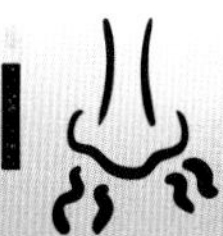

Pregnant women often complain of a **heightened sense of smell** which is why they feel like vomiting if they smell something bad. It is a very strange phenomenon. Not all pregnant women experience this super smell.

When a woman becomes pregnant, her hormones (or estrogen) react in a way that she achieves a heightened sense of smell. In fact, even before testing for pregnancy, a woman can tell if she is pregnant by getting this super smell symptom. But nobody knows exactly why this happens.

It is possible that women have this sudden super power because the body instinctively is trying to protect the mother from smelling toxic or harmful things that could harm the baby.

215. Autism

Do you know what **autism** is? Autism Spectrum Disorder (ASD) or autism is a disorder that affects the brain's development. Children with autism have trouble with social interaction. They might also have trouble with interacting through verbal and nonverbal communication or understanding it.

For every 100 people, one person has autism. Why autism affects people is unknown. Scientists believe that it could be caused because of faster brain development in some children. It could also be a result of overstimulation in the brain. Once we find out what causes autism, it will be easier to find personalised treatment for every autism patient.

216. Laughter

One symptom of autism is sudden and unexplainable laughter. But actually, why people laugh is still a mystery. **Why do people laugh and have fun**? You might say it is because they heard a joke, but the psychological reason behind laughter is unknown.

Laughter is an involuntary reaction, which means that people cannot control themselves when they laugh. Everyone laughs for different reasons. Two people might not find the same joke funny. Scientists think that laughter is necessary so that people can balance their mental processes and relieve their stress. When a person laughs, antidepressant hormones are released in the body. Laughter makes it easier to fight worry or anger. So, it is important to know why people laugh. Most emotions are connected to the brain. So the more we find out about it, the better.

217. Sleep Jerks

When you are almost asleep, you suddenly jerk awake. Have you ever experienced this? Nearly 70 per cent of people wake up from their sleep because of sudden jerks or twitches. This is called **'hypnagogic jerk'** or 'hypnic jerk'. It is an involuntary action and forces the person to wake up for a few seconds.

The hypnic jerk causes a person to have rapid heartbeats and quick breathing. They might wake up sweating. Scientists don't know why this happens. Those who have a bad sleep schedule tend to experience this more than others. Could it possibly be a reaction, to some ancient signal, that a primate had of falling off a tree while sleeping?

218. Speech Evolution

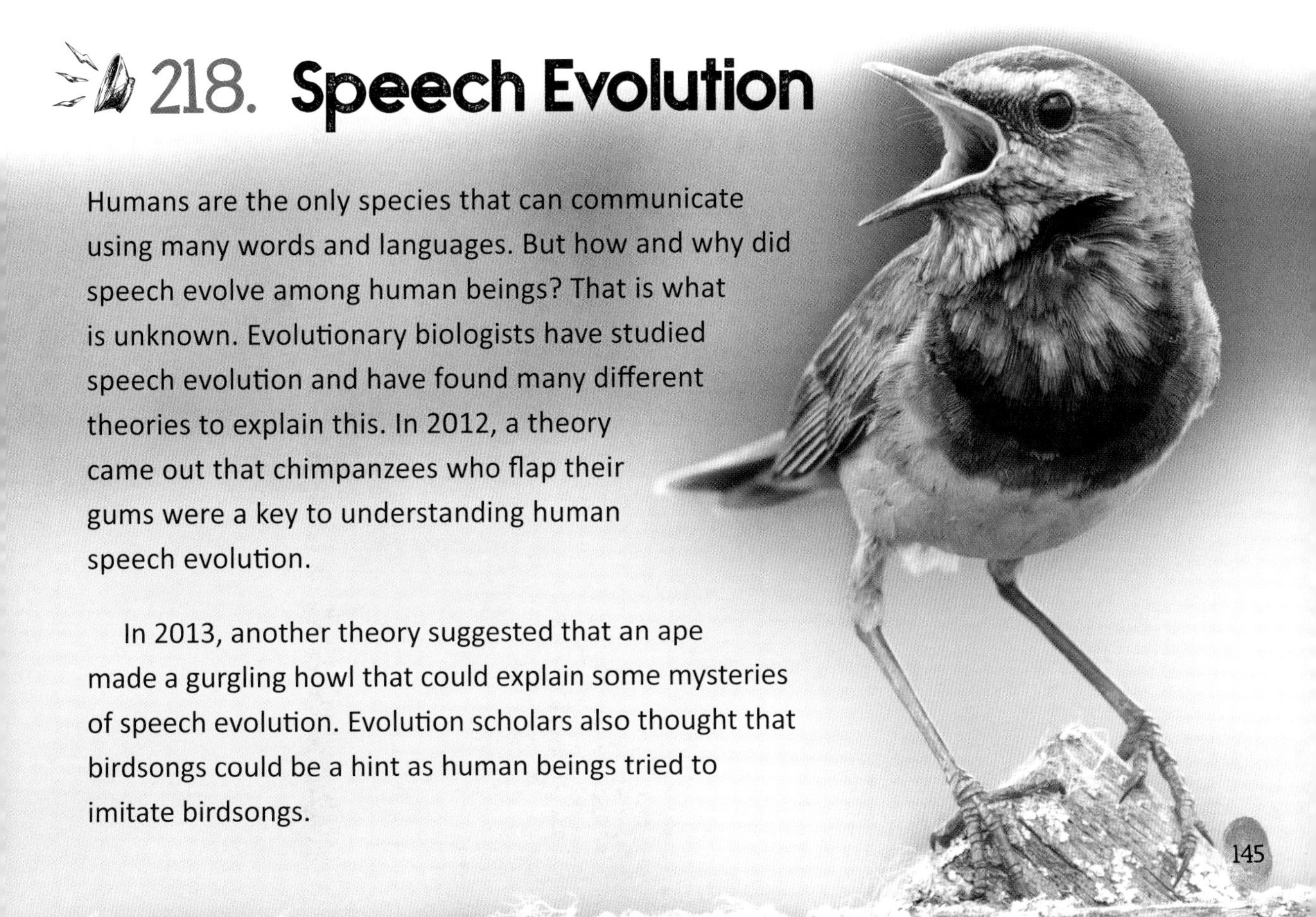

Humans are the only species that can communicate using many words and languages. But how and why did speech evolve among human beings? That is what is unknown. Evolutionary biologists have studied speech evolution and have found many different theories to explain this. In 2012, a theory came out that chimpanzees who flap their gums were a key to understanding human speech evolution.

In 2013, another theory suggested that an ape made a gurgling howl that could explain some mysteries of speech evolution. Evolution scholars also thought that birdsongs could be a hint as human beings tried to imitate birdsongs.

219. Sneezing at the Sun

Some people sneeze when they look at the Sun's light or at bright lights. It is called the **photic sneeze reflex**. This is a condition where a person cannot control a sneeze, and they might sneeze many times. It is an involuntary reflex to a stimulus like a bright light.

It is said to affect 18 or 35 per cent of the entire world's population. This is a very old phenomenon that even Aristotle wrote about in 350 BCE in his *The Book of Problems*. According to him, the Sun's heat causes a person to sweat inside the nose, thus making them sneeze. This theory however, has not been confirmed.

Aristotle was proven wrong in the 17th century, when Francis Bacon, an English professor, stood before the Sun and didn't feel like sneezing. He said that instead of the nose, the reason for the sneezing reflex must be the eyes. If you look at a light for too long then the eyes water, and the moisture seeps into the nose. This moisture irritates the nose and causes a person to sneeze in response.

Later, another person named Henry Everett proposed that the nervous system transmits a lot of signals quickly at the same time which causes confusion. However, why this confusion results in a sneeze is unknown.

While this problem is not very harmful, it still is a big mystery why the body reacts in this way. Those who cover their eyes with hats or sunglasses can avoid the problem.

FACT FILE

A photic sneeze reflex patient might sneeze while getting anaesthesia during an eye surgery.

220. Why Do We Dream?

All humans, and even some animals, **dream when** they sleep. We all have different dreams. But why do we dream? Is there some useful purpose behind it?

One theory is that dreaming is a way for our brain to sort through the information it has collected during waking hours. This information can be anything from the smell of a flower to the date of someone's birthday. Whatever information is useless is forgotten, and whatever is important is remembered. This is also how we form memories.

Another theory says it is just like our brain is putting up a screensaver when it is working in the background. None of the suggested theories have been confirmed.

221. Nightmare Reign

A bad or scary dream is a nightmare. It might even cause a person to wake up in the middle of their sleep. Nightmares usually happen when a **person is scared or worried** about something in their life.

However, it is possible that nightmares have a beneficial purpose. There are two types of nightmares. One is when you have nightmares after experiencing something horrible in life. Another is simply a nightmare that occurs at night, unrelated to daily life. Scientists think it is better to interpret your dreams and nightmares than to try and forget about them.

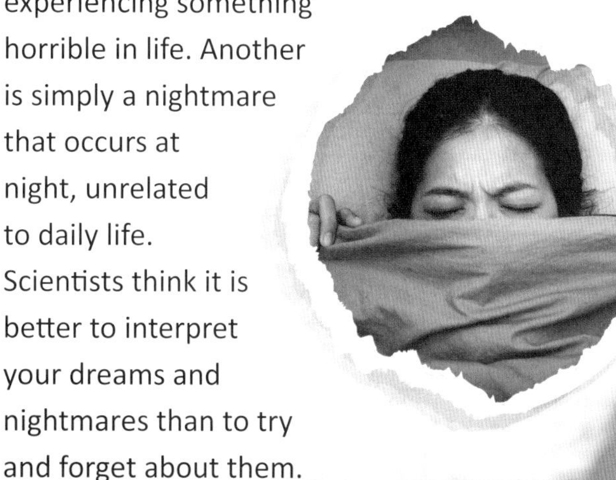

222. Ebola's Hiding Place

A little boy named Emile Ouamouno from an African village suffered from some intense symptoms like high fever, black stools and constant vomiting. After his death, his sister, mother, neighbour and a nurse died of the same symptoms. This contagious disease spread to other parts of the village. And that is how the world was introduced to a disease called 'Ebola'.

It is a **virus that disappears** for many years at a stretch. After 1976, it disappeared for 17 years. Recently, in 2013, it spread to three continents and killed many people. All viruses need a host. So, what does the Ebola virus consider a host? And where does it hide? That sure is a mystery!

223. Yawning

Yawning has been discussed by scientists for over 2500 years. You would think that by this time human beings would know everything about yawning. But not much is known about it including **why people yawn**. Yawning is an involuntary action. An average person's yawn lasts for six seconds.

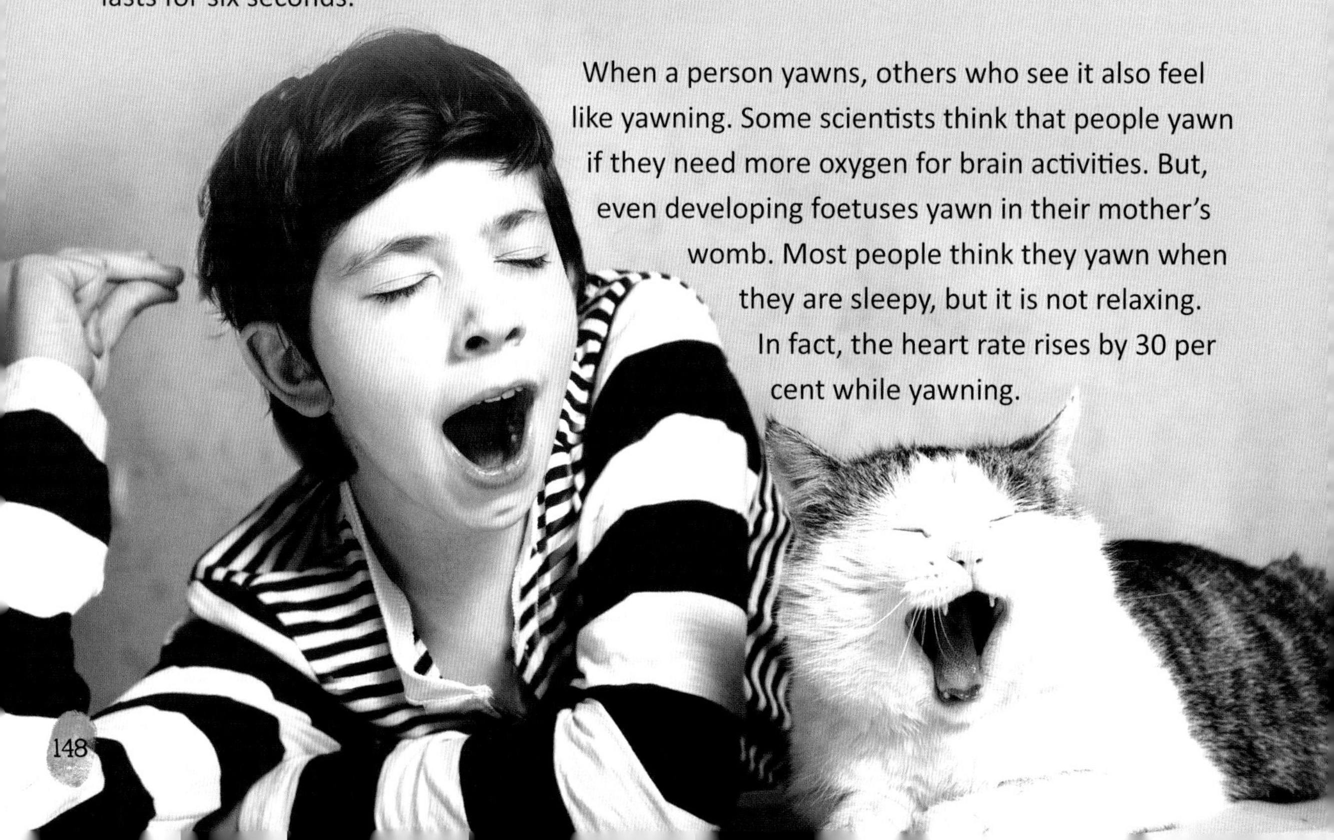

When a person yawns, others who see it also feel like yawning. Some scientists think that people yawn if they need more oxygen for brain activities. But, even developing foetuses yawn in their mother's womb. Most people think they yawn when they are sleepy, but it is not relaxing. In fact, the heart rate rises by 30 per cent while yawning.

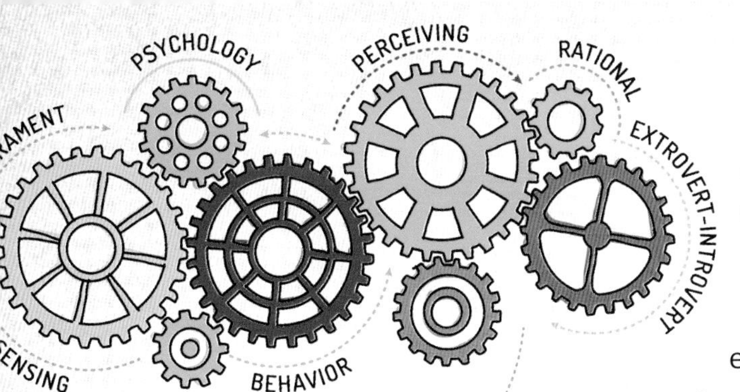

224. Personality

Scientists have always debated the effect of **nature or nurture** on a person's development. A scientist named Steven Pinker believes that all human beings are born with certain personality traits or abilities. Other scientists think that a human being is born like a blank slate, and their surroundings and circumstances are what define their personalities. While still another side believes that people are born with certain traits and preferences passed down through their genes.

What exactly shapes ones personality? Is it the impact of genes or the environment or a mix of both? And where does the effect of genes start and end? To find out, scientists study twins who were separated at birth.

225. Adaptation

Adaptation is the process in which animals like chameleons, or plants like the mimosa **adapt to their surroundings**. It is the change in the physical feature or behaviour of a living organism to adjust to its environment. Adaptation is a process of evolution. A gene in a living organism might change by accident or even 'mutate'. Mutate means to change, to survive or reproduce. This changed trait is passed on to the offspring.

That is how adaptation works. It occurs over many years. But the mystery is that there is no clear model on adaptation that defines how it takes place or when it is complete. Some scientists think living organisms are constantly adapting. Of course, when we do stop adapting we might become extinct.

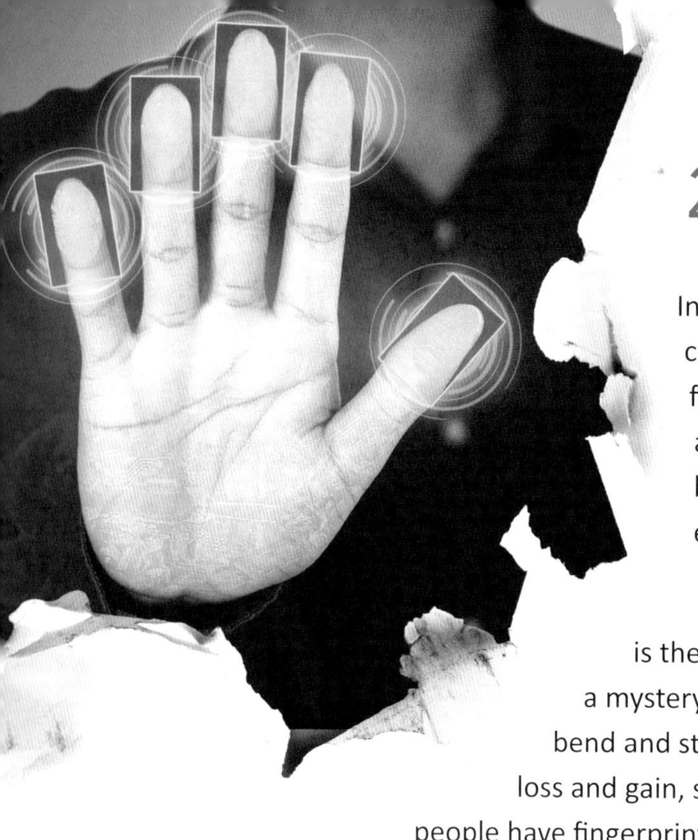

226. Fingerprints

In almost every spy movie, detectives come closer to solving the crime, when they take fingerprints of all the suspects. **Fingerprints** are unique to every person. People even believe that they have a meaning that can explain different personalities.

But why do we have fingerprints? What is their function in terms of biology? That is a mystery. A person has wrinkles because they bend and stretch their skin over time through weight loss and gain, smiling or other such activities. But why people have fingerprints and how they get them is still unknown. Scientists believed that fingerprints helped humans grip objects but that was disproven. Now no one knows what fingerprints are for.

227. Free Will

Free will is not just an option in video games. Human beings have free will. This means that a person can act and do things that they want to without being interrupted by an external force like fate. A person's actions are up to their decisions and abilities.

Scientists do not know how and why human beings and other living beings have free will. Even philosophers have been trying to figure it out. The question is, is free will real or is it just an imaginary concept? Once people understand what free will is and how it works, there could be other breakthroughs in understanding how the complex mechanism of the human body works.

228. Art

Do **human beings create** art to impress others or to share knowledge? That is the question. Scientists think it might be a way for people to display their own talents and make themselves look good before potential mates. But the better reason could be because they want to share their knowledge with other people.

There are several art forms in the world. Political art is supposed to enlighten people about the injustices of the world, religious art is supposed to teach people about religious practices, functional art is supposed to look beautiful and also serve a purpose. Art is also one way to learn about history, either by learning from the paintings made by ancestors or by recreating scenes from history in art.

229. Blushing

Why do humans blush? It could be a fight or flight response. Women try to recreate it with makeup. When people lie, or feel embarrassed, their cheeks turn red and **become warm**. Charles Darwin observed this in humans and tried to figure out why it happened. He called it the 'most peculiar and most human of all expressions'.

Blushing could make people feel uncomfortable if they notice it. It is an awkward social reaction as it reveals when a person is lying. Blushes are more obvious on fair skin than dark skin. According to Darwin, blushing is a reaction to adrenaline, causing capillaries to carry blood to the skin. The skin widens.

230. Gravity's Effect

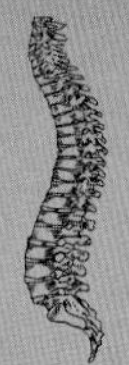

According to NASA, astronauts grow **taller by 2 inches** when they are in space. But when they come back to Earth, they go back to their normal height. NASA explained it by telling people that the vertebrae form something like a giant spring that is pushed down by gravity. There is no gravity in space, so the vertebrae elongate to their maximum extent which is about 7.6 cm or 3 inches.

Something similar happens to people every night when they go to sleep. While lying down, it is difficult for gravity to push down on a person's vertebrae. Therefore, a person who has been lying down for a while is taller in height compared to when he or she is standing. There is no fixed theory that can explain this mystery.

I'm taller in space.

One theory says that the spine is elongated which causes this change in height. It does not affect other parts of the body. The spine has discs that can be compressed by gravity. Other parts of the body have rigid bones. The spine also has a natural curve or a pronounced slump which is checked in space. Without gravity, the spine can relax and elongate to its maximum height.

The other theory says that the discs that are placed between each vertebrae press together because of gravity on Earth. Just like we cannot float on Earth because gravity pushes us down, the spine too is pushed down by this gravity. In this way, the discs can hold less spinal fluid and become compressed.

FACT FILE

Astronauts took 10 days to go back to their normal height when they returned to Earth.

231. Late Growth

Puberty means that a boy or a girl reaches sexual maturity. For human beings, they start to undergo puberty when they are teenagers. Our primate relatives, transition from childhood to adolescence and then to adulthood when they are five years old. They skip the 'teenage' phase of life. Their transition period is not too long either. For human beings, it takes several years. The period of adolescence in human beings is usually 11 to 20 years. It might start earlier for boys.

Why do humans have a **longer period of adolescence**? According to scientists, the more time it takes to develop social skills, the longer it takes for puberty to end and maturity to begin.

232. Picking the Nose

It is an uncontrollable urge to begin **picking one's nose**. It is also an unhygienic habit that people dislike, then why do so many people do it? According to scientists, picking the nose is a way to remove little nostril hair that filter the dust from the air that we breathe in, and massage the nose. This habit might not be helpful.

Another mysterious thing about this habit is that some children (and even adults) pick their noses and then eat the mucus that they pick out. This apparently builds the immune system of the body because the bacteria in it work like a vaccine in the stomach. However, this habit could also harm the nose.

233. Superstitions

A superstition is an irrational belief in **supernatural forces** or concepts like bad luck, bad spirits and so on. Many people around the world believe in superstitions regardless of their religious and spiritual beliefs. Despite being the smartest living species, human beings are the only ones who believe in superstitions.

It is a way for people to have control over situations that they cannot control. This might also be a way to alleviate blame. You cannot control having 'bad luck' or 'good luck'. But you can make sure that you take a step back when you see a black cat. But what are the psychological reasons for believing in superstitions? This is still an unsolved mystery.

234. Generosity Genes

People want to help others in times of trouble, be it friends or complete strangers who need help in any way. **Altruism** is a word that means to live an unselfish life. But what makes people unselfish or generous? Why do they want to help others in times of need? Scientists think that generosity is a way for people to show others that they are good. This is how they attract a mate.

Scientists also think that altruism is one of the reasons why people want to become parents and raise their children well. It is possible that a good person will pass their 'good genes' forward so that their children are also altruistic.

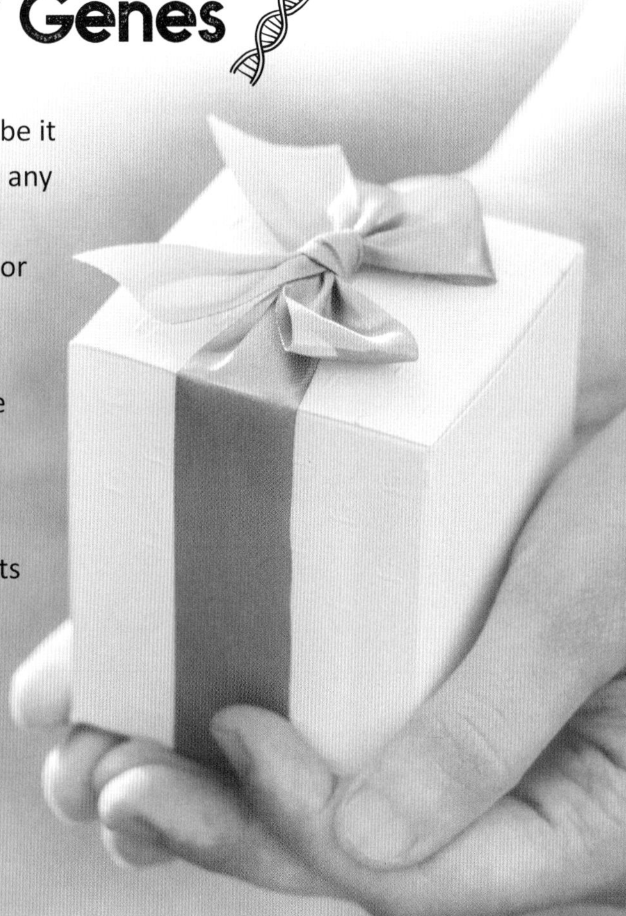

235. Time

One of the important things we learn in school is to **tell the time**. But how does our brain sense and understand what is time and how it passes? Nobody truly knows. Scientists believe that there is an "internal clock" just like there is an external clock. But this concept is still to be proven. There might be distinct neural systems in our brain that specifically help us process time.

Without such ability, a person could shower for hours or drive for a longer time than necessary and miss the next turn. Scientists think that the brain recognises that there are different types of time and that is why we don't eat breakfast for hours.

236. Music and Emotion

You might feel sad when you **listen to a sad song**. If you listen to something peppy, you might feel energised and ready to dance. Music could also affect how we see others. But why does music affect our moods and control our emotions?

We attach an emotion to every song that we listen to with or without our realising it. We even display certain expressions or do certain actions while listening to songs. Music triggers emotional responses in human beings. Music also triggers a physical response. Scientists believe that music is relaxing but other than that it has nothing to do with survival. So how does it alter our moods and emotions? That's a mystery!

237. Neural Codes

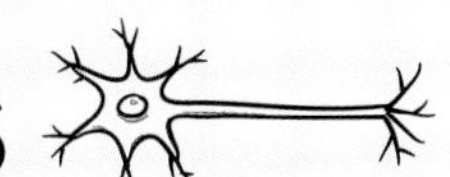

Neurons are the cells of the brain that specialise in certain tasks. They give out electrical pulses that can travel to different sections of the brain to send messages or information. The things we recognise with our five senses, as well as the feelings we might have such as hunger and thirst, are communicated through neurons.

This is very similar to how computers send signals to different parts. But while we know the code that a computer uses, we do not know the **coding system of neurons**. Once we understand how information is received, stored, processed and shared with different parts of the brain, we will be able to solve many diseases.

238. Hiccups

When you have hiccups, it is **difficult to get rid of them**. Imagine having continuous hiccups for two years nonstop. Christopher Sands was a young man who had to live with hiccups for two years. Chronic hiccuping started for no apparent reason.

Sands complained that he could hiccup for 14 hours in a day without stopping. Suddenly, the hiccups would start and just as

suddenly, they would disappear. To get rid of them, Sands tried every type of treatment he could think of. But nothing seemed to work. He was finally cured when a tumour was removed from his brain stem. So why did Sands' hiccups last for so long? That is a mystery.

239. Human Intelligence

What does being intelligent mean to you? For some it means getting good marks in exams. For others, it means being able to create a painting or write a book. Even scientists don't know in biological terms what intelligence means.

The mystery about intelligence is how neurons in the brain can work together to process information and use learned lessons as knowledge to deal with new situations. The brain can even erase or forget information that becomes useless over time. The brain can mix two learned concepts and put them together to solve the situation.

240. Brain Stops Working

Some brain diseases cause the **brain cells to die off due to degeneration**. Very little is known about why and how these cells degenerate. Once the cells degenerate, they leave behind some build up that is sticky and accumulates. This is called amyloid plaque. These might be big clues to understanding why brain cells degenerate.

It is possible that these plaques are the cause of degeneration. They could also be a reason to understand how to cure the problem of brain cells degenerating.

241. Dark Matter

Dark matter is a big mystery to scientists who have been trying to figure out what it is, for decades. It is invisible material that could make up nearly 80 per cent of the matter in the universe, which also includes human beings.

More than 10 years ago, scientists sequenced the human genome. 'Genome' is the set of genes or genetic material that is present in the cells of the human body or other organisms. While they knew what the different things might be, they could not understand how to explain a lot of things that they found.

Scientists found that nearly 80 per cent of our DNA has dark matter. Earlier, the major chunk of our DNA was thought to be 'junk' which does nothing and has no effect. Now, it is possible that the dark matter has a huge impact on how the body evolves and the kind of diseases the body might have.

Like the dark matter in the universe, people are no closer to finding out what the dark matter in the human body or DNA is and what it does.

There are variations in the DNA that can cause diseases. These diseases might not be connected to the genes themselves but with the chunks of DNA that control those genes.

FACT FILE

The Human Genome Project is called 'Encyclopaedia of DNA Elements" or "ENCODE'.

242. Déjà Vu

'Déjà Vu' means to **see something again**. If you have ever had a feeling that you have seen or experienced something without any memory of it before, then that is called déjà vu. It is a creepy feeling that many of us experience. That is why neuroscientists have been interested with it. But it is difficult to understand why people have this feeling.

One of the challenges of solving this mystery is that people dismiss it immediately. It is short-lived and fleeting. The feeling of déjà vu cannot be triggered. It is just a feeling people have unpredictably. Interestingly, déjà vu about a person and déjà vu about a place come from different regions of the brain.

243. Snappy Beats

Is it possible that a song can cause a seizure in the listener? That is what happened to a woman named Stacey Gayle when she was listening to her favourite song by Sean Paul, a singer. She was listening to a fun rap song when she had her first seizure. The experience was repeated many times. Gayle kept having seizures until she got treatment.

Seizures occur when the part of the brain that processes emotions overlaps with the part that might trigger a seizure. But this experience of having a seizure after listening to a particular song is so rare that doctors don't know the real cause of the seizure.

244. Baseline Activity

Did you know that brain activity can be represented in a laboratory as a picture or a sound? When the brain is at rest, which is also an activity, it is called **'baseline activity'**. What this is and what it represents is still unknown. Figuring out what this is might be the most important finding about the brain.

When the body is awake and the brain is at rest, 20 per cent of the total oxygen and nutrient consumption of the body is used up by the brain. But the brain only makes up for two per cent of body mass. It is the most demanding organ of the body. So, what exactly is baseline activity?

245. Integration

Different parts of the brain focus on different functions. While we don't know everything that the brain is capable of and everything that each part does, we do know that **all the parts of the brain work together** in harmony.

The question is how do specialised parts of the brain integrate with one another? Only when the brain works together can we get one perspective on the world. What are the parts of the brain that are involved in making the different sections integrate? How exactly is this done? And what happens in case of a discrepancy? These questions have been unanswered for years.

246. Computer Brain

The **brain is said to be the CPU** of the body. Alan Turning, a computer scientist, said that the computation that the brain does can be used as a model to create processes in computers and other machines. That is when people started to look at the human brain and its functions like a computer.

Other scientists think that this idea is far-fetched and that human beings cannot replicate how the brain works in machines. The major case for this argument is that machines don't have 'consciousness' and 'free will', which human beings have. Humans don't know why they have these as well. So, can the brain be computerised? That is a mystery.

247. Movement

Typing on a keyboard might seem mundane, but it is an accomplishment that human beings have made through evolution. Our bodies can **move through space and time**, but how do we control our bodies to perform actions and react to external things?

Our brain has nerves that help us with movement. They are called 'motor nerves'. But they are quite slow and unpredictable. There is another part of the brain that helps us work faster and smoother. But the link between these parts of the brain is unknown.

248. Alzheimer's Disease

Solving the mysteries of the brain, as well as the mysteries of the other parts of the body, will help us understand why certain diseases are caused. It will also help us cure several diseases. Alzheimer's disease is one such disease whose cause and **cure is a mystery**.

Scientists suspect there is a protein called 'tau' that stabilises microtubules. Too much of these proteins could build up inside the nerve cells. The cells then die off and cause Alzheimer's. But why the tau protein negatively affects the brain or seemingly attacks it is unknown. Treatment can manage the symptoms, but it cannot cure the disease entirely. That is why solving this mystery is very important.

249. Water Allergy

Have you heard of an allergy to water? Seems impossible to be allergic to water because 60 per cent of a human being's body is water. But one in every 360 million people are allergic to water. The condition is called **aquagenic urticaria** and was first discovered in 1964.

More accurately, it is the skin that is allergic to water. So even if people with this condition can drink water, they cannot wash their bodies with it. Just a few minutes under a shower would make their skin feel itchy, and the skin would break out in red marks. Ion sensitivity might be the reason for the allergies.

250. Foreign Accent

Imagine waking up in the morning and **suddenly speaking in a British accent** or a thick Jamaican accent. What is even stranger is that this could happen even if you never heard these accents before. This is called 'foreign accent syndrome'.

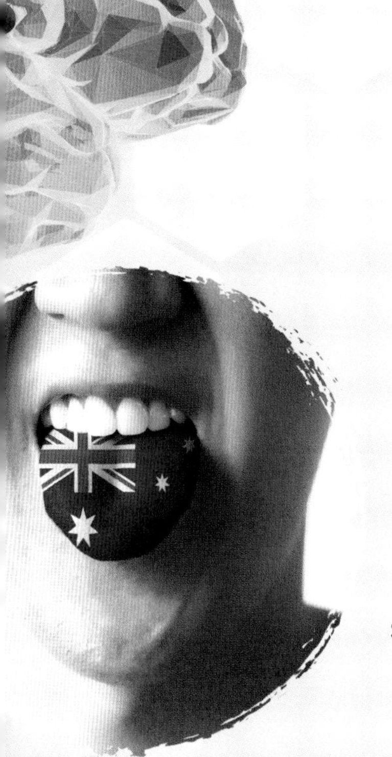

Once, in 1941, a woman from Norway was socially ostracised when, after a bad accident, she began to speak with a thick German accent. Scientists thought that this was a psychological disorder in response to a bad accident, but later discovered that it was because of injuries to the part of the brain that controls speech. This speech disorder is a problem from start to end.

251. Morgellons Disease

Morgellons disease is a **rare and mysterious skin disease** where fibres grow out of the itchy abrasions on the skin. There is also a funny sensation of parasites climbing and biting the skin. The cause of this disease is unknown, but thousands of people suffer from this problem.

Those who complain of Morgellons disease are rarely diagnosed with it. Doctors instead diagnose them with 'delusional parasitosis' which is a psychological disorder where a person is convinced that a parasite is crawling under their skin even if no such parasite is found. But doctors are now taking complaints from these patients more seriously and trying to figure out what causes this disease.

252. Arsenic

King George III, died years ago, but the reason for his death has interested many scientists and doctors. The British King had mental derangement and was forced to be restrained by a straitjacket and tied to a chair. Scientists thought that he had **'porphyria'** which is a genetic defect.

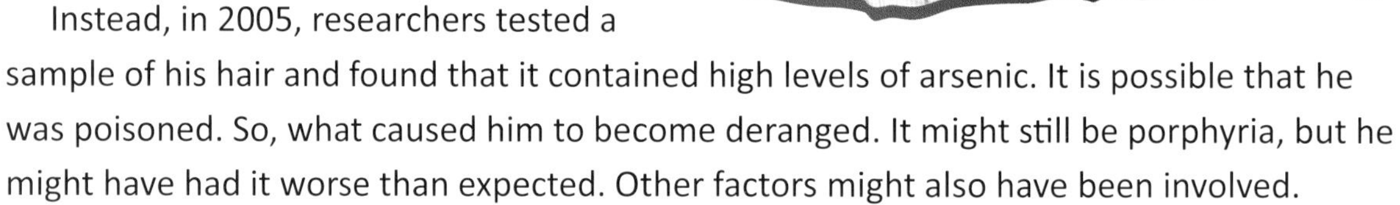

Instead, in 2005, researchers tested a sample of his hair and found that it contained high levels of arsenic. It is possible that he was poisoned. So, what caused him to become deranged. It might still be porphyria, but he might have had it worse than expected. Other factors might also have been involved.

253. Tree Man

A Bangladeshi man named Abul Bajandar was diagnosed with an extremely rare and mysterious disease. He was called 'tree man' because he had scaly warts all over his body, and his hands and legs resembled the branches of a tree. Another man who was diagnosed, died at the age of 42.

The cure for this disease is unknown and until recently, people did not know what caused it either. A few scientists came up with the idea that it is a rare immune deficiency which spreads the human papilloma virus that causes the warts. Dede lost his job, family and friends. He even had trouble feeding himself.

254. Painless Disorder

When you prick your finger with a needle, you feel pain. When you fall, and hurt your knees, you feel pain. So, while you might not appreciate pain, it is important, because if you don't feel pain it can be extremely dangerous. A girl named Gabby Gingras has a rare condition called **'hereditary sensory autonomic neuropathy'** or HSAN.

Her father discovered the problem when she was a baby. He was feeding her with something when she bit on his finger hard. When he pulled his finger out, her tooth came out with it. But she did not cry or make a fuss. She continued playing happily. Much later, when they visited a doctor did they discover the problem.

Slowly, Gabby lost all her teeth and even scratched her cornea so many times that the doctors had to remove her left eye. To prevent her from damaging her eyes further, doctors recommended she wear goggles and a helmet. Gabby's parents have had to watch her constantly to make sure that while growing up, she does not do anything to herself that might harm her.

The HSAN condition is said to have arisen because of a genetic disorder that stunted the development of the nerve fibres in her brain that are needed to detect temperature and pain. Very few people diagnosed with this problem make it to adulthood, because it is difficult for them to understand when they are harming themselves. So far, less than 40 people have been found with this condition. Finding the cure to this condition requires us to first understand how the brain processes pain.

FACT FILE

Gabby's parents started a foundation called 'Gift of Pain' to find a cure.

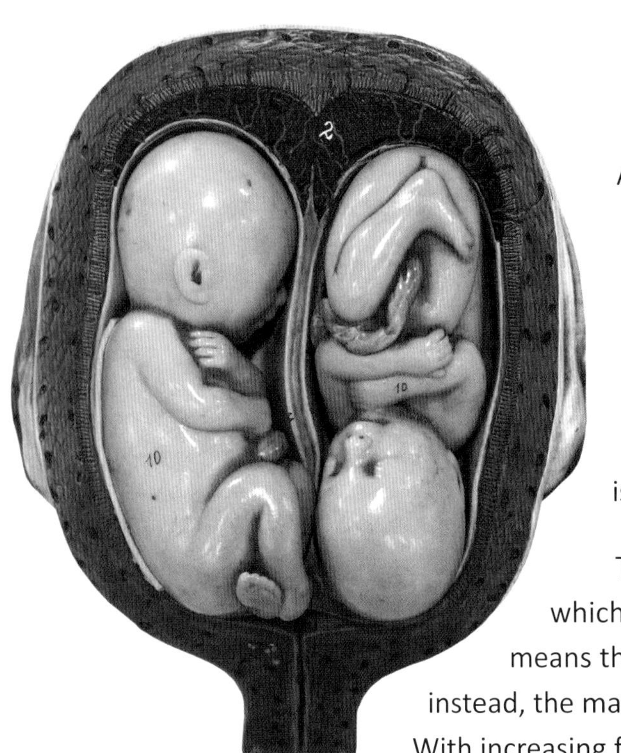

255. Chimera

A mother took her daughters to get genetic tests done, when she found out that she was not actually their mother. This was a bigger problem than it might seem because she clearly remembered giving birth to them. She did not need tests to prove she was their birth mother. So, why did the tests fail? That is a mystery.

The mother was declared to be a 'chimera', which is a **'mix' of two different people**. This means that her mother was supposed to have twins, instead, the material fused together in the womb to form her. With increasing fertilisation techniques, it is possible that this rare disorder might eventually become common.

256. Putrid Finger

In 1996, a man was cooking chicken when he suddenly pricked a finger on a bone and his life changed. He suffered from an infection that made him **smell horrible**. The smell came from the finger that was infected. Even if you stood at opposite ends of the ballroom from the man, you could still smell him.

Antibiotics did not work nor did any medicines. For five years, doctors could not figure out what caused this horrible smell. Scientists felt that a particular organism was living in his body but could not figure out where it was. The man tried everything, when out of nowhere, the smell and infection cleared up on its own.

257. Allergy to Cold

If it is too cold, you use a blanket. But what will you do if you have an allergy to cold? This is a condition called **'cold urticaria'**. A person with this condition feels allergic to cold temperatures. If you rub an ice cube on the skin of someone with this condition, they develop a sudden rash on the area.

If an ice cube causes such a reaction, imagine being around during an angry blizzard. If a person with this condition faces a strong blizzard or enters chilly waters, they could die because of the sudden allergic reaction. Patients need to be treated quickly, so this is a very rare and a very serious problem, and no one knows what causes it.

258. Uncool

Those with a cold allergy would be jealous of a person who **cannot feel cold**. This is a rare condition experienced by a man in the Netherlands named Wim Hof. He is extremely resistant to cold. Scientists have been able to conduct several tests on him but have found no reason as to why he is able to endure extreme cool temperatures.

He has taken full advantage of this condition. His name has been entered in the Guinness World Records twice. He was able to swim for 80 m under ice in the North Pole. He ran for 1000 m bare foot in the Arctic Circle. If anyone else did this, they would die.

259. Memories

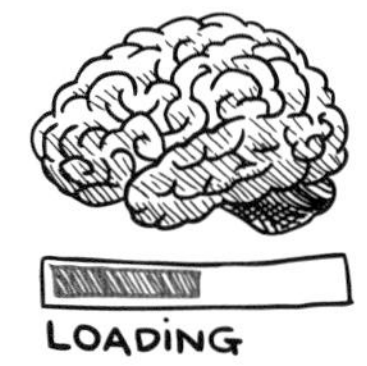

You can think of a memory, as a photograph. Our brain is like an app on the phone that stores useful photographs for a long time. But, it gets rid of useless photographs. Of course, the brain does this on its own without assistance. How does the brain store, handle and save different **types of memories**?

Not all memories are good and happy. Some are unpleasant, some are scary, some are useful like remembering the phone number of a friend, some are long-term, like the date of your mother's birthday. Some memories are unique and without any 'classification', like the first time you rode your bicycle.

260. Short Memory

Some people have a very good memory and some people have a very bad memory. A woman named Beki Propst experienced a seizure that left her without her memory. Now, she cannot remember what she was like before the seizure. Her family and friends feel she behaves in the same way.

Doctors don't know why her memory disappeared so suddenly. They know that the seizure must have affected a part of her brain that stored things like her identity, important life events, dates and facts about herself. But that part of the brain is intact and not causing more problems other than the fact that she has no past memory. Doctors are not sure what treatment will bring back her memory.

261. Long Memory

They say elephants **never forget anything**. But human beings can be forgetful. In fact, while we sleep, the brain clears away useless information. But some people can remember every moment of their lives from newspaper articles to passing conversations. These people are almost like a human Google search feature for their family as they can recall anything that happened in the family.

A man in Wisconsin named Brad Williams, and a woman in California named AJ both have this condition. It is called 'hyperthymestic syndrome'. They have both tried to find out why they have this condition, and if there is a cure for it. The solution can only be found by understanding the memory system better, especially the mystery about how and where the brain stores memories.

So, neuroscientists are very interested to learn how the brains of AJ and Brad Williams can be so good at memory and recall. However, they are still at the step of trying to understand the condition itself.

FACT FILE

'Hyper' stands for 'more than normal', and 'thymesis' means 'to remember'.

262. Shut Eyes

Imagine if you woke up one morning, and you couldn't open your eyes. That is what happened to a woman in Australia who was **unable to open her eyes for three days**. She regularly experiences this condition. When she is getting ready to sleep at night and her eyes feel heavy, she knows that she has to prepare for three days of closed eyes.

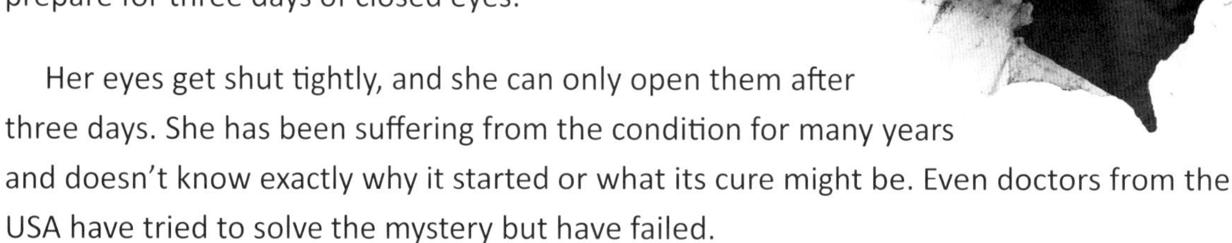

Her eyes get shut tightly, and she can only open them after three days. She has been suffering from the condition for many years and doesn't know exactly why it started or what its cure might be. Even doctors from the USA have tried to solve the mystery but have failed.

263. Sleepless

When your eyes are shut for three days, the best you can do is sleep. But what if there is another condition where you just **cannot sleep** no matter how much you try to close your eyes? This happened to a four-year-old boy named Rhett Lamb who stayed awake throughout the day and night.

The sleeplessness began very early, right after he was born. His mother took him to the doctor several times, but at first the doctors did not believe that was possible. Slowly, they came to realise she was telling the truth. They diagnosed the baby several times but were not convinced that any of the diagnoses were correct. To this day, no one knows what happened to the baby. Sleep deprivation is linked to heart disease.

Unsolved Mysteries of Science

In 1900, a British scientist named Lord Kelvin proudly declared that there are no new discoveries to be made in the field of physics. Now all we have to do is find more precise measurements.

However, within years of that declaration Einstein and other scientists changed that view. Now we know that science is full of unsolved mysteries and puzzled scientists.

264. Modern Corn

Did you know that corn feeds 21 per cent of the population? But little is known about its **past and its history**. Modern corn was first developed in ancient America. The plant it was developed from was named 'teosinte'. But the teosinte plant had very little nutrients. That is not the case for corn, which is quite rich in nutrients if you compare it with teosinte.

Why did people decide to take teosinte, which has little nutrients and is relatively useless, and develop it into a very important artificial plant? How was this process conducted? These questions are left unanswered.

265. Moving Out

One of the biggest mysteries of evolution is, why did human beings leave Africa? Human ancestors are said to have started leaving the African continent nearly 50,000 years ago. Even this date is not confirmed as yet. At the time, human ancestors did not have cars and airplanes. They had to walk on foot for days.

What did our human ancestors expect to find when they set off? Why did they leave Africa, a continent that surely was not getting overcrowded at that point? In fact, they might have had plenty of food and water to survive. Some biologists think it could have been climate change or a random outbreak of diseases that caused this move.

266. Wing Mutation

A man named Richard Dawkins once proposed that a creature evolved wings from partial wings that allowed animals to glide towards the ground after jumping from a height. In this way, over time, mutations took place so that the animal could survive and reproduce. That is how some animals got wings.

But some scientists don't think that is possible because partial mutations itself cannot be possible. Remember, dinosaurs are linked to birds in the study of evolution. That means a bird had to first lose most of its body mass and bone marrow. It is not just about changing their scales to wings. So, which theory is correct? Do animals develop partial wings or lose bone marrow?

267. Whale Evolution

Did you know that the **hippopotamus is the whale's cousin**? That is what the research of a few biologists have revealed. They had developed a way to find out how animals have evolved in the past. To do this, they inspect the DNA of the animal they want to learn more about.

There are bits and chunks in the DNA of animals that help scientists study their past. When scientists compare the DNA of different animals, like hippos and whales, they can redraw the family tree of the animal. Whales are more like cows than dolphins. So, why did the whales decide they like swimming more than walking? That is a mystery!

268. New Life

Scientists believe that **new life can be found on Earth** just like it could be millions of years ago. By new life, a new species, or a completely different type of life, could suddenly generate if the conditions are right.

Scientists have pointed to different places to suggest that new life could form there, because they have an ideal weather or climate conditions and suitable land. They could be ponds with stagnant water or hydrothermal vents in oceans. But other scientists think that there are lots of bacteria that will eat up any protocells before they can even develop. It is unknown if global warming is helping or hurting the development of new life and species.

269. Molecules

When an atom joins with other atoms to form chemical bonds, and forms a larger particle, it is called a **'molecule'**. We all know that a molecule is represented in diagrams with three or more balls with connecting sticks. But this is only what they show in textbooks.

Scientists have been trying to understand molecules and atoms since the 1920s. Around the world, scientists are trying to figure out how molecules came together and how atoms form bonds with other atoms. There have been several theories to understand this. One scientist thought that the electric charge of the atoms caused them to form bonds. Another thought that they mix together. None of these theories have been proven correct.

270. Protons

Life is mortal, as in, there is a definite end to all life on Earth. But, is that also true for protons? Protons are extremely small particles – much smaller than the tiny atom. In fact, proportionally, if an atom was the size of a cricket stadium, the proton would be as small as a pebble on the grass.

We cannot see protons even if we use a very powerful microscope. So, there are mysteries about the proton that still need to be solved. Like **are protons immortal**? Even after several experiments, scientists cannot be sure. Protons can be broken down under extreme pressure. It is also possible that the lifespan of a proton is very long.

271. Biofuels

Biofuels are eco-friendly. Unlike solar energy, biofuels require plants. The energy that plants store from the Sun is converted into fuels. Ethanol and biodiesel are two important examples, where ethanol is made from corn and biodiesel from seeds. The problem here is that in developing countries, there might not be enough food if we use edible food items to make fuel.

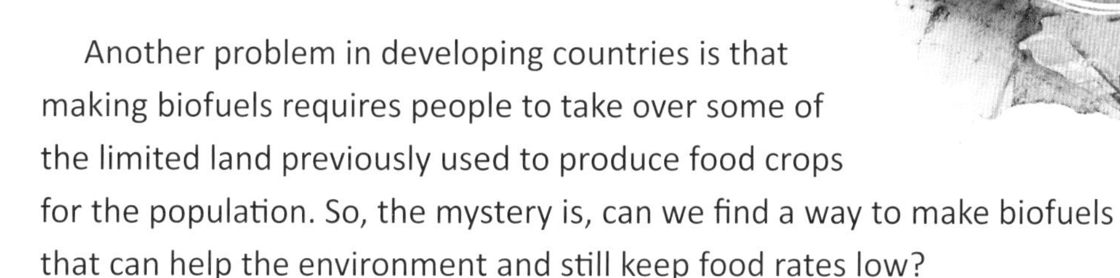

Another problem in developing countries is that making biofuels requires people to take over some of the limited land previously used to produce food crops for the population. So, the mystery is, can we find a way to make biofuels that can help the environment and still keep food rates low?

272. Saving Solar Energy

Scientists have been trying to **harvest solar energy** in a way that it could improve efficiency and not just be an expensive alternative to coal and other sources of electricity. For a long time, the way to do this has been a mystery. Life is powered by solar energy, so why can't machines be? To find the solution, scientists looked to leaves and the process of photosynthesis.

The idea is to harvest or store solar energy into a material that can handle really high temperatures. This material would store energy in a cell. The cell, like a battery or an electric cell, can be used to run machines big or small. But everything about this process is still to be worked out.

273. Booming Life 

Earth is very old and it might seem like life has existed forever but that's not true. Over the 4 billion years that life first began to exist on Earth, there were very small organisms like bacteria, plankton and algae. These were single or multi-cellular organisms. Scientists can keep track of when **life began to bloom** by observing fossils.

Fossils show that around 600 million years ago, there was a big boom in diverse life. First, there were some strange creatures that lived in the fauna of Australia. Then, between 570 and 530 million years, the first variations of the animals we see today appeared on Earth. It's called the 'Cambrian explosion'. No one knows what caused it.

274. Chemical Sensing 

In the 1960s, biosensors were used to monitor diabetes in a way that we could check on the amount of glucose in the blood. That is the inspiration for 'chemical sensing' which is still t**o be developed to its full potential**. The goal is to find out if there are contaminants in food and water, even if these contaminants are in very small concentrations.

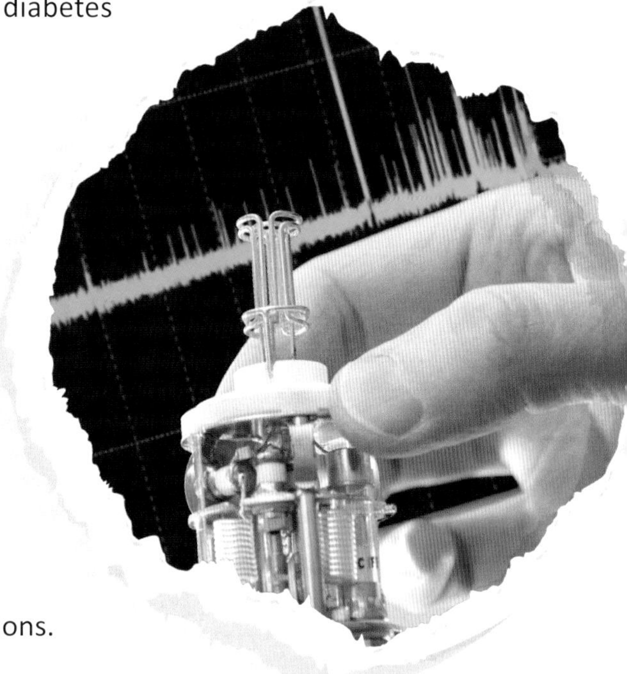

Another goal of chemical sensing is to monitor pollutants in the air or other elements. Chemical sensing could also be a big deal in biomedicine as it could detect the genes that cause cancer and exist in the bloodstream even when they are present in small concentrations.

275. Cicada Evolution

Cicadas have troubled the residents of USA for decades. Eastern USA expects to receive migrating cicadas **every 13 years**. But why did cicadas suddenly decide to spend some of their time in Eastern USA? How did they collectively decide on this migrating pattern? That is an unsolved mystery.

Cicadas are not that great at survival when they are left alone. That is why they have come up with a unique way to save themselves from predators. They just group up so that there are many cicadas together. Hungry predators are quickly satisfied and move away, leaving the majority of them safe. This might be a reason for their group migration to Eastern USA.

276. Dark Energy

The universe is said to be increasing continuously. In the 1990s, scientists found that the universe might eventually stop increasing and collapse. It might have very little energy. In the second scenario, the universe would never stop the continuous increase, but it would slow down with time because of gravity.

But later people found out that gravity in fact fastens the speed with which the universe increases. This did not add up with what scientists knew about the universe so they realised there is a missing factor that is causing this increase in speed. This missing factor was called 'dark energy'. It is one of the greatest unsolved mysteries of science.

277. Carbon Computers 

All computers use chips. These chips are not edible but small chips inside the CPU that store data. These chips have been made of a material called silicon. The problem is that silicon is not very environment friendly. So, is it possible for scientists to find a material to make this chip that could also be good for the environment? That is exactly what they are trying to do!

In 2010, a physicist invented **graphene**, which is made of a web of carbon atoms. This is what got people thinking of the possibility that computers could be made of carbon. Or did we still need to stick to silicon? But so far, no progress has been made with it.

Many people have been trying to figure out how to use carbon in computers, because the computers can then turn out to be much faster and much more powerful than the ones with silicon. So, in 1985, a man discovered 'buckyballs' which used carbon. With the discovery, the computer world was supposed to be changed entirely.

Several scientists got excited, but little progress was made. Nearly six years after the discovery, someone arranged carbon material into tubes. These tubes were shaped in a hexagonal pattern held together by chicken wire. Basically, they were carbon sheets made of graphite. Like the earlier chips, they were stiff but very strong and could conduct electricity well.

The problem here is that scientists don't know yet how to use these hollow tubes in a way that they can build a circuit to carry enough electricity to run a computer for any purpose.

FACT FILE

The practical way to use graphene is still unknown.

278. Wave or Particle?

Light is in the form of rays. But, they create patterns that are usually seen as waves. They also reflect off surfaces like glass. That is why some beginners get confused and think that light could also be a wave rather than a particle. It could also be both things at the same time.

There are certain properties of lights that match particles and some that match waves. How can light have these properties? It is quite possible that light can act as a wave and as a particle in different circumstances even though it travels in rays. The mystery is, what determines this behaviour?

279. Reverse Law

We all know that time travels in only one direction. People can grow older, they cannot get younger. Seeds can grow into trees and not the other way around. And the end of time for most living things is death. But time keeps moving forward.

Only in science fiction novels and movies does time move backwards. Scientists have been trying to figure out why time only **moves forwards and not backwards**. There is no real law that says that time cannot move backwards. Even though Newton doesn't say things can happen in reverse in his laws, he doesn't say that it is impossible. That is the problem with all physics laws.

280. Cancer

A study received instant negative feedback from people when it stated that **cancer is determined by luck**. In fact, many doctors say that cancer is detected or left undetected because people do not take regular tests. Detecting cancer, in that case, can be difficult and mostly comes down to luck. So, could the study be correct?

What causes cancer? Is it random mutations, which can be seen as luck? Is it bad genes passed on by parents? Is it an unhealthy lifestyle or exposure to a bad environment? The answer to this is pretty much unknown. So, it still remains a mystery if cancer is caused by bad luck or not. Luckily, several scientists are trying to find the answer.

281. Animal Cancer

One theory of why people get cancer is that human beings have a lot of cells. More cells means more chances of getting cancer. Every cell in the body has a chance of becoming cancerous. But have you heard of whales or elephants getting cancer? They don't seem to be prone to cancer like human beings. Larger mammals and animals have a greater number of cells.

More cells means cancer has a greater chance of affecting larger mammals or animals. But this is not the case. This is called **'Peto's paradox'**. The mystery is what the relation between body size and getting cancer is.

282. Gall Wasps

Gall wasps cause **gall formation** in plants. These are little structures that form because of abnormal growth activities of plants. These formations are induced by gall wasps. Nobody knows exactly how these formations appear on the plants. There are several theories that try to explain these formations.

Normally, other types of galls are caused by insects and mites. Some galls are caused by fungi, viruses and bacteria. Galls can appear on the leaves, buds, roots and stems of plants. We don't know much about how any of these galls are formed. The only gall formation that is clearly understood is the one caused by a bacterium called *agrobacterium tumefaciens*.

283. Flowering Plants

We have no idea **where flowering plants came from**. You might think, so what? They are good to look at! But that is not what scientists feel. Charles Darwin, the father of evolution, wanted to know where exactly flowering plants evolved from. When Darwin checked fossils for records, he found that flowers appeared about 100 million years ago. They were present in many sizes and shapes.

Does that mean that as soon as flowers evolved, there was a wide variety of them? This was a confusing problem for Darwin who thought that evolution was a slow and gradual process. But there are more recent theories that suggest flowers evolved gradually from angiosperms. That again raises more questions than it answers.

284. Apes and Humans

Not only historians, but scientists too are known to find fossils useful. Fossils help biologists understand evolution. We all know that human beings evolved from apes. But at some point, there was a split in evolution between apes and human ancestors. Where and how this divide took place is the mystery that still has not been solved.

A fossil was found in 2008, in South Africa, that showed feet that resemble an ape's, but knees that resemble a human being's knees. At least, to a great extent, they looked like a human being's knees. This must explain the walking patterns of human beings. But scientists still need to verify if they are the fossils of our ancestors.

285. Homing

Have you seen many pigeons sitting together near a fountain or an abandoned corner of a road? It might be their home. Pigeons fly long distances and then **come back to their home**. This ability that pigeons have to find their home even after flying far away, and to unfamiliar places, is called 'homing'. That is why you hear the phrase 'homing pigeon'.

Several animals have this strange ability. The location that animals return to could be a safe place or a spot where they breed with other animals. The reason why animals have this ability is unknown. It could be something in their neurological processes. One theory suggests they use sound waves.

286. End of the Universe

Many scientists and conspiracy theorists have been predicting the end of the universe. It has been a big mystery in the world of science and space. **When and how the universe will end** is an unsolved mystery.

One theory is called the 'big crunch'. It says that the universe is constantly expanding. Suddenly it will stop and collapse. The theory suggests that the universe will end in an exact opposite way to how it started. Gravity will be the culprit that will make the universe collapse on itself. Another theory called 'big rip' suggests it will expand and get pulled apart when it clashes with another galaxy. Which one is true? That is the mystery! Will the world end in a big crunch or a big rip? When will it happen?

287. Lithium

3
Li
Lithium
6.941

When the universe first began, temperatures were extremely high. **Isotopes of lithium**, helium and hydrogen were synthesised at these temperatures. Today, helium and hydrogen greatly add to the mass of the universe. The amount of lithium however, has reduced a lot.

There is only a third of the lithium left. Why did the level of lithium reduce? Scientists do not know what happened for certain, but there are several theories. One theory is that lithium axions (imaginary particles) were trapped in the core of exploding stars. But nobody can see these axions through telescopes. This is the only popular theory, but it still has several missing links in it.

288. Gravity

Jump up. You won't float in the air because **gravity 'pushes you down'**. There is very little gravity in space. Every single object in space has a gravitational pull on every other object in space. The path in which the planets and all other bodies travel in space are influenced by this gravitational pull. That is why gravity holds galaxies together.

Gravity also makes it possible for us to live on Earth because it traps gases and liquids in the atmosphere. Earth's gravity holds everything down. The Sun also has gravity which keeps our planet moving in an elliptical orbit.

While we understand, what gravity does, we also need to understand how gravity works. Not much is known about how gravity works, but powerful things have been invented from the little that is known about gravity. For example, we know that heavier the mass of an object, greater is its ability to attract other objects. That is because gravity's force is derived from matter. The more matter there is, the greater the force. There are several other such properties about gravity that need to be found.

Atoms mostly are empty space. They are held together by ionic and covalent bonds. So, why is the force that holds atoms together different from gravity? Why does gravity exist? Was it always present in our environment? What is the origin of gravity? We also don't know if gravity itself is particles.

FACT FILE

The moon's gravity causes tides on Earth.

289. Life in Space

Do you know what the observable universe is? As the name suggests, it is basically what can be seen from Earth. Since the beginning of space expansion, whatever light has reached Earth can be seen. The observable universe is spherical or ball-shaped, but that doesn't necessarily mean that space is of this shape.

Observable universe is different from different places in space. So, the observable universe seen from Earth will be very different from the observable universe seen from another planet or an asteroid. We don't know how much these observable universes overlap.

The observable universe from Earth is estimated to be nearly 92 billion light-years in diameter. There are a billion or more galaxies in this diameter alone. There are billions of stars and planets that are yet to be found. Scientists have long believed that there is life elsewhere in space but have been unable to find it. So, this is one of the biggest mysteries of science and space – is there life elsewhere? This is called the **Fermi Paradox.**

The only evidence of life is found on Earth. Other planets within our solar system seem inhospitable or unsuitable for life to exist. Scientists are trying to figure out if Mars can be a 'home away from home' or a second Earth. But there is no life found on Mars yet. Scientists have come up with many theories to say why they have not been able to find life as yet, but few say that life doesn't exist elsewhere.

FACT FILE

Fermi Paradox was named after Enrico Fermi, who invented the first nuclear reactor.

290. M-theory 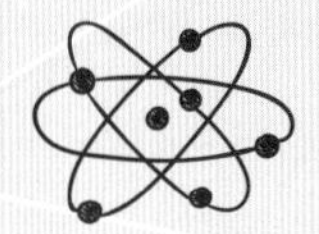

M-theory is a **superstring theory**. Superstring theory refers to the theory, that tries to explain, about particles and forces that exist in nature as vibrations on symmetric strings. It is a small-particle physics concept invented by Edward Witten. It challenges the idea that all the objects in the universe are like dots. Instead, it says they are like large and thin pieces of string.

The problem with this theory is that it is impossible to test it in the practical world and see if it is true. So, it is a topic of dispute between scientists. However, if the theory is proven to be correct then a lot of progress can be made from it. M-theory is a part of a series of theories called string theory. It is a heavily disputed topic of physics. Many students of science write their assignments on this topic in particular.

291. Supersymmetry

Supersymmetry is an idea that each particle has a **'superpartner'**. A superpartner is a bigger subatomic partner to its twin that can be observed by us. However, not a single superpartner element has been found by scientists so far.

This idea comes from thinking that all forces of the universe are in unity and act together. Scientists already know that there are certain particles that are the building blocks, which created everything in the universe. Each of these particles are said to have twins. They are called 'sparticles'. Once we find this sparticle, then we can solve several mysteries in the field of physics.

If these two forces compete, which one will be the winner? Which is more powerful? The answer could be found by understanding these forces better.

292. Measurements

Scientists are divided over two opinions—**everything can be measured or everything cannot be measured**. So, which of these opinions is correct? Einstein thought a lot about this conflict. He also wondered if all measurements came into existence by chance. If everything has a measurement, then that means everything has a measure. That also means that everything has a relative measure, just like how we measure the length of curtains to match our windows.

Scientists have started out with one 'pure number' called 'alpha'. They have calculated this alpha measure using a concept called 'Planck's Constant', which always has the same value. It is the measure for how much energy a photon can carry.

293. Gravity vs Electromagnetism

Gravity is what holds you down. Electromagnetism is the powerful force that explains the relationship between magnetism and electricity. **Gravity might seem weaker than electromagnetism**, but several scientists think otherwise.

Scientists think that if all the gravity in the universe is brought together, it can create a mini black hole. But several scientists disagree and think that electromagnetism is the more powerful force. It is the glue of the universe. Stars even emit their electromagnetic energy as light.

If these two forces compete, which one will be the winner? Which is more powerful? The answer could be found by understanding these forces better.

294. Earth's Capacity

Earth's population keeps growing. In 2012, Earth's human population was more than seven billion, but in 1960 it was just three billion. By 2050, there will be nine billion people on Earth. Can all of them be **sustained by Earth's resources**?

India is the second most populated country in the world, and many claim it will become the most populated country and overtake China. However, the growth of human population affects the finite resources of Earth like gold, iron and petroleum. These resources in turn, also affect the human population. So, scientists often wonder what Earth's carrying capacity is. This means the maximum number of a particular species that can exist on Earth and be supported by its resources.

295. Measuring Evidence

Scientists conduct experiments to understand a subject. They then analyse the results and infer conclusions from the results. Many repeat the experiments several times to check that they have the right results and thus are able to come to the **right conclusions**. However, is this evidence solid or can it be taken as luck? Would the evidence change if someone else performed the tests?

Game theory is trying to solve this mystery. It is a mathematical concept that analyses strategies of competitive situations. Each outcome of the action taken by a participant depends upon the actions of other participants. This theory has been used to understand biology, war and business.

Game theory is a unique way to solve problems in science. With game theory, it might become easier to understand the impact of luck on evidence and scientific findings.

296. Periodic Table

The periodic table as you know it today is not final. It most definitely could change. Scientists have long accepted this fact as more and more elements get added to the periodic table. The **number of elements in the periodic table keeps growing**. So, nobody really knows how many elements are there in the world.

Scientists themselves can create new elements in laboratories using particle accelerators to crash the atomic nuclei of two different elements together. While there are 92 elements found in nature so far, scientists have found a few more that have more protons and neutrons than the natural elements.

Obviously, since they are artificial and heavier than natural elements, they are also unstable. They are called 'synthetic elements'. You can see element 108, hassium on the periodic table, to understand what synthetic elements are.

The synthetic elements are also called 'super heavy elements' because they are heavier than other natural elements and have more protons or neutrons. All these elements have fixed chemical properties and behaviours.

If you want to control an unstable element, you can add or remove some of the things that make up the element. Another challenge with synthetic elements is, can their size be increased without limit? In that case, is there a limit to the periodic table itself? Will we ever stop finding and inventing elements to add to the periodic table, or will there be an end to it?

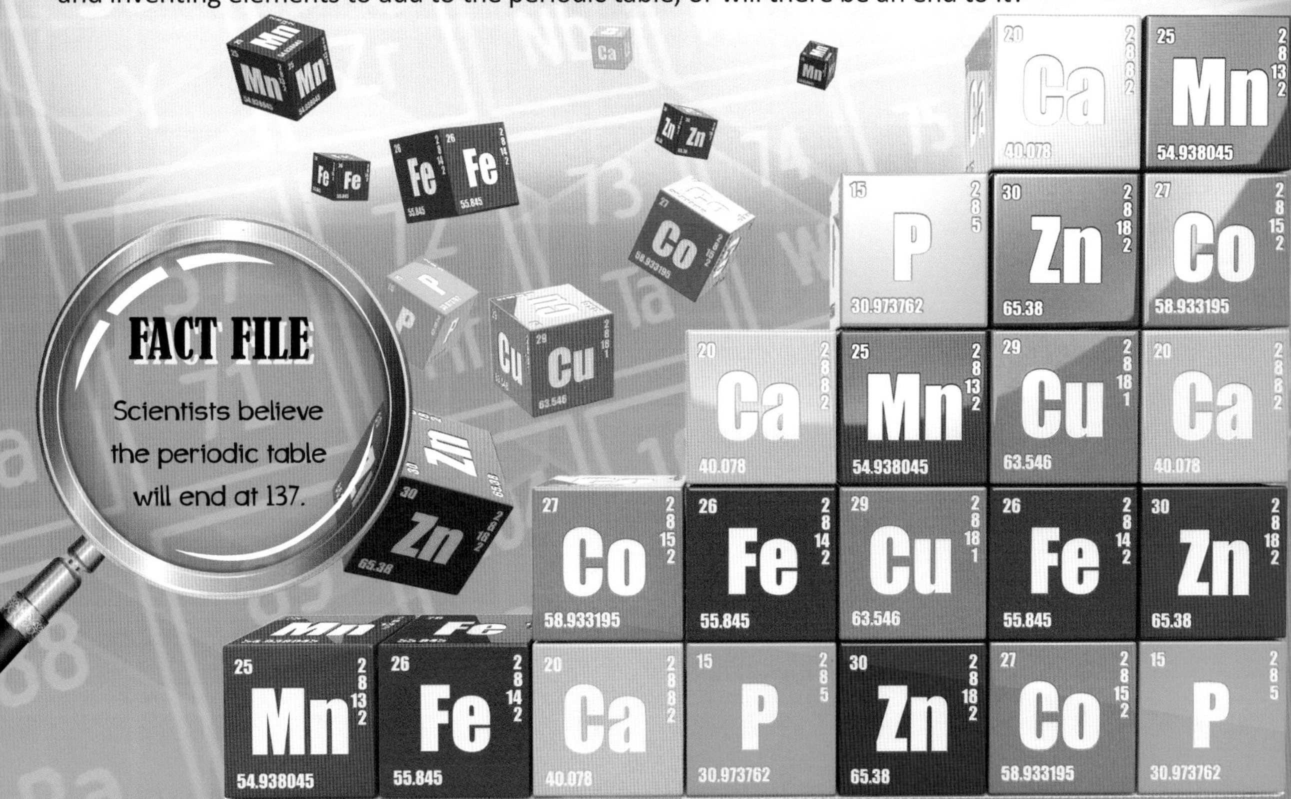

297. Magnetic Poles

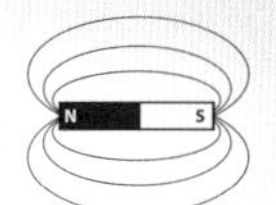

Did you know that every hundred millennials, the magnetic poles of Earth flip? It is a radical change that puzzles many scientists. So right now, a compass will point to the north. After the **big magnetic flip**, it will point to the south which is our current north. So, you might wonder, what kind of changes will Earth undergo if its magnetic poles are flipped?

That is what scientists are trying to figure out. When will the poles flip and what will happen? It is not wrong to be a little worried about this flip. In fact, it is a popular doomsday scenario where people suggest that the magnetic poles will flip in one single day. If this happens, the world will stop spinning for some time, and all life on Earth will be destroyed. If Earth stops spinning, the magnetic field would briefly allow deadly cosmic rays to pierce through, thus making Earth inhospitable.

However, many scientists think that this scenario is simple fear-mongering because they don't understand how Earth's magnetic field works. Scientists know that Earth's magnetic poles have been flipped many times since its creation. The last time it happened was estimated to be 800,000 years ago.

They also think that there shouldn't be adverse effects if magnetic poles were reversed. In fact, this whole pole flipping business took place even before Earth settled down nearly 20 million years ago. One interesting fact that comes out of this theory is that the giant magnetic Earth does not have constant poles like a bar magnet.

FACT FILE

Scientists think magnetic pole reversal will be great for magnetic compass manufacturers.

N

S

298. Neutrinos

Neutrino is a **subatomic particle** that exists in the universe in large numbers. Scientists think trillions of neutrinos were created after the Big Bang. They are present in stars. Due to radioactive decay, they can be found in reactionary bodies of space. They also flow through the celestial bodies.

Neutrinos are neither protons nor electrons. But scientists don't know much about neutrinos, including their mass. The answers to solving this mystery could solve many more like, why does a supergiant star explode with a brightness that outshines 100 billion stars, and why does the universe have matter?

299. Sleep and Rest

If you don't sleep for at least a few hours every day, you will feel very tired. That is because you might have an internal clock that helps you follow an awake/asleep cycle. But why do living things **need to sleep** or rest? An average human being spends one-third of their life sleeping.

It has already been proved by scientists that animals that sleep have been able to evolve, to protect themselves from their predators. There are some organisms in the world that do not need to sleep at all, but they do get rest in other ways. They need to stay alert from attacks from their predators. Sleep also benefits brain plasticity.

300. Multiverse

When you say 'uni', you mean 'one'. So, universe means there is only one of its kind. The universe is all of space and everything that is in it, like the stars, galaxies and planets. A multiverse means there are many such universes because 'multi' means many. 'Multiverse,' was a word that was invented by a man named Andy Nimmo who thought that there are many universes like the one we live in, and this makes up an entire, bigger universe.

The reason he thought of this is because he wondered if the universe is without limit or is it infinite. Does it keep going on and on? If someone figured out how to travel to all parts of the universe, will they find out that there is an end to the universe? All of these questions are unanswered. The most important unanswered questions are, do other universes like ours exist, or are there other universes that are different from ours?

Another theory among those who believe in multiverse is parallel universe. We don't know yet if parallel universes exist. In 1954, Hugh Everett III had this idea. He claimed that there could be parallel universes exactly like our universe. Each parallel universe is then related to our own. It could also be possible that these parallel universes are branches of our own, and there are more that are branches of those universes.

For example, a parallel universe could have dinosaurs or even one-horned rhinoceroses and other extinct animals. In another universe, human beings could be extinct.

301. Multiple Dimensions

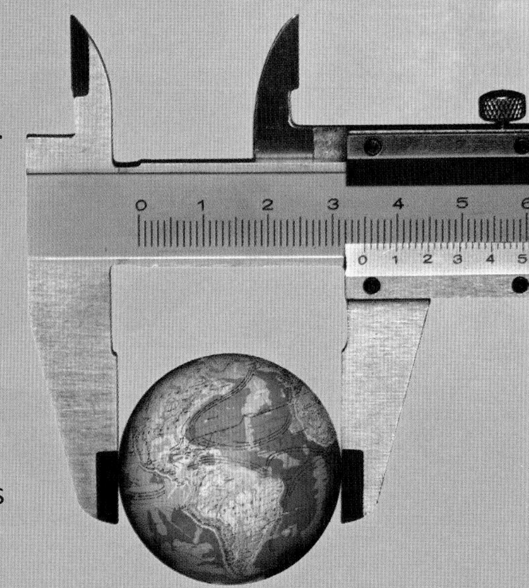

Some scientists argue that Earth is two-dimensional. Others say it is three-dimensional. There are some scientists who think there are four **spatial dimensions** and not two or three. In fact, there are theories in physics that require there to be 11 dimensions.

More and more theories are coming up that deviate from the two-dimension or three-dimension limit that was set in the past. Now, scientists want to either prove these are correct, or they want to find the missing dimensions and find out how they are a part of our reality. Some think that time is the fourth dimension.

302. Bicellular Organisms

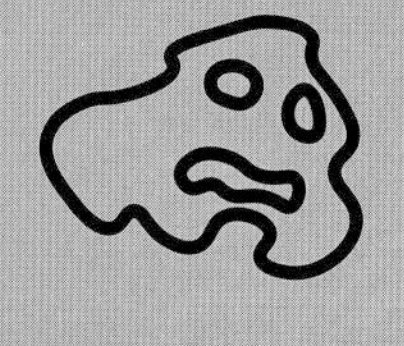

As human beings, we have many cells in our body. 'Unicellular organisms' are organisms that have only one cell. Can you imagine such organisms? They cannot be seen without a microscope. Then, there are organisms that have two cells. They are called 'bicellular organisms'. Over time, organisms evolved to have multiple cells.

There is a mystery related to bicellular organisms. There is a certain characteristic about them that doesn't allow them to adapt. Their cells cannot multiply and that is why they cannot survive for too long. They are not even that common today. So, solving this mystery becomes more difficult.

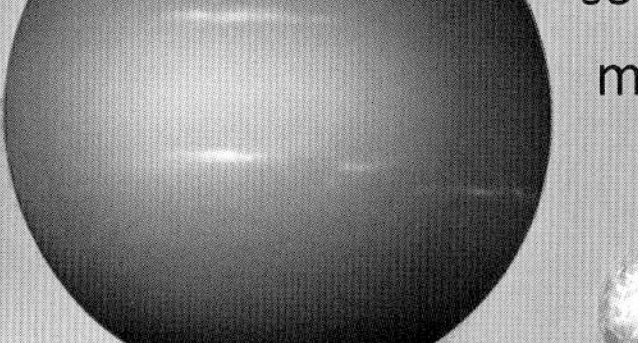

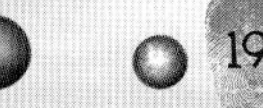

303. Rectangular Galaxy

When billions of stars, gas and dust are held together by a powerful gravitational force, it is called a galaxy. Our Earth and solar system are a part of the milky way galaxy. There are said to be trillions of galaxies out there and not all of them have been discovered by us. The few that we have discovered have been identified and named.

Each of the galaxies identified by scientists can be classified by their shape. The elliptical galaxy is egg-shaped or elliptical in shape. It can be flat or slightly spherical. The spiral galaxy is the most common type of galaxy. It is flat and has a bulge at its core. It is called the 'galactic bulge' and can be easily identified because it is extremely bright. There are long spiral arms that emerge from this bulge.

The barred spiral galaxy is another shape where lines or bars of stars run across the centre of the galaxy. The irregular galaxy has no specific shape.

But it is possible that scientists have found another galaxy that is shaped like a rectangle. In 2012, astronauts found a galaxy that was 70 million lightyears away from Earth. It is a part of the observable universe. It was named the galaxy LEDA 074886. Unlike other galaxies, it is not shaped like a disc. Instead, it looks kite-shaped or rectangular with a flat appearance. No one knows if this is a unique galaxy or if it was created after collisions from two spiral galaxies.

FACT FILE

Earth is about 27,000 light years away from the core of the Milky Way.

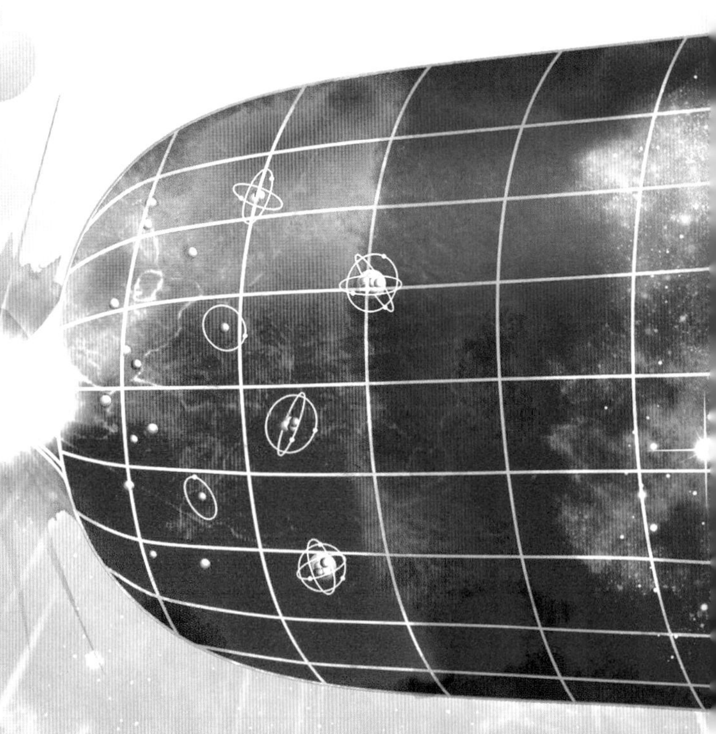

304. Before the Big Bang

We know that the **Big Bang explosion** took place nearly 13.7 billion years ago. Then there were inflations and fluctuations. Afterglow light patterns appeared nearly 3,80,000 years ago. Then there was the Dark Ages for some time. Nearly 400 million years ago, the first stars appeared. Galaxies and planets developed. Dark energy accelerated expansion. And now Earth is in its current state.

The common assumption is that there was no universe before the Big Bang.

In fact, some scientists believe that there was no matter at all that existed before the Big Bang anywhere at all. Scientists use powerful telescopes to verify this belief. They can look back in time to approximately 700 million years after the big bang. Better equipment is in the process of being invented so that they can look back even further.

But scientists are looking back to figure out what started the big bang and what matter was like during the big bang. Many scientists believe that any evidence to say that there was matter or no matter before the big bang has been destroyed because of the big bang itself.

A scientist recreated a model that suggests that a spontaneous explosion occurred that was a once in a lifetime event. This model even suggested that our universe is like an infinitely oscillating cycle where several big bang events will occur, expand, collapse and then another big bang will occur. But the question remains, what was there before the big bang that caused it?

FACT FILE

Scientists think there was no dark matter, dark energy or antimatter before the big bang.

305. Placebo Illusion

Have you heard of the placebo effect? It means that someone is **being tricked or fooled** into thinking that they are getting better. Placebo is a type of medicine that is not healing the body but tricking the mind into thinking you are getting better.

But strangely, the placebo effect has worked on sick patients. So, when people take placebo medicines thinking that they will be cured because of it, they really do even if the medicine does nothing for their body. This suggests that the mind can trick our body into healing. Placebos are mainly used as painkillers and they work more than 50 per cent of the time. Most countries try to ban placebos regardless of their results.

306. Nocebo Illusion

The **opposite of the placebo effect** is the nocebo effect. How this works is also a mystery. While the placebo effect has a positive impact on a sick person, the nocebo effect has a negative impact. Sometimes, a person is prescribed some medicines. The doctor tells the patient about some negative effects. The patient then begins to experience the negative effects in much higher proportion than they should.

Basically, the nocebo effect is perception that something will cause a negative impact even if it shouldn't. So far, scientists think this happens because of psychological reasons. The extreme effect of the nocebo effect is death. Even anaesthesia doesn't work if the patient believes it won't work on them.

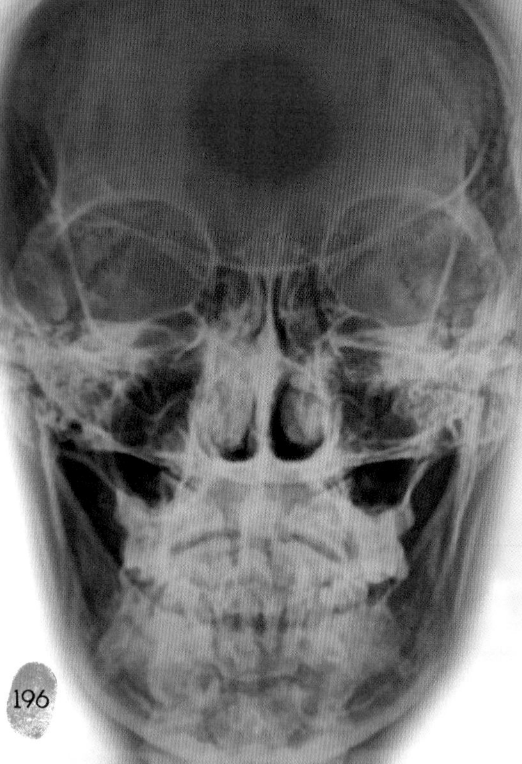

307. Moon Illusion

When the **moon is closer to Earth's horizon**, it appears much larger than it does when it is further from the horizon. This is called the 'moon illusion'. Like many scientific mysteries about celestial bodies, the moon illusion has been a mystery since the fourth century BCE.

If you get a chance to see it, it would feel surreal. There is a gigantic moon that appears closer and right next to the horizon, then as it climbs overhead the size of the moon shrinks tremendously. The moon is not really changing its size. But scientists don't know what the real reason for this illusion is.

Aristotle suggested that Earth's atmosphere was influencing what we see and that is why the moon appears enlarged. It is similar to immersed objects that look bigger in water. Ptolemy thought that it was the atmosphere's influence coupled with the distance of the moon. Today, scientists know that Earth's atmosphere has no such influence. It can appear to change the colour of the moon but not the size.

Many scientists claim that the moon's size is just an illusion we create in our own minds with our imagination. They have asked people to take photos of the moon when it seems to be the largest. Then when the moon is overhead, compare the photos to the size of the moon in the sky. There will be little difference in size. Why this illusion occurs is anybody's guess.

FACT FILE

An ancient Arab mathematician claimed that the brain can perceive distances and objects incorrectly.

308. Tardigrades

Do you know what tardigrades are? They are **microorganisms** present in large numbers in nature. They can survive in almost all climatic zones in the world. They can even survive in high and low altitudes from the seven continents. Tardigrades are extremely capable of surviving. They can live in low temperatures below freezing point and above boiling point. It is like they have some super powers!

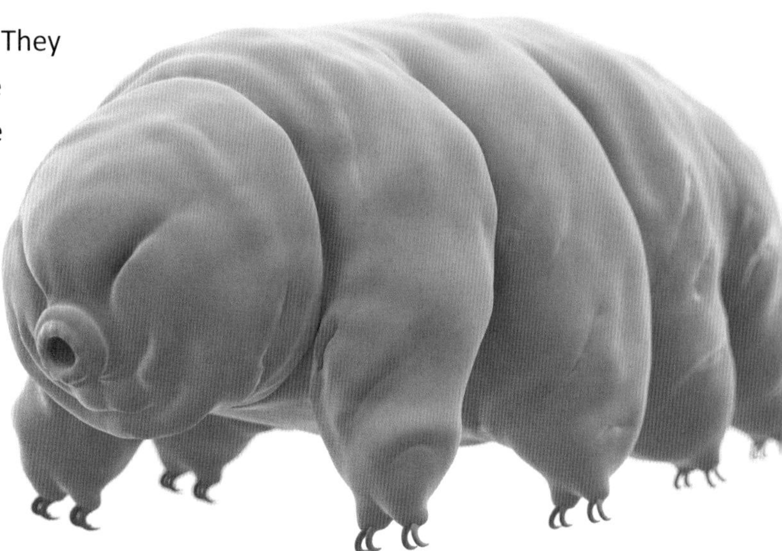

Scientists even tested to see if they could survive in the vacuum of space and they did! They were orbiting outside a rocket and could fight off all the cosmic radiations that came their way. They then travelled back home happily to survive here. They can even survive in the Mariana Trench. The question is...how?

309. Protein Folding

If you have ever read about nutrition, you would know that proteins are called the building blocks of life. When we eat eggs or drink milk, we get protein, and our body breaks down the protein molecules. This allows us to grow.

Each molecule of protein contains sequences of **amino acids** that shape the molecule's structure. Amino acids also dictate what the protein molecule's function will be. This shape and function can change depending on where the molecule is applied. It is called protein folding and how it works is a big mystery to this very day. In fact, it is called one of the biggest unsolved mysteries of science. Understanding the mystery of protein folding can change the world of genetically modified food.

310. Dighton Rock

The **Dighton rock** was found in USA in the Taunton River in Massachusetts. It was half submerged and is considered one of the most important finds in the field of science. There was cuneiform-style inscription whose real meaning might be lost forever. There has been extensive research done on this inscription to no avail.

The rock itself weighs around 40 tonnes and has a width of 2.9 m. It is 1.5 m in height and 3.4 m in length. Incidentally, an Inca stone was found in Brazil and is nearly 6000 years old.

311. Cicada 3301

Since 2012, an **organisation** started posting, extremely difficult and complex, puzzles and alternate reality games. They called themselves Cicada 3301. They claimed that their goal was to attract and hire hidden codebreakers from the public. Almost every year, since 2012, the group posts new puzzles for the codebreaking community. In 2015, they released several new puzzles at once.

Then another organisation asked its members to try and solve the puzzles of the Cicada 3301. The puzzles were called 'Liber Pimus'. After trying hard, almost all the members had given up on it. While the puzzles themselves are mysteries, even the organisation is unknown. People have linked it to the American NSA, CIA and the British MI6.

312. Seismic Hum

The seismic hum is a continuous and distinct sound. Do you know how it is recorded? Earthquakes are measured by seismic instruments, and the seismograph records the force and duration of the earthquakes. But while they are picking up the details of an earthquake, they also pick up some **vibrations** from storms that are moving over the Earth's surface at the time. Vibrations are also picked up from the waves crashing on coastlines. These are the seismic hum vibrations.

There are some other sounds that remain mysteries to this day. There is a rhythmic buzz picked up coming from the Gulf of Guinea in the Atlantic Ocean. The source of this sound is unknown. Nor is the reason for this sound.

313. Naga Fireballs

Have you been to the Mekong River in Thailand? There is one time of the year, where this river becomes simultaneously dangerous and beautiful. Each year, nearly **one hundred fireballs explode** right out of the river. It is called 'Naga fireballs'. According to local legend, these fireballs explode from the breath of a mythical serpent. This serpent is said to haunt the River Naga.

But naturally, according to scientists, this is not the reason that the river has these explosions. Instead, they believe that the fireballs are explosions from pockets of methane on the floor of the river. The methane bubbles up and explodes.

Mysterious Unsolved Crimes

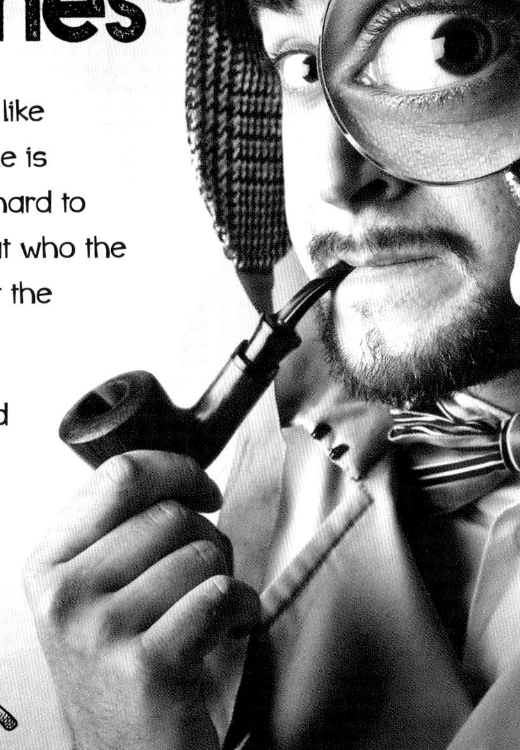

The newspaper is full of reports about crimes like murders, robberies or takeovers. Once a crime is reported, the police work on the case. They try hard to find all the evidence they can and then figure out who the suspects could be. They build up a case against the suspects and arrest them.

Sometimes however, the police try their best and still cannot crack a case. This could be because they cannot find any evidence, or the culprit has outsmarted them, or they are missing something. As a result, some crimes remain unsolved.

314. Ken Rex McElroy

Most crimes are committed at night or at a time when there is nobody to see what happened. But there is a strange case where a killer committed his crime, **in broad daylight**, while several people were watching. People who watch a murder or robbery happening are called witnesses.

The killer murdered a man named Ken Rex McElroy by shooting him. Several people saw him, including the dead man's wife. Besides her, everyone else claimed that they did not see the murder. McElroy happened to be the local bully who committed many crimes in the neighbourhood. The town people hated him and worked together for more than three decades to keep his killer's name a secret.

315. Beaumont Children

In 1996, three siblings **went missing** from their home in the suburbs of Adelaide, Australia. They were Jane, a nine-year-old girl, Arnna, a seven-year-old girl and Grant, a four-year-old boy. All three of them had got into a bus to go to Glenelg Beach, a place they had visited several times before.

When they never returned, their parents filed a police report. The case has never been solved. Witnesses claimed that they saw the children playing with a tall, thin man with blonde hair. Jane was even seen buying a pie with some money, but her parents had not given her any. A mailman even saw them walking home. But nobody knows what happened to them on the way.

316. William Desmond Taylor

William Desmond Taylor was a film director who made silent movies. In 1922, he was found **dead in his own home**. He was wearing a diamond ring and carrying cash. The police ruled out robbery, because his expensive items were still in the house. As he was a Hollywood director, the case received a lot of interest.

The police made a long list of suspects. They suspected his valet, who had been hired recently. They also suspected his previous valet, who had stolen from him, which was why he got fired. They even suspected his girlfriend, Mabel Normand, who was a movie star. The case was never solved.

317. Edgar Allen Poe

Edgar Allen Poe was an American writer and critic. He also edited written work. He is famous even today for his unusual style of writing. He wrote many poetries and short stories on mysterious and dark themes. He is considered the inventor of the detective genre and an inspiration for science fiction.

He had a very unusual life, and even his death was extremely unusual and mysterious. It is said that in the year 1849, he was travelling to Richmond from New York City. However, his trip ended at Baltimore, when on October 3rd, he was found before a bar, slouched and confused. He appeared to be delirious. He was immediately taken to a hospital and four days later proclaimed dead.

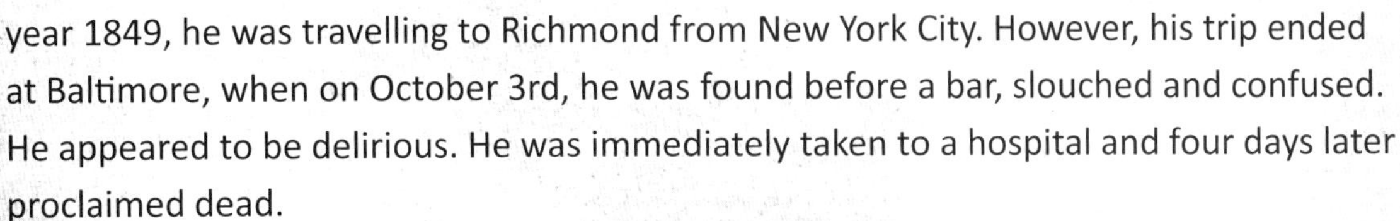

His death was publicised in the newspapers. Doctors claimed that he had a congestion of the brain, which was the old term for alcohol poisoning. During his life, many claimed that he used drugs and drank a lot of alcohol. But researchers later found out that these were just rumours from his enemies whose work he had criticised in the past.

What is more bizarre is that no one could find his death certificate. So many conspiracy theorists rule out common theories about his death, stating he was suffering from rabies, syphilis even cholera. Instead, they believe that was the work of some politicians. At that time, during the election season, politicians were known to drug people and take them to the polls to vote for them. This might explain why he was in Baltimore in a different set of clothes.

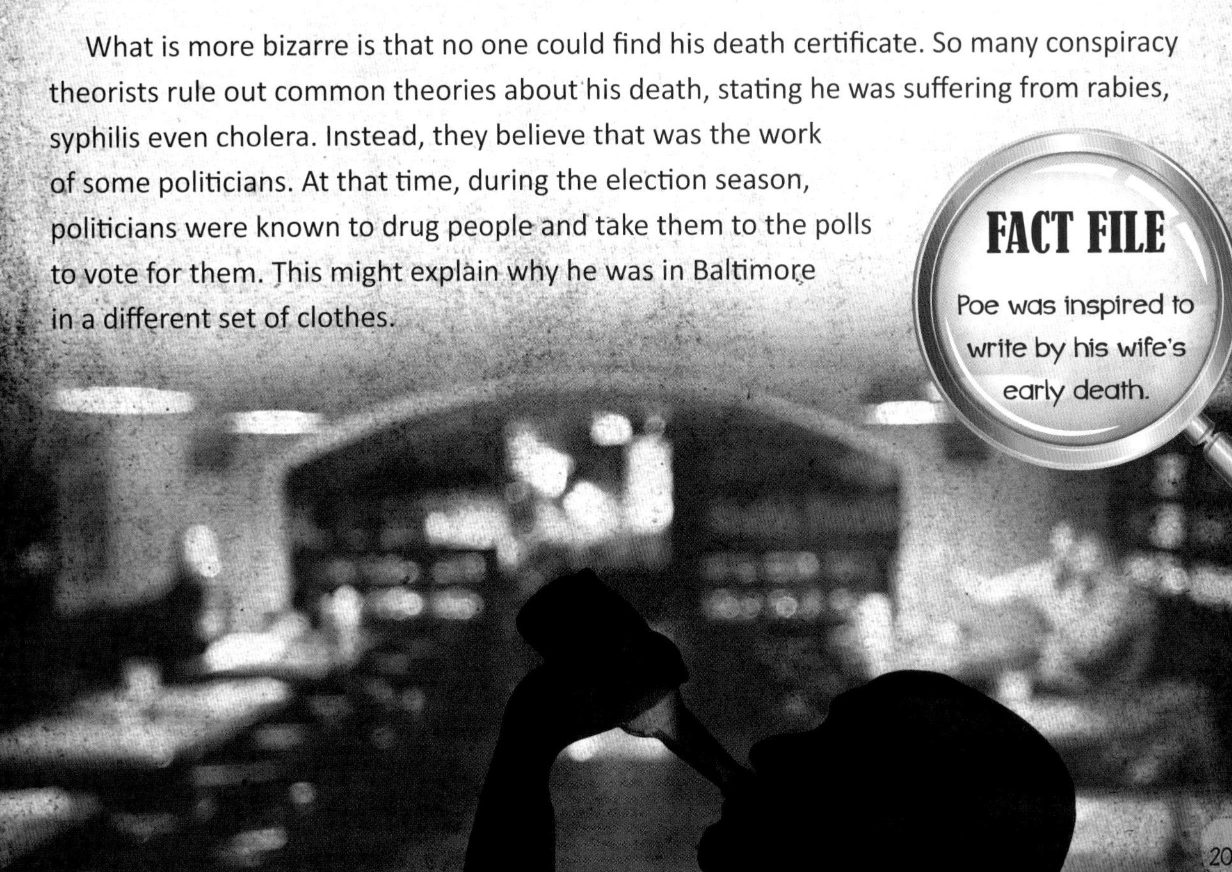

318. Beirut Bank Robbery

In January 1976, a bank named **'British Bank of the Middle East'** was robbed. It was in Beirut, Lebanon. The police reported that the robbers stole gold bars that were worth a 100 million US dollars. As a result, this robbery is one of the biggest bank robberies in world history. But the robbers were never found. So, it is also one of the biggest unsolved crimes in the world.

There were eight soldiers who conducted the robbery. They had brought with them, a M16 assault rifle and pistols. Just their weapons, gave the police a clue that they were not regular military folk but that they held high positions. They couldn't however, tell where these soldiers were from because they wore unmarked military uniforms that didn't even display their rank.

The soldiers were led by a commander who gave instructions about when to start the attack. The bank had already undergone attacks previously, because of fights that broke out between two opposing communities. The entire country was chaotic and fighting off a civil war.

The robbers were not as smart as bank robbers usually are. Instead of using clever tactics, they used their guns and strength. They did not sneak into the bank. They blasted down a wall that it shared with a church and forced themselves in. They cracked open the bank vault and carried out its contents. Besides the gold bars, they also stole jewels and currency. Then they disappeared without a trace.

FACT FILE

The robbers are said to have been with Yasser Arafat's Palestine Liberation Organization.

319. Geezer Bandit

The Geezer Bandit is the nickname given to a mysterious man who is said to have **robbed 16** banks in California, USA. Witnesses have described him as an old man, but some policemen who were investigating the cases felt that he was a young man wearing a mask.

His last robbery was in 2011. He might have stopped because he 'retired' from this strange occupation or because he died. But the police would still like to find out who he is. He always entered a bank as a normal customer, holding a leather case, and then demanded money from the teller. He threatened a teller's life if the money was not handed over.

320. Baghdad Bandits

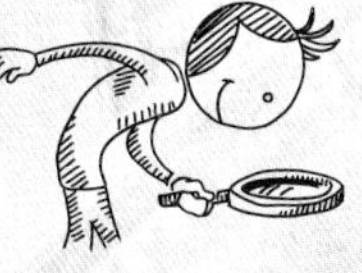

Banks have a lot of security, so criminals spend a lot of time planning their crimes. Sometimes, they get help from the people who work at the bank or from the police. That is possibly what happened in 2007, when nearly 250 million dollars were stolen from a bank in Baghdad, known as the **bank robbery capital**.

The robbers escaped into the nearby desert, despite the fact that police had put up check posts for all travellers to check their vehicles. It is also possible that the robbers were helped by a rebel organisation. The robbers got away and were never found again. Nobody even knows what happened to the money. Who was it that worked from inside the bank? Who were the robbers? These remain a mystery.

321. McCann Disappearance

Kate and Gerry McCann had taken their three children and a few family friends to their holiday apartment in Praia da Luz. Their eldest daughter Madeleine was only three years old at the time.

On May 3, 2007, they went to dine with their friends at a nearby restaurant while their children were sleeping. Around 10 o'clock, Kate went to check on them.

That's when she realised that Madeleine had disappeared! The family then rushed to the nearest police station to lodge a complaint. At first, the police thought that Madeleine had been abducted.

After a thorough search of the apartment and taking DNA tests, they believed that Madeleine had been murdered while Kate and Gerry were away. However, they later realised that they had misread the results of the tests and Madeleine could still be alive.

Four years on nothing had turned up. People around the world wanted to know what happened to Madeleine. In 2011, feeling desperate, Madeleine's parents sought help from Scotland Yard.

By this point, the police had found some clues, but not enough to find Madeleine or her abductor. Footage from CCTV cameras had shown a man carrying a child wearing pyjamas. He was taking her to the beach at around the same time that Madeleine was suspected of being abducted.

Could he have abducted Madeleine? Is she still alive? Nobody has seen or heard from her yet.

ABDUCTED

FACT FILE

Madeleine's parents were accused of faking the abduction.

322. Poison

In 1982, seven people in Chicago took Tylenol pills. What they didn't know was that they contained cyanide. Usually, **Tylenol pills** are taken by people who might experience chest pains. A man named Adam Janus took them and collapsed an hour after that, then died.

Few other members of his family, not knowing the cause of the death, took the pills as well and died. A young girl took some Tylenol to cure her cold and she died as well. The police took immediate charge and travelled across the state in police cars, warning people to stop taking the pills. The drug was temporarily discontinued. Nobody knows who started this mess.

323. Tara Calico

Tara Calico was 19 years old when she rode her bicycle down Highway 47. When she didn't return for several hours, her mother went looking for her and eventually filed a missing person's report. Tara has never been found since her **disappearance in 1988**.

Tara was listening to music on her Walkman, a portable music device, which was later found near the area where she went missing. Like Tara, her bicycle has still not been found. Her mother later saw a photograph of a girl who was tied up in the back of a truck. While her mother believes it is Tara, the police disagree.

324. Yen Robbery

In 1968, Tokyo heard news of the biggest robbery of Japan. It all happened on the 10th of December when the robbers stole 300 million yen from a vehicle that was being guarded by four men. The money was to be transported to a factory to pay bonuses for the workers.

A policeman pulled over the guards on the way by convincing the driver that the car had an explosive device right under it. The guards got off the car and the policeman got into it. Suddenly, before the guards knew it, the policeman drove away with the stolen car and the stolen 300 million yen. He was not a real policeman and was never to be seen again.

325. Tucker Cross

A group of researchers recovered a valuable cross made of **22-karat gold and imbedded with emeralds**. They found it from a sunken shipwreck off the coast of Florida. The ship, San Pedro, was reportedly heading to Spain from Cuba. The cross was called the 'Tucker Cross' after the explorer Teddy Tucker who dived down and found it.

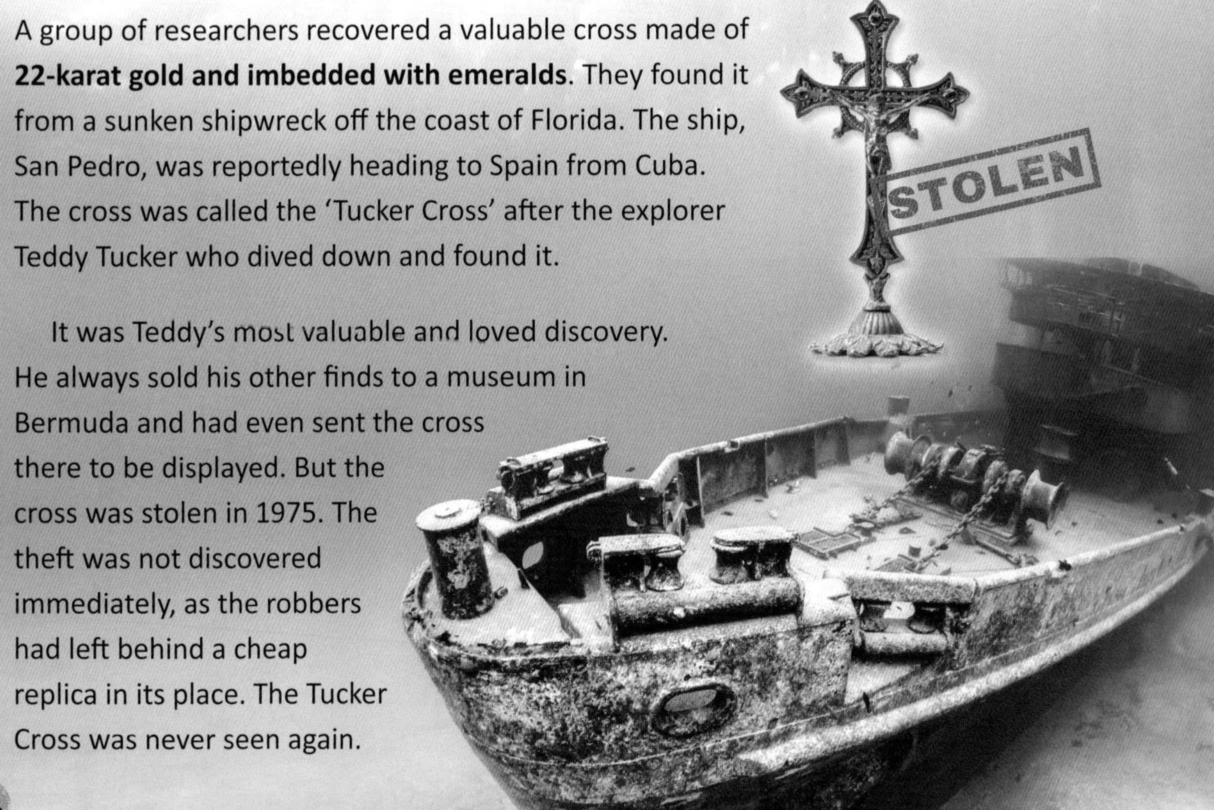

It was Teddy's most valuable and loved discovery. He always sold his other finds to a museum in Bermuda and had even sent the cross there to be displayed. But the cross was stolen in 1975. The theft was not discovered immediately, as the robbers had left behind a cheap replica in its place. The Tucker Cross was never seen again.

326. Baker Street Robbery

In 1971, a robbery took place in Baker Street, London. The culprits were never caught however, many mysteries and theories emerged from this robbery. A group of **robbers dug an underground tunnel** weeks before the robbery. The tunnel led to the Lloyds bank on Baker Street.

Then on September 11, 1971, the robbers broke into the bank using an explosive to tear up a part of the floor. They then began robbing the place by threatening the workers and scaring the customers. A customer got the police on the line but did not tell them the name of the bank. Just that a robbery was taking place in a London bank.

The police took a long time to figure out which bank in London was being robbed. They visited 750 banks before they got to the right one, by which time the robbers had escaped with nearly 3 million pounds.

It has been nearly four decades since the robbery. The amount of money stolen can be estimated to around 5 million pounds in value today. The robbers have not been caught yet. At the time, the case was all over the newspapers for several days. But suddenly, it was out of the papers because of a government order to stop covering the story. The public which was already outraged by the delay the police caused in getting to the scene, felt there was something suspicious about the order.

FACT FILE

A man named Robert Rowlands claimed to have heard the robbers digging the tunnel.

327. First National Bank Robbery

It was a peaceful summer day of April, 1981. On the 13th of the month, a customer entered the **First National Bank of Barrington**. He made his way to the safe deposit box vault and asked an employer to give him a key to his own customer box. All of a sudden the lock fell into the unopened box. The customer was confused and was immediately sent out.

The FBI was called. A few agents came into the bank to check the locks of the customer's boxes. They gently pushed another customer box's lock, and it fell into the vault. They opened all the vaults and found that nearly 1 million dollars had gone missing. Several gold coins and other valuable items that were stored in 74 safe boxes were missing as well. To this day, none of this loot has been found.

A federal jury even convicted a man named William Smarto at the age of 44, years later for conspiring and robbing the bank. This was a very confusing arrest, because while Smarto insisted that he was just a hairdresser, the FBI claimed he was a criminal mastermind to be able to stay in the bank deposit vault and walk away with the money.

Finally, the truth came out and Smarto's arrest led to finding out how exactly the robbery was committed. Smarto was sentenced to spend time in prison. He appealed to the court to cut his sentence short. But Smarto never shared where the loot was even while appealing to reduce his sentence. Nobody knows where the money is.

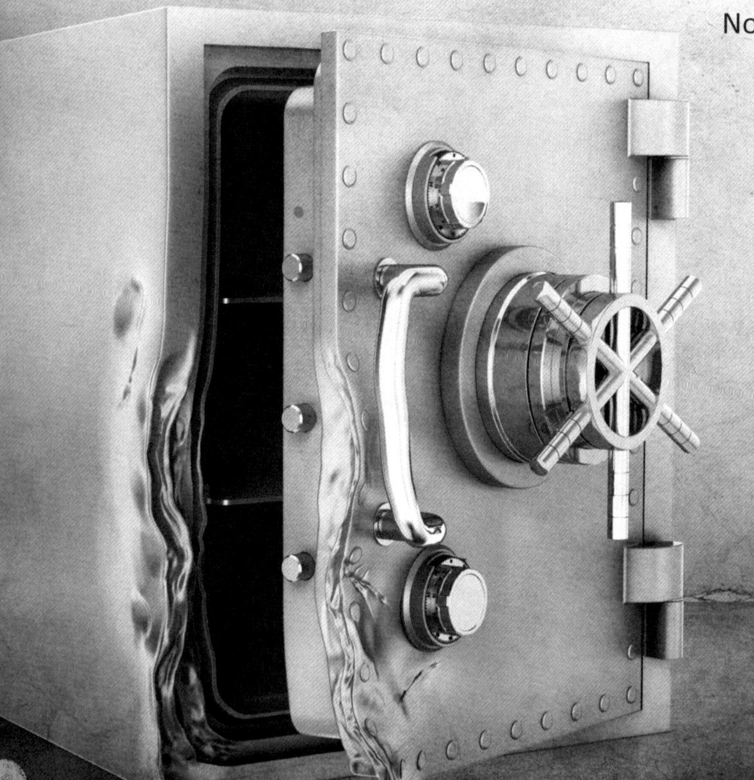

FACT FILE

This was the first successful bank vault robbery in world history.

328. Northern Bank

On the December 20, 2004, 26 million British pounds were stolen from one of the biggest banks of Ireland called 'Northern Bank'. The robbery was considered to be the greatest and the most mysterious bank robbery in Ireland. This branch of the bank is located in Belfast. To this day, none of the group of young robbers has been found.

The robbers had planned in advance by holding the families of two different bank officials at gun point. They forced them to go to work the next day and do as they had instructed. The officials allowed the robbers to enter the area where the money was stored and happily take away the money.

329. Annie Borjesson

Annie Borjesson's body was **discovered in 2005** on the west coast of Scotland. The police thought that it was suicide and informed her family. Her family were against the idea, because they felt something odd had happened. On her last day, Annie had travelled nearly 129 km away from her home to the Prestwick Airport.

Nobody knows why. She withdrew cash from her bank twice even though there was not enough money in the bank. Then she went to the airport and stayed there for less than five minutes. Her family thought something fishy was going on and started a private investigation to look for answers.

330. Mark Devlin

A rebel group of boys once ran wild and robbed and rioted in a small town. There were only a few policemen at the time, so they had trouble catching the boys. Finally, they caught Mark Devlin while he was trying to conduct a robbery. To scare the other boys, the judges sentenced him to **death by hanging**.

Nobody in the small town wanted to do the job, so they sent for someone from Edinburgh. On the day, the hangman didn't show up, but someone else volunteered and gave his name as James Livingstone. Turns out it was not his real name because the real James Livingstone had refused to do the hanging. Who was this man? No one knows.

331. Clayton Murder

A man named John Middleton Clayton had a terrible day on January 29, 1889. He had just lost the elections that he had been campaigning for. He was supposed to win the senate seat in the Congress of Arkansas, USA. He was graciously giving his concession speech when suddenly **he was shot**. This was right in front of his own home.

The killer or any witnesses never came forward despite the police offering 5000 dollars as a reward. The local detectives got involved and ran through a long list of suspects. They found nothing to implicate anyone in the murder. Once his opponent died, people found that he had committed voter fraud. Could he have been the killer?

332. Marilyn Sheppard

A 30-year-old doctor returned from work on July 4, 1954, and found his wife murdered in the bedroom in their home in Ohio. He fought the killer who then escaped. He described the killer as a bushy-haired man. **Sam Sheppard** was the husband of Marilyn Sheppard who was murdered.

Marilyn was in their Bay Village home on the shore of Lake Erie when she was murdered. The police believed this was an open and shut case. Obviously, the husband had done it. Many people became interested in the court case. Sam Sheppard was found guilty of the crime. But 12 years later, another jury declared that he was not guilty, because by then the police were able to use new technology to prove he was not the murderer.

Even a third jury found him not guilty in 2000 and asked that he and his family be granted some penalty fees for so much inconvenience and wrong doing on the part of the previous jurors and police officers. As for Sam Sheppard, he kept looking for the real killer for several years through private investigation officers. After his death, his son took over but the real killer was never found.

Sam Sheppard was represented in the courts by a young lawyer named F. Lee Buckley who later became famous in the US justice system. The case also inspired a landmark Supreme Court decision in the US on the right to fair trial for all.

FACT FILE

Excessive media coverage might have influenced the first trial's verdict.

333. Jack the Ripper

In 1888, between August and November, the London police found the bodies of five women. They suspected that each of the women was killed by the same person. The police knew that the murderer was a man who called himself 'Jack the Ripper'.

Jack the Ripper was a **'serial killer'** The police had not heard of such killers before and were unable to solve the case. He had even sent them a bloody letter ridiculing them because they were unable to catch him. They never found him but suspected three people; a mad barrister, a barber and another man who had been put in the asylum months after the murders took place.

334. Zodiac Killings

It was a quiet evening in December 1968. A couple had parked their car by lover's lane in the Bay Area of San Francisco. Suddenly, they were **shot to death** by a mysterious man. While the police were investigating their murder, the killer had struck again. This time, he had shot a couple in a park.

Over the next 10 months, the killer would go on to shoot more couples as well as a taxi driver. The police were under a lot of pressure, because they had not found a single suspect. The killer kept teasing them by sending letters to the local newspapers. He had named himself the 'Zodiac'. The case was called 'The Zodiac Killings'.

335. Michael Rockefeller

THE NEWS
Governor's Son Is Missing Off Coast of New Guinea

A young man named Michael Rockefeller disappeared in 1961 while collecting indigenous art in Netherlands, New Guinea. He was working with the Asmat tribe at the time. Michael was the son of the New York State Governor, who was preparing to become the Vice President of the United States of America. After his son's disappearance, he launched a long and powerful investigation but nothing ever turned up. The search lasted for two weeks with ships, airplanes and helicopters looking for the young man.

Nobody knows what happened, but an author named Carl Hoffman went to the area where Rockefeller disappeared and investigated what happened. He had a theory that Rockefeller was killed by a local tribe who practiced cannibalism. There was also a possibility that Rockefeller unknowingly disturbed the tentative peace between two warring tribes and was punished as a result.

This theory sometimes sounds odd, because outsiders had visited the area before and had a peaceful time. The tribes were known to either cooperate with outsiders or just kept their distance.

At the time of his disappearance, Rockefeller was just 23 years old. He worked as a photographer as well. Even the locals were involved in searching for him after his disappearance, but to no avail. Since the water was close, some people believe he drowned while boating. This was quite possible, because the waters were uncertain, and one slip could have cost him his life.

FACT FILE

Rockefeller was accompanied by a Dutch researcher.

336. Collar Bomb Heist

In 2008, a **pizza delivery person** walked into a bank and demanded 250 thousand dollars in cash. He had a bomb strapped to his shirt and this made all the bank workers nervous. He convinced them that it would explode in 15 minutes if he was not given the money. The bank workers only managed to give him eight thousand dollars.

The pizza man left the bank, but unfortunately, the police had made it in time and surrounded him. The bomb exploded before he could escape. The bomb was tied to his neck collar. Police think that a group of unknown men had forced him to commit the crime and lured him by ordering pizza.

337. Militant Robbers

In 1972, a **group of robbers** broke into the British Bank in the Middle East. They managed to steal nearly 25 million pounds in cash and other items. The PLO was behind this operation and they were a militant group. The robbery was intended as a means for them to riot as well as to fund their group.

This case is like the robbery that took place in 1972, because the robbers used a grenade to get into the bank and used brute force rather than intelligence and stealth. They even escaped into the Lebanese countryside, after the robbery and were never caught. The police still wonder if they had help from some bank workers to conduct the robbery.

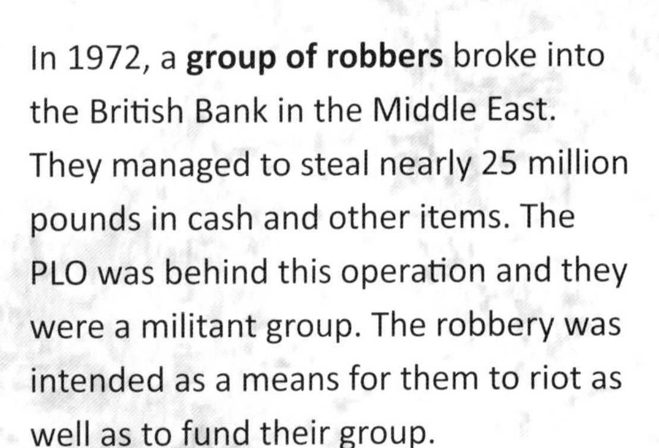

338. Plymouth Robberies

A **mail truck** was a means of transportation for banks to transfer their money to different branches. In August 1962, when a mail truck made a stop in Plymouth, Massachusetts, a state in USA, a group of thieves robbed the truck and took away 1.5 million dollars in small bills. The mail truck did not carry too many bills on that day (even though 1.5 million dollars seems a lot). It was travelling from Cape Cod to the Federal Reserve Bank in Boston, Massachusetts.

Two gunmen stopped and threatened the driver of the mail truck on Route 3 in Plymouth. The gunmen were dressed like policemen. That is why the driver had at first willingly cooperated with them. But he quickly noticed that something was not right.

The driver was not alone. He had a guard to accompany him. The guard was also threatened. The gunmen tied up the guard and put him in the back of the truck, while they forced the driver to take them to another location to drop off the money.

Luckily, the driver and guard were left off in a place called Randolph, on the side of the road. The thieves and the money were never heard of again. The police and the United States Postal Inspectors investigated the case for five years. They got very little evidence which frustrated them deeply. They offered 150,000 as a reward for anyone who could get them more information. This is nearly 10 per cent of the amount stolen by the thieves. Still, the case remains unsolved.

FACT FILE

A mobster named Vincent Teresa claimed one of his men conducted the robbery.

339. Diamond Heist

Did you know that Antwerp in Belgium is called the diamond exchange capital of the world? That is why it attracts so many diamond robbers. The vault at the **Antwerp Diamond Centre** was broken into in February 2003. The vault is not so easy to break into. It has seismic and heat sensors. It has a lock with one combination and 100 million possibilities.

The thieves were able to break in and escape, something that has never happened before. They stole diamonds worth 100 million dollars. A man named Leonardo Notarbartolo was arrested. He was the ringleader, but he never told anyone who his partners were and where they hid the diamonds. He now gives interviews and is consulted for movies for profit.

340. Relic Heist

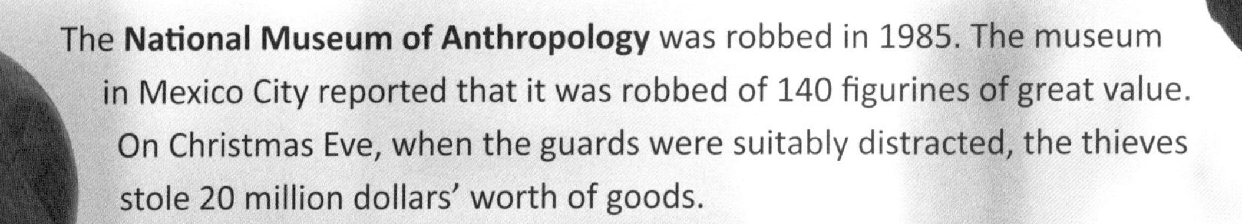

The **National Museum of Anthropology** was robbed in 1985. The museum in Mexico City reported that it was robbed of 140 figurines of great value. On Christmas Eve, when the guards were suitably distracted, the thieves stole 20 million dollars' worth of goods.

The museum's security system had been damaged for several years, and someone must have known, because the thieves had easily been able to break into the museum and sneak out even though the museum had a 7 foot fence. In addition to the relics, they also took valuable things like gold, jewels and small bags to fit these into. Besides the value, the history of these items was lost as the items came from Aztec and Mayan cultures.

How did the robbers know about the weakness in the system? Was it possible that someone from the inside was involved in the robbery? Did they help the robbers find the right time and the right items to steal? These questions remain unsolved to this day.

Mysteries in pop Culture

Famous people sometimes are the victims or perpetrators of unsolved mysteries. Either they write or sing something that later becomes a mystery, or they themselves are the mystery. And because they are so famous, many people get involved and try to solve the mystery only to keep failing.

In this last section, let's read about all the mixed bag mysteries that are a big part of popular culture. This section is about authors who go missing for days, old classics whose real-life counterparts are unknown and codes that are yet to be cracked.

341. Man in the Iron Mask

Alexandre Dumas wrote "The Man in the Iron Mask" about a **prisoner** who lived in the Bastille in Paris, from 1698 until 1703, where he died. He was said to be the twin brother of the royal French king, Louis XIV. He was put into prison from birth.

His face was hidden from soldiers and prison guards as he wore an "iron mask" whenever he left his isolated cell in Bastille. But, he was given respect by the guards. This is a true story where the man in Bastille could have been Louis XIV's twin brother, older brother or even his father whose legitimacy Louis XIV always questioned. Recently, people thought it was Eustache Dauger, a valet to the Chief Minister.

342. The Hitchhiker's Mystery

"The Hitchhiker's Guide to the Galaxy" is a **popular science fiction** series written by Douglas Adams. He had originally spoken about the subjects of the series on a radio comedy show on BBC Radio 4 in 1978. He later adapted it into novels, plays, comic books, TV shows, computer games and even a 2005 movie. It's a series loved by young and old alike.

The subject of the series is a man named Arthur Dent who is the only man who survived the end of planet Earth. It seems Earth was destroyed by an alien constructor fleet in order to make way for a hyperspace bypass. The reason that only Dent survived is that he was rescued by an alien named Ford Perfect who writes "The Hitchhiker's Guide to the Galaxy".

Dent uses the guide to explore the galaxy along with Ford Perfect and meets another person named Trillian who is a human being taken from the planet right before its destruction. He also meets several other characters.

Through his adventures he comes across a designer who speaks of super-intelligent people who invented "Deep Thought" which was a machine useful to calculate the Answer to the "Ultimate Question of Life, the Universe, and Everything". Apparently, the answer is 42.

But what does 42 signify? While it might be the answer, how did anyone come up with it? Why is the answer to such a complex question a two-digit number? How can it be applied in the practical world? These questions do not have answers.

FACT FILE

Scientists predict the universe will end 10 or 22 billion years from now.

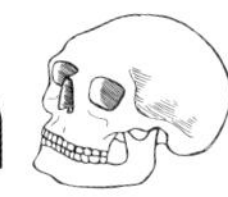

343. Lois Duncan

Lois Duncan was a popular suspense author. His books like "I Know What You Did Last Summer" and "Killing Mr Griffith" became instant hits and were also made into movies. But, one of the books written by her was quite personal. It was titled "Who Killed My Daughter" and was a non-fiction novel released in 1992.

The book was about Duncan's eighteen-year-old daughter Kaitlyn Arquette. She was **shot to death in 1989** on the way home from a friend's house. Lois later found out that her daughter's ex-boyfriend was involved in an insurance fraud that Duncan's daughter tried to expose. She thought that was the reason why her daughter was killed while the police just thought it was an accident.

344. You're So Vain

Maybe you are too young to have heard this song called **"You're So Vain"** written by a woman named Carly Simon. It was a mean song that tore apart her subject. It was released in 1973 a month after her marriage. Carly later confessed that the song was dedicated to Warren Beaty and a few other men. It sparked an interest about who the song was for.

Carly's old boyfriends were looked at with the song in mind. Some people thought that it was about her then husband James Taylor, but Carly adamantly denied it. Now there are theories that name several men but no one knows who it could be besides Warren Beaty.

345. Agatha Christie's Disappearance

Agatha Christie was a world-famous author of mystery novels. Her novels have helped many of us become pseudo detectives in our spare time. So, it's only natural that she would make it to this list of pop culture mysteries because of **an incident in her own life**.

She disappeared on the 3rd December 1926, from her own home in Berkshire, England. After some investigation, detectives found her car a few miles down the road from her home. Inside the car, they found a few suitable clothes and identification, but none of them could give an idea about where she might be.

Her family was worried because they thought it was a delayed reaction to losing her mother a few months prior to her disappearance. She was still coming to terms with her mother's death. She had also learned that her husband was having a secret affair with another woman, so she was in a depressed state of mind.

The news of her disappearance had been published in the newspapers and several people began to keep an eye out for her. She was found eleven days later in a hotel, and it seemed as if she had been staying there since the day after her disappearance. She was identified by her husband and taken home. She had signed her name "Teresa Neele" and had written several letters to friends before the disappearance. People thought she had a nervous breakdown. No one knows why she chose to disappear.

FACT FILE

Her husband's girlfriend was named Nancy Neele.

DISAPPEARED

346. Ambroce Bierce

Ambroce Bierce was an eccentric journalist who is best known for his short story "An Occurrence at Owl Creek Bridge". He also wrote a famous book titled "The Devil's Dictionary". He had a very different personality. He would make things up about other people and write them in the newspaper. That is why he made many enemies.

He **suddenly disappeared** in 1914, and no one knows what happened to him to this day. He was supposed to travel to write about the Poncho Village's in Mexico. He wrote letters, and his last one was dated December 26, 1913. He wrote that he was going to an unknown destination, and truly, no one knows where this is.

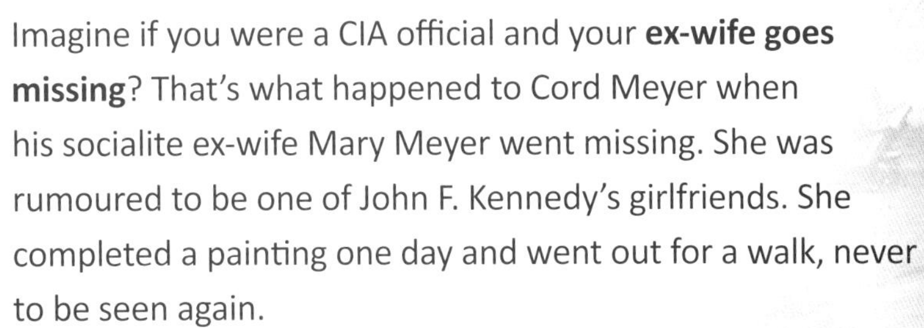

347. Mary Meyer

Imagine if you were a CIA official and your **ex-wife goes missing**? That's what happened to Cord Meyer when his socialite ex-wife Mary Meyer went missing. She was rumoured to be one of John F. Kennedy's girlfriends. She completed a painting one day and went out for a walk, never to be seen again.

A man, named Henry Wiggins, claims he heard a woman crying for help and then heard two gunshots fired along the same road where she had walked. He ran over to a wall that stood above the area and noticed a man standing over the body of a woman. He later felt that Mr. Kennedy could have been the murderer, but the police suspected Mr. Meyer. The case was never solved.

348. A Passage to India

"A Passage to India" was a novel released in 1924 by the author E. M. Forster. The novel ends in a strange mystery where the reader just cannot tell what happened to **Adela Quested**, the protagonist, who travels to the Marabar caves. She claims to have been a victim of assault which then starts a trial. During the trial, there is a lot of visible animosity between the British and the Indian characters. Slowly, as the trial progresses, Miss Quested changes her story and says that she does not know what happened in the cave.

In her new story, she doesn't know why her field glasses are on the ground or if anyone tried to assault her. She also claims that she might have had a hallucination because of the extreme heat.

Some people claim that these events don't present a mystery. Some readers feel that the mystery of the book doesn't matter. It's how the other characters react to the mystery that matters. The verdict would matter to the readers involved in supporting either side of the argument.

However, some believe if the mystery was not solved or if the verdict was reached without the reader knowing exactly what happened, it would leave a feeling of emptiness and frustration. The readers don't know why the mystery even exists and why they can't be privy to it. Today, "A Passage to India" is studied by students around the world. It is an important read for those who want to know English Literature. This mystery is open to the readers.

FACT FILE

The story's main characters were Dr. Aziz, Mr. Cyril Fielding, Mrs. Moore, and Miss Adela Quested.

349. The Unconsoled

The novel "The Unconsoled" was written by Kazuo Ishiguro and published in 1995. It was a story about random events that take place over three days to a **famous pianist named Ryder** who travels to central Europe for a concert. He wants to complete all his commitments before Thursday but cannot seem to remember them or take control. The reader is left with a baffling mystery that remains unsolved to this day.

In fact, the novel received a lot of negative reviews because the readers felt the author himself had made the novel bad by adding in such a long and winding unanswered mystery. The reception to the book was mixed, because it won several awards.

350. Hanging Rock

"Picnic at Hanging Rock" is a 1967 historical novel written by Joan Lindsay. The story is about a **group of schoolgirls**, belonging to a woman's college, who travelled to Hanging Rock for a Valentine's Day picnic only to disappear without a trace. The novel is based in Australia and focuses more on the effect the disappearance has on its people.

It only took four weeks for Lindsay to write this novel and is now known as one of the most important Australian novels of all time. The mystery of what happened to the girls and why they disappeared remains unsolved. The author has never revealed what happens to them as that wasn't the point of the story.

351. Anna Nicole Smith

Anna Nicole Smith was a famous American socialite, model and actress. She was an enigmatic personality who attracted attention. Today, she is most remembered for her **mysterious death**. Nobody knows exactly what happened to her to this day despite the fact that the media had constantly reported on it and also garnered it a lot of interest.

Some people believe that Anna Nicole Smith was depressed and was driven over the edge by the death of her son in 2006 when she broke down in tears. Her death came just six months after. However, while some believe she committed suicide, others think that she was poisoned.

352. Jack Nance

Jack Nance was an American actor who worked with a director named David Lynch on his biggest hit movie, Eraserhead. He died in California on December 30, 1996. Before his death, on December 29, Nance told his friends about a **young homeless man** who had beaten him up outside a doughnut shop.

Later, he ate lunch with his friends and showed them his bruise that was visible right under his eye. He then complained about a headache and died, because of complications that arose from his injuries. However, when police investigated his body, they found no evidence of a fight!

353. Henry Hudson

A man named Henry Hudson went missing in James Bay in Canada in 1611. He was a famous **British navigator** whose many discoveries led to a river, bay, bridge, strait and an entire town being named after him. He was said to be a tough guy to work for as his own crew would always be homesick, hungry and cold. They were trapped in ice for so many months that they revolted and refused to continue explorations.

Hudson, his son and seven other sailors decided to continue the exploration anyway and took a small boat and set off in the middle of the day. Sadly, they were never heard from again. The mystery about what happened to Henry Hudson is of great interest to people who live in and outside the Hudson town and other Hudson named areas.

This incident took place back in the 1600s so very little detail is known about the case. What happened to the mutiny that revolted? What happened to the crew that survived and went back to England? Some of them appeared for a trial in England and were charged for murder of the captain but escaped all punishment.

Hudson is said to have drowned while reaching the shore on a tiny lifeboat, and this scene is painted by John Collier in his famous painting. An author named Peter Mancall wrote about Hudson's last trip in a book "Fatal Journey: The Final Expedition of Henry Hudson".

FACT FILE

Hudson might have changed his hair colour and escaped to Rio de Janeiro.

354. Tallahatchie Bridge

Who jumped off the Tallahatchie Bridge? It is apparently **Billie Joe**, and this was known to us after a song named "Ode to Billie Joe" was released by Bobbie Gentry, a famous American singer. The song has such a casual tone to it that it is almost creepy.

Billie Joe was spotted by a man named Brother Taylor while he was trying to chuck or throw something off a bridge. It could have been a wedding ring. It could also have been a baby. There were many other possibilities as were discussed in the song. But, no sooner had Billie Joe thrown it off than he jumped off the bridge himself. So, what did he throw? That still remains unknown.

355. The Riddle

In the 1980s, a popular song was released by **Nik Kershaw** named "The Riddle". It had twisted lyrics like "Near a tree by a river, there's a hole in the ground; Where an old man of Aran goes around and around; And his mind is a beacon in the veil of the night..."

In the 80s, people were obsessed with "The Riddle" and wanted to know what the lyrics meant. The record company took advantage of this interest and held a contest asking the fans to solve the riddle. Several people tried. The singer himself later confessed that it was just a bunch of unrelated words that rhymed well together. But many believe that there is a darker secret behind it.

356. Fatty Arbuckle

Fatty Arbuckle was the loving nickname given to a comedian who worked in Hollywood movies in 1921. He went to a Labour Day Weekend party with a screen actress named Virginia Rappe who was famous for her work in silent movies. The party was held by Arbuckle himself , and it was also celebrating his recent contract with Paramount, a movie studio that offered him one million dollars.

As the party went on, Rappe suddenly became ill and went into Arbuckle's hotel room. Much later, when Arbuckle entered the room to change his clothes, he found the actress lying unconscious and thought that she had too much to drink.

Later, Rappe went home but continued to remain ill. After three days, she was admitted into a hospital. Rappe died in the hospital , because of a ruptured bladder. Another guest who attended the party named Bambina Maude Delmont claimed that it was Arbuckle who hurt Rappe and that Rappe herself claimed that he was hurting her. Arbuckle was immediately arrested and tried for murder.

FACT FILE

Fatty Arbuckle was so popular that people would ask him to perform for political campaigns.

People claim that Arbuckle had assaulted her and that led to her injuries. He was later found not guilty after undergoing three trials, with two different set of juries, all the while battling against a pushy media. The final jury apologised to Arbuckle because his personal life and career was completely destroyed and there was no evidence to link Rappe's death to Arbuckle. Someone else might have murdered Rappe or it might have been an internal disease.

357. Marilyn Monroe

Marilyn Monroe, whose real name was Norma Jeane Mortenson, is an iconic figure even today. She was at the very peak of her career when she was **found dead in her home** in Brentwood, California. She was lying dead with an empty bottle of sleeping pills. The conclusion was that Marilyn Monroe had committed suicide.

It looked like the court would give it a suicide ruling as it seemed like the actress was undergoing problems. On 4th August 1962, the actress was sent to a psychiatric facility to fight depression. But her loyal fans felt that she had not committed suicide, instead she had been murdered. After all she was only 36 at the time of her death and it seemed like her career could only move upwards.

After investigation, the police found some items missing from her home, including a personal diary that she maintained. There was also a note that went missing and people believed it was from the White House itself. People felt that either the mafia or President John F. Kennedy was involved in the murder. It could have been that Marilyn Monroe was dating Robert Kennedy.

Even after more than five decades, the murder of Marilyn Monroe sparks a lot of interest. People refuse to believe the suicide verdict and feel like there is evidence hidden by the FBI. In fact, the FBI reported that certain files about her death had gone missing. Once they are found, the rumours about her might just be put to rest.

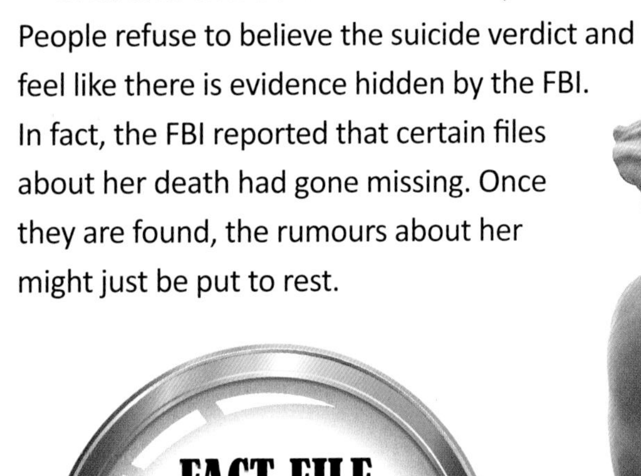

FACT FILE

Ben Hecht and Marilyn Monroe wrote her biography "My Story" about her life.

358. MKUltra

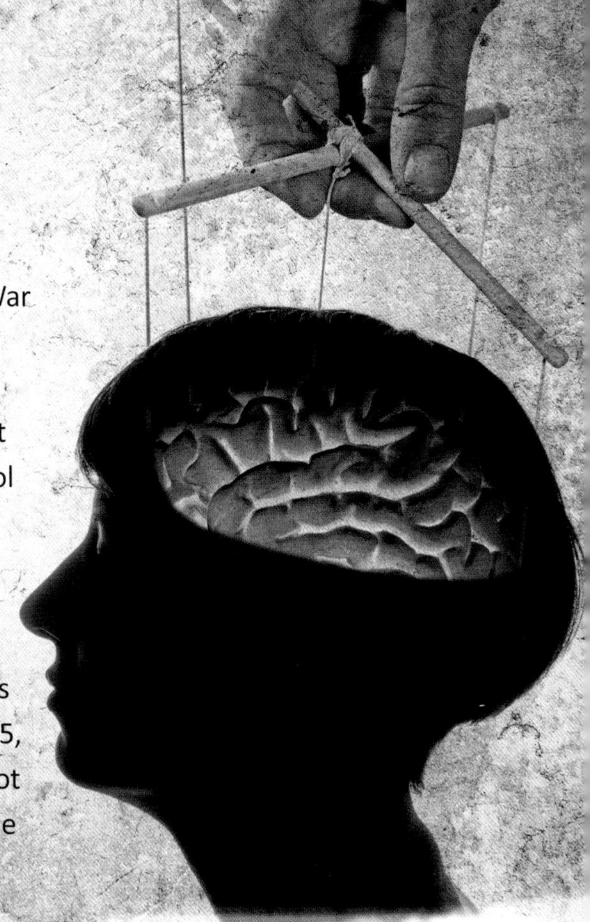

MKUltra was a mysterious **government program** sponsored by the CIA. It was set up during the Cold War between the USA and Russia. The entire operation of MKUltra was to find, research and develop materials useful for controlling the brain or human behaviour. It was meant as something that could be used to control the mind of the enemy.

The CIA had kept the program a secret and ran it covertly in hospitals, prisons, drug offices and universities. In fact, they sometimes used prisoners as test subjects with or without their permission. In 1975, details about MKUltra were released even though a lot of information was destroyed two years ago under the orders of CIA director Richard Helms.

359. The Majestic 12

During the 1980s, there were **many leaks coming from the US government**. President Harry Truman, who was the 34th President of the United States, served his term from 1948 to 1949. The leaks revealed that President Truman had signed a legislation to allow a government operation called “Operation Majestic 12” to be set up. It was supposed to be a twelve-man committee that would go undercover and investigate the “Roswell Incident”.

The Roswell Incident was the name given to a UFO crash. Apparently, there was some strange technology found there and the twelve men were to investigate it. Many people believe that these leaks were fakes or hoaxes while others think they were real.

360. George Reeves

George Reeves was best known for playing the role of Superman in the 1950s hit television show. He later died in 1959 on June 16 after a bullet was shot and hit his head. He was in the bedroom of his Los Angeles home. His fiancé, Leonore Lemmon was entertaining some guests downstairs in the living room. That's when he was shot.

The police thought that Reeves had killed himself, because he wasn't able to get more work after the Superman show ended. He was also undergoing financial problems. So, at the young age of 45, unable to get ahead in his career, the depressed actor had taken his own life.

FACT FILE

In 1999, a publicist spread rumours that Mannix had confessed to the murder.

It was Reeves' mother who felt that something was missing in the case. She did not believe that her son was capable of killing himself. She claimed that the evidence found did not naturally lead to the conclusion of a suicide, because the guests themselves had waited sometime after hearing the gun shot to report the murder. There were some stray bullet cases near the body which is unusual if George Reeves had shot himself. The news quickly spread that it might have been a murder.

It is believed that before he met Leonore Lemmon, Reeves was secretly dating the wife of a powerful Hollywood personality called Eddie Mannix, who was the head of MGM studios. He then left Toni Mannix for his fiancé. That was why she probably shot him dead. There is no proof to confirm this theory.

361. Moscow Coverup

There was a very famous competition that took place between America and USSR during the Cold War. It was a battle to develop a superior space program. It was called the "**space race**". While the USSR was ahead of America, America finally won the race.

In 1957, USSR became the first to launch an artificial satellite in space called the Sputnik 1. America was the first to send a man to the moon in 1969. But, there are rumours that USSR had sent two men to space and that this program ended in great tragedy. Embarrassed, Moscow tried to cover-up the program. No one knows if this is a true incident.

362. Prime Numbers 

A key property of prime numbers is a big mystery among mathematicians and several theories have come up to explain it. **Do prime numbers ever end**? Basically, prime numbers can be divided without a remainder by only two numbers – one and itself. The first prime number is 2, followed by 3, 5, 7, 11 and so on.

Every positive integer can either be a prime number or a product of primes. For example, 36 is a product of the primes 2, 2, 3 and 3. A basic observation will tell you that the higher the number, the lesser there are prime numbers. Euclid said the prime numbers don't end. But there is no proof either way.

363. Van Gogh

Vincent Van Gogh was a famous painter who lived in Paris. He was later said to have suffered from mental health issues. He was found dead in his home on July 27 with a **bullet in his stomach**. Everyone thought it was a suicide. But according to a historian named Steven Naifeh, Van Gogh would never have killed himself. There was no gun found on the premises.

Van Gogh did not leave a suicide note, but the historian felt that he would have wanted to live longer as he had ordered a fresh stock of paints. He had also sounded positive in a recent letter to his brother. No one knows if Van Gogh's death is a suicide or murder.

364. Hemingway

Any author or artist would be troubled by the news that his **work was stolen or copied**. And that is exactly what happened to Ernest Hemingway while he was on a Paris train in 1922. He was going to meet his wife who lived in Paris. Hemingway travelled Europe as a reporter. He had written to her to meet him in Geneva with a few unpublished manuscripts of his.

She took his manuscripts written over the course of four years and boarded a train in Paris. The suitcase she carried them in, contained the copies as well as the originals. She stashed them in the luggage compartment and went to get some water. The work was stolen and never retrieved.

365. Bruce Lee

Bruce Lee is known around the world as the **master of martial arts**. He has starred in many movies where he shows off his superior fighting skills. His first big break was acting in a television show named "The Green Hornet" where he played the role of "Kato". Since then, he has gone a long way and has starred in several more martial arts movies. Today, he is a household name, like Jackie Chan.

On the 20th July, 1973 , he went to visit a producer friend named Raymond Chow. He was supposed to discuss his role for the new movie he had been offered.

The movie's name was "Game of Death", and after 4 p.m., Bruce Lee travelled with Chow, to an actress's house to read the lines. Her name was Betty Ting Pei. They worked until they had to leave for a meeting. As they were leaving, Lee complained of a headache so the actress gave him a painkiller.

At around 7.30 pm, Lee went to lie down as he was not feeling well. The next thing anyone knew, the doctors had come to check him and said that he was in a coma. Before he could be taken to a hospital, Bruce Lee died in his coma. After performing tests, the doctors said that his brain had swollen to 13 per cent of the normal size. There were no external injuries. Doctors don't know if he was poisoned or if it was all an accident.

Bruce Lee's death, though shrouded in controversy, came as a shock to his fans around the world. Some of his fans, to this day, are keeping the interest alive to find out what really happened.

FACT FILE

Bruce Lee's son died while shooting a death scene.

OTHER TITLES IN THIS SERIES

ISBN: 978-93-84225-33-9

ISBN: 978-93-84225-31-5

ISBN: 978-81-87107-53-8

ISBN: 978-81-87107-52-1

ISBN: 978-93-80070-79-7

ISBN: 978-93-84625-92-4

ISBN: 978-93-83202-81-2

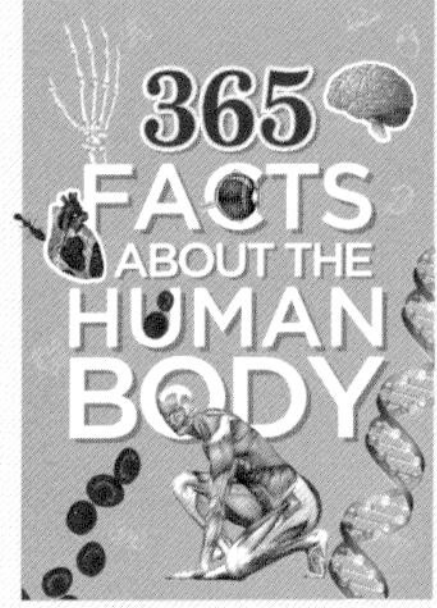

ISBN: 978-93-84625-93-1

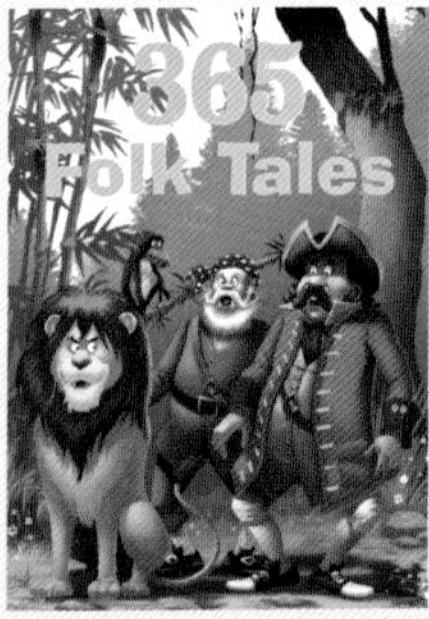

ISBN: 978-81-87107-56-9

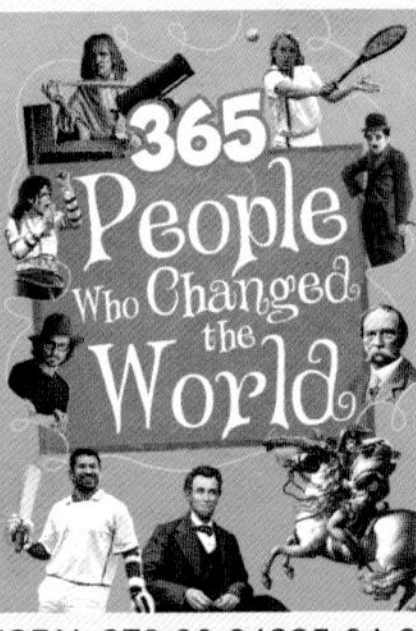

ISBN: 978-93-84225-34-6

ISBN: 978-93-84225-32-2

ISBN: 978-93-81607-49-7

ISBN: 978-81-87107-55-2

ISBN: 978-93-80070-84-1

ISBN: 978-93-80070-83-4

ISBN: 978-93-80069-35-7

ISBN: 978-93-80069-36-4

ISBN: 978-81-87107-57-6

ISBN: 978-81-87107-58-3

ISBN: 978-81-87107-46-0